CHILDREN OF THE GRAVE

EDITED BY MONIQUE SNYMAN

Crystal Lake Publishing
www.CrystalLakePub.com

INTRODUCTION

Welcome to Purgatory.

It's a post-mortem *Hunger Games*, where zombies are the least of your problems. This dangerous, arid plain is, however, escapable. A reprieve from the constant hunger and thirst is possible. Getting out of the clutches of the sadistic overlords is achievable. You simply have to tally up an impressive death count ...

That's right.

What lies ahead, dear reader, is no picnic. It's a kill or be killed world, where every man and woman needs to fend for themselves.

Before you jump ahead, though, there are a few things you ought to know:

The opening scenario is where you'll meet Blaze, the newest addition to Purgatory. You'll also be introduced to the dusty plains and its mountainous surroundings. At the end of this opening section, though, you'll not only have the choice of which direction you want to take Blaze, but which author you'd like to journey with.

Each author has chosen a different past, present, and fate for Blaze, and brings their own vision of this world to life. There are also a few exciting surprises in store for you, all thanks to the imaginations of these wonderful authors.

This is truly an interactive, shared-world zombie anthology, reminiscent of choose-your-own-adventures from yesteryear.

And what waits at the end of Purgatory?

Some say if you fight hard enough you'll be reincarnated. Perhaps you'll end up in Heaven. Then again, Hell might be closer than ever . . .

Monique Snyman
Editor of
Children of the Grave

CHILDREN OF THE GRAVE

OPENING SCENARIO

And Satan, who is the beast, was thrown
    into the lake of fire,
which is the second death.

Revelations

TOO SCARED TO open his eyes for another look, the man continued to feign unconsciousness. He had woken in semi-dark catacombs only moments earlier, alone and without shoes, and after brief moments of nothingness now realized he was being carried out of the cave by what appeared to be four tall men, draped in black robes.

Even though he had no idea who they were, or for how long he had been down there, he knew there was something different about himself. Perhaps it was the stiffness in his joints or the compressing ache in his lungs that indicated he'd been dead for quite some time.

With every passing second he became more attentive to the cold, bony hands cradling his limbs.

Sharp fingernails ran long lines across his skin, cradling him with their razor-like edges. He was afraid; afraid to breathe, afraid to tighten the smallest muscle. Who knew what they'd do to him if they found out he was awake?

The creatures stopped as if they'd reached an intended destination. They placed his body on the ground, and retreated into the catacombs.

The man forced his heavy eyelids open, and like two squeaky coffins they opened for their master to see the world.

The world?

What world could this be?

The sky above was a calm black-and-purple haze, easy on the eyes yet heavy on the nerves. It held no moon or stars but was filled with phosphorous-like clouds illuminating the world below.

A soft breeze proved to be a lot cooler than the heat within the catacombs.

He contemplated the consequence of sitting up: *I'm alive,* he thought, *and I need to stay that way. I need to get up.*

He breathed in the sulphurous air and struggled to sit upright.

The wasteland surrounding him seemed a lot less peaceful than it first appeared. Except for the partly illuminating sky, darkness hung over the semi-desert, like fog. Even the clouds had taken on a more menacing palette, much like that of a fast brewing storm.

With his mind numb from confusion, and an apparent lack of use, the stranger rose to his feet, his fallow legs close to collapsing. This only strengthened his initial thoughts about being dead for a long time.

Now what? What the hell did I get myself into now? Fuck . . . Who am I?

Crunching footsteps echoed in the distance, growing louder. Loose rocks scattered in their wake.

The stranger turned his head to see two figures charge toward him from the shadows.

He froze.

His limbs tightened from the chill running through his body, yet his mind kept note of every inch of the approaching men's movements: The snarl forming on the closest man's face, his fingers tightening around a knife; the second attacker staying three paces behind.

They were close enough for him to see their savage faces, ragged clothes barely covering their skeletal bodies.

Calmness eased over the stranger's body, like he'd done this before. He instinctively turned sideways, making his body a smaller target to the attacker. He lowered his stance and focused on the first attacker, who'd picked up speed. It was a rookie mistake that would prove his undoing.

The attacker raised his arm.

The stranger watched the blade barrel toward his face and he turned his hips forward. He shot his right arm out and twisted it to slap the man's wrist, attempting to parry the attack.

His attacker stumbled.

The stranger used the momentum to swing his left elbow around, catching his bewildered target just above the left eye.

The assailant faltered on wobbly legs, knife still in hand.

What the . . . What's happening to me?

The stranger stared at his open hands, briefly wondering where he'd acquired these deadly skills. Though, now was not the time for distractions. In the back of his mind he could hear someone screaming at him to focus, someone who had once taught him how to fight.

The attacker turned to face him again, but before his charge could pick up momentum, the hero widened his stance and shot his right foot straight into the guy's chest.

His opponent doubled over, cranium first into the dirt. Their entire exchange took less than two seconds from beginning to end.

The stranger turned in time to see the second attacker approach, his knife aimed for the stranger's chest. With a quick turn of the hips the stranger sacrificed his left shoulder instead. The blade penetrated the soft tissue, cutting through his flesh like butter. Adrenaline overpowered fear and pain, and the stranger grabbed the man's wrist, using all his strength to slowly pull the blade out of his flesh.

Once the blade was clear, the stranger thrust his open left hand toward the attacker's flattened elbow. There was a brief barrier of resistance before the arm hyperextended and snapped.

"Who are you?" the stranger shouted as the other man screamed in pain.

He held onto the dangling arm, wrenching it as he picked up the dropped knife with his free hand. Blood dripped from his shoulder as he bent over. It was the most painful thing he had ever experienced.

Boots crumbled on dirt behind him; the first attacker was back on his feet again—charging.

He pushed the wounded man back, to face the first attacker once more. They exchanged several blows, the stranger doing his best with only one arm, before plunging the knife into the man's neck. Blood sprayed over his shirt as the aorta severed. He pulled the knife out and flipped it over, dipping his fingers into the warm blood layering its surface.

A mysterious surge of energy coursed through him, like the man's lifeblood had somehow rejuvenated him.

With little more than a second to spare, he swung around and flung the knife through the air at the other approaching attacker. It sunk into the other man's skull, between the eyes. The dying man managed two faltering steps before he crashed to the ground, a puff of dust hovering into the now quiet air.

Another surge of energy flitted through his body. He felt the pain in his shoulder dissipate.

I've never felt so alive!

The stranger scrambled toward the knife, not knowing if he might need it to fend off another attack. He was quite fit, and fast, for a dead man.

Finding only sparse, leafless bushes around him, he ducked down for cover to catch his breath.

That's when he noticed the drying blood on his hand; it tightened around his skin and pulled at the tiny hairs. The exertion of the fight had caused a sweat to break across his brow. He wiped his hand in the dirt and then against his jeans, trying to wipe away the evidence, but even his shirt was soaked with the other man's blood. Bile pushed higher and higher in his throat.

Relief came with the revulsion.

Revulsions meant he *wasn't* a killer, even if he knew how to fight and kill. It meant he *wasn't* used to the act he'd just performed. That said something about him, at least.

He checked his shoulder and found the wound closing. He stretched the skin just to make sure he wasn't dreaming.

What's going on?

A grey layer of dust now covered his hand. He looked up at the large plain stretching out before him, and the eerily dark mountains encircling it.

Two odd shapes standing to the side caught his attention. The one was tall and skinny while his friend was short and muscular. They were staring at him, mouths agape like he was some sort of caricature.

A rush of cold air swept through the awkward silence. The breeze stemmed from the central plain, a brief relief from the heat emanating out of the caves behind him.

The stranger rose to his feet and turned toward the two men. He twisted the knife in his hand until it felt more comfortable. When he felt balanced enough, he leaned forward, and charged.

He picked up speed, dodging several shrubs and small boulders.

The eyes of the two men grew larger with every meter the stranger advanced, until the tall one raised both arms to show his empty hands. "Whoa!" he protested. "We come in peace!"

Reluctantly the stranger slowed to a stop. The men looked sincere enough, but he wasn't about to let his guard down.

"We . . . " the shorter man said as he pointed to the

dead and dying men in the catacombs, "we're not with them."

"Yeah," the tall guy said, "we're the good guys."

The stranger recognized the anxiety they garnered toward him—he was scared of himself right then—and approached the men.

They retreated.

The stranger tested them by taking another step forward, to which they replied with another step back. *I can get used to this.* "Who are you?"

The taller man forced himself to take a step forward. His jeans, which looked like they used to be a dark shade of blue, sagged over worn-out shoes which proudly displayed his toes. His shirt appeared to be different shades of grey. Hell, everything in this place seemed to be grey. "My name is Scrubs. This fat fuck next to me is Bones."

The stranger inspected Bones, who wore nothing but torn shorts and a once-white vest. The man wasn't fat at all, but from the eyes of his tall and skinny companion, everyone could be seen as fat. In fact, nobody he'd seen so far had sufficient meat on their bones.

"You've got some nice moves, man," Bones said with a smile.

The stranger refused to lower the blade. "Thanks, I think."

Bones looked over his shoulder, growing noticeably uncomfortable. "Now that that's over, I think we should start moving along."

"Considering we know each other so much better now," Scrubs added, "I second that motion."

The stranger shook his head. "You don't think I'm gonna come with you, do you?"

Bones stared at the stranger. "There are worse things than hunters out here, my nameless friend. If you want any information from us, you'll have to come *with us*. 'Cause we're leaving. Now."

"Of course," Scrubs said as he elbowed Bones in the ribs. "He doesn't know anything. How could we forget? You didn't even know you could fight, did ya? Or what your name is, right?"

Bones eyed the stranger from top to bottom. "That's it, we'll give you a name and it'll be like you've always been one of us. Let's call him . . . Blaze."

"Why?" the stranger asked.

"Your hair, man. In case you don't know, it's red."

"Yeah," Scrubs added, "for now. Until the dust in this place sneaks into every corner of your body and turns you grey like the rest of us."

The three men stared at each other, wondering what to say or do next.

The stranger nodded, accepting his new name, for now. "How do you know all these things?"

"Well, Blaze, we've been here pretty long. We all started out just like you, and no one remembers anything when they first wake up. It'll come back in a few months."

"Months?"

"If you live that long," Bones added.

Blaze's muscles tightened, his grip squeezing the knife.

"Wait," Scrubs interrupted. "Forgive my stupid friend. He just means this is a dangerous place. There are a lot more of these hunters out here, and they'd just love to kill the three of us. Especially someone with your skills."

"What? Do they want me for bragging rights?"

Scrubs smiled. "You felt that energy surge after killing those guys, right?"

"Yeah, what was that?"

"It's like you're stealing their life force. You even get their strength and skills. The more you kill the better, and stronger, you become."

Bones spat on the ground. "And there's no food here, my friend, only hunger. But each time you kill someone, you not only become stronger, but you fend off the hunger pains."

"You also heal faster when you're injured," Scrubs said.

"Can we get out of here now?" Bones moaned.

With a new found curiosity in the two men, Blaze wiped the dust from his eyes. He didn't know what to do or where to go. He needed more information about this world, and its so-called rules. Who or what were these things that carried him out of the caves? Besides, he couldn't help but feel exposed just standing there. "Okay, I'm in."

"Great," Scrubs said.

Bones pointed to the dead men. "You might want to check if their shoes fit you. You're going to do a lot of walking from now on. If . . . if you don't mind, I'll quickly check them. Take them with us."

Blaze watched Bones circle the bodies, wondering if he could trust him. What kind of man steals from a dead guy? A thief? Scavenger? Or perhaps . . . a survivor?

Bones approached Blaze with two sets of shoes raised shoulder-height. "I take it you're about a size ten?"

Blaze nodded and took a pair of shoes with one

hand, cradling the knife like a cowboy priming for a quick draw in his other. "Okay, looks like you guys know a lot," he said as he laced up the runners. "So, tell me everything."

Scrubs raised his dust-layered forearm to show thumbs up. "On the way out of here."

Blaze hesitated for a few more seconds before trailing them at a safe distance. They crossed over parched earth and rocks, around barren trees pointing toward the ominous sky like skeletal fingers, further and further away from the caves. They walked hunched most of the way, trying to stay low and out of sight, whispering whenever they needed to talk.

Every now and then they'd hear a distant cry for help, or the deafening scream of the dying.

Bones turned sideways, trying his best to maintain eye contact with Blaze. "Bet you'd like to know what the hell's going on, right?"

Scrubs shook his head. "Why else would he be following us, you dimwit."

Bones pulled a comical face behind Scrubs. "Well, we don't know everything, but what we do know is that we're all dead."

"What?" Blaze said.

"Yip," Scrubs added. "Sorry, my friend, but you managed to get yourself killed in the real world. Now you're stuck here with us."

"How do you know for sure?"

Scrubs stopped, his cheeks scrunching into an expression of uncertainty. "'Cause in a few days you'll start remembering how it happened."

"If you live that long," Bones said again, continuing to walk ahead.

Scrubs scooped up a small rock and hurled it at Bones. "Fuck, dude. Sorry about that," he said as he turned to Blaze, "this guy's a fucking idiot."

"Birds of a feather, nutsack," Bones retaliated.

"So this is—"

All three men simultaneously heard voices off to the side and ducked down, scrambling for cover behind whatever availed itself to them. Blaze's heart thumped against his chest, louder and louder the closer the voices came.

It was two women, audibly arguing. The argument quickly turned heated and one of the women screamed in pain. Blaze impulsively made to go and help, but Scrubs reached out to push him back. "Don't get involved," Scrubs whispered. "It might even be a trap." They waited a few more minutes after the voices ended and moved away in the opposite direction. Scrubs turned to Blaze. "Sorry about that, but you'll have to make some hard decisions if you want to survive."

"So this is like some kind of Purgatory?" Blaze continued.

Scrubs snapped his fingers. "There it is. I can never remember that damn word. Purgatory, although it feels more like hell sometimes."

As they continued on, Blaze stared toward the distant mountains encircling them, wondering what lay beyond—how he got to this barren wasteland. "So why are we here?"

"As far as we can tell," Scrubs answered, "everyone used to be some sort of criminal, but instead of going straight to hell, we came here. Some sick version of a second chance."

"For what?"

"Life. You kill enough people, or zombies, and you get to leave. Whether you go to Heaven or you're reincarnated back on earth, no one knows for sure."

"Did you say zombies?"

"Yeah," Bones said. "Nasty buggers. Bit slow, but don't let them bite you, or surround you."

"You guys aren't shitting me, right?"

"Nope," Scrubs continued. "Best of all, if you stay here too long, you decay into one of those brain-dead zombies yourself. Then you'll never go back. You'll just get yourself killed and be sent off to hell, or whatever comes after this world."

"Fucking hell!" Blaze said.

"Pretty much."

"Why haven't we run into any zombies yet?"

Bones answered, "They tend to get stuck in the middle, since there are a lot more trees and bushes over there. And people. It's like everyone wants to stay as far away from where the Gatherers first dropped us."

"Damn, so I was some sort of criminal back on earth. That sucks." With that thought came the realization that his companions were admitted criminals too, and unlike him, they could remember exactly who they once were.

Scrubs looked up at the sky. "There's no day or night, no food. But since we're already dead, you just stay hungry the whole damn time. You'll get used to the darkness eventually."

"Yeah, and don't try to eat someone. Last guy who tried that turned into a zombie within two days. Like some sort of virus or food poisoning took hold of him. Guy was oozing puss from every hole you can think of. You'll get used to the hunger pangs as well."

Blaze shook his head, overwhelmed with the urgency of his situation. His chest felt like someone was sitting on it, slowly increasing the weight. He hadn't been given a second chance, none of them had. It was a prison, a torture chamber for lost souls and nothing more. Souls that weren't accepted into Heaven or Hell—a fucked-up no man's land.

"Whatever you do," Scrubs started, "stay out of the forest beyond The Commons. It's like the zombie mother ship over there."

Blaze parted his lips, but words failed to follow.

They walked in silence for another half hour, the area growing rougher with big rocks turning to small boulders and thorny bushes reaching out at them from all angles. Thank God for the shoes. He was about to ask more about The Commons when the guys stopped at the edge of a slight hollow. It was a few meters to each side, deep enough to conceal anyone hunkered down.

Scrubs surveyed the area and motioned for the others to get down. "This is our spot. Nice and hidden if you keep low."

Blaze joined them and lay down. The surface had been cleared of rocks, and the ground was soft beneath them. It was quite cool here, away from the scorching caves, safer as well. And although he'd finally managed to still his anxiety, he started experiencing the first pangs of hunger.

Bones lay back, his hands cupped behind his head. "Home sweet home."

"How big is this place?" Blaze asked.

"Uhm," Scrubs answered, "about two days walk from end to end, one if no one bothers you, which is impossible. We probably only covered a third now, and the quiet third at that."

"Damn."

"So," Scrubs continued, "any more questions?"

"How do we get out of here? That's a good start."

"Well, you've got a few choices . . . That is, if you're a killer, but not everyone is." His voice grew hesitant. "You can either kill zombies, or humans. But you'll have to kill a lot more zombies to earn a ticket outta here."

Blaze turned onto his side, propped up on his elbow. "So I have to prove myself worthy of a second chance at life by killing people? Doesn't that sound a bit off to you? And who judges us?"

"Yeah," Bones said, "messed up."

"No one really knows, but those dudes in black who brought you here are pretty much in charge. We call them Gatherers, and this world, suspended between Heaven, Hell and fuck knows where else, is theirs to rule."

"So that's it? That my only choice?"

"Well," Bones said, "some people decide to just settle down and wait it out. For that, you could join The Commons. You'd be better off joining us, but if you're really psycho, you could always take down a Gatherer." He chuckled.

"Yeah," Scrubs said. "That'll get you out of here real fast."

Blaze bit his lower lip in thought.

"Fuck, man. We're just joking. Wanna get yourself killed? Or *worse*?"

"Just imagine how strong you'd be," Bones said more to himself than the others. "Those things aren't even human."

"How would you know?" Scrubs scowled.

Bones shifted closer. "Ever seen one of those fuckers close up, so close you can smell the sulphur on their hot breath? I have."

"Blah, blah . . . whatever." Scrubs turned to Blaze. "Don't listen to his nonsense. He's full of it, if you haven't noticed."

"Seriously. They've got no flesh underneath those hoods, just bright red eyes with smoke and shit coming out of it. They're like the guardians of this place. It's like they keep watch over the plain from high up in the mountains."

Scrubs added, "Seriously? *Shit* coming out of their eyes?"

"You know what I mean," Bones said.

"Anyway," Scrubs continued. "They live in the caves, but I'd stay far away from them if I were you. They like to torture people. They even come out sometimes to catch a stray. Some brave yet foolish souls have tried to storm the caves, looking for a way out. Their screams echo over the plain for days after."

"So they allow certain groups to survive?"

"In a way," Scrubs said.

"Like The Commons?" Blaze asked.

"Oh, yeah. Good point," Scrubs said. "I forgot to tell you about them, just weird to see someone with your skills right off the bat not being a contender. We call the guys who've been here a while contenders. You see, there are some people, unlike you, who can't kill, so they just try to survive as long as possible. For those people there are lots of small communities around if you get lonely, groups of three to five taking turns to watch over the others. On the other side of all this, damn close to the mountains and that zombie forest, is a big community with about fifty people living inside a walled village. You could always try to join them."

"That's not a bad idea," Bones said. "That's if you don't want to stick with us, of course. We tried to join them once, but we just didn't have enough to offer. Not like you have."

Scrubs mumbled "Yes" as if his mouth were filled with food. "You're more than welcome to join us, but each guy has to make his own decisions around here."

"Aren't the folks in The Commons too close to the Gatherers? How can they even be safe?"

Scrubs mumbled over unrecognizable words, either uncertain of the truth or doing his best to hide it, " . . . knows for sure."

"What do you guys do?"

They looked at each other and nodded. "We hunt zombies," Scrubs said with a smile. We take turns killing them so that we both get to leave this place relatively together."

Blaze eased onto his back and sighed. Time crept on as he contemplated his choices, staring at the purple haze above. He could join his two new 'friends', but could he trust them? Really trust them? How could he know for certain they wouldn't kill him once he fell asleep?

Perhaps getting to know them better would be a good start. He peered over to see if they were still awake. Upon seeing their eyes open he said, "Why are you called Scrubs?"

"Ah, I used to be a doctor."

"Aren't doctors supposed to go to Heaven? Seeing how many people you save and stuff."

Bones laughed softly, not wanting to attract unwanted attention. "Not this guy. Nope."

"Yeah," Scrubs said sheepishly, "I ripped people off every chance I got. Started out with a few extra dollars on their accounts, ripping off their medical aids, then things quickly grew shady. I ended up stealing a couple of organs here and there. Never would've done it if I knew I'd end up here."

Blaze didn't need to ask Bones how he got his name. You just had to look at him to know. He didn't want to admit it, but he was growing quite fond of this duo.

"Rest, my friend," Scrubs said. "Then let us know of your decision in the morning. Choose what comes natural to you, since you can't remember anything from who you used to be."

Blaze bid them a good night and slid closer to a dry, leafless shrub behind him and curled up underneath. He wasn't as scared as he perhaps should've been, but he knew the smaller he made himself during the night, the better his chance would be of waking up in the morning. Sleep would be difficult.

He peered up at the sky and then over the edge of the hollow at the unpromising mountains. He noticed for the first time the red and orange glow emanating beyond them.

I wonder if it's Heaven, or hell? Perhaps it really is the way back.

His mind raced with the choices laid out before him:

VALLEY OF THE SHADOW

AURELIO RICO LOPEZ III

He could not imagine anyone being able to sleep under these conditions. The faint, yet unmistakable stench of decay lingered in the soil. Like walking into a bathroom minutes after someone had taken a shit. Didn't matter how much air freshener you used, the scent hung around like a jealous ex.

The ground was hard and cold, and the ditch Bones and Scrubs called *home* was about as comfy as an outhouse. Smelled like one, too.

Blaze wasn't sure he could trust his new acquaintances. They seemed all right, but so did Norman Bates. Appearances, he knew, could be deceiving.

He thought sleep would be impossible.

He was wrong.

***

"Blaze! Hey man, wake up!"

Blaze woke up with a start. He scrambled to a crouch, prepared to attack at the slightest provocation, business end of his knife at the ready. Bones stumbled backwards and fell in a plume of grey dust.

"Jesus, take it easy," Scrubs said, holding out his calloused hands. "It's just us."

Bones backed away. "Christ, I thought you were going to kill me."

"He's just edgy, that's all," Scrubs said and turned to Blaze. "Ain't that right, Blaze? Tell him."

Adrenaline coursed through his body like a live current. Blaze looked around and remembered where he was. How long had he been asleep?

"Why did you wake me?" he asked.

Scrubs carefully poked his head out of the trench and got back down. He flashed his yellow teeth, which might have passed for a smile.

"We've got zombies."

"How many?" Blaze asked.

"Four," Bones answered, still eyeing Blaze with caution. He got up and brushed the seat of his pants. "Normally, Scrubs and I can handle one or two on our own. Maybe three . . . "

"That's a load of crap, Bones, and you know it," Scrubs snorted. "Three is too damn many, and the two of us taking on a group of four is suicide. The truth is, we need your help. Bones and I figure with your skills, it'll be a cinch."

Blaze stuck his head out the trench, just enough to glimpse the four shambling figures a hundred yards away. Their movements were awkward, their putrid stench wafting toward him. It reminded Blaze of stale milk and dog shit.

"Zombies," Scrubs grumbled, covering his nose, "I swear if I didn't need to kill them, I'd want nothing to do with them."

Blaze's mind raced. Was it true? Did you really have to kill to get out of this place? Bones and Scrubs certainly thought so. They'd been on the level about everything else so far, and he certainly didn't see what they had to gain by lying to him.

He returned to a crouch and adjusted the grip on his knife. He gazed at his companions. They stared back, waiting.

"Okay, I'm in. What's the plan?"

***

The plan was stupid. Bones and Scrubs guaranteed it would work, but that didn't change the fact.

Bones crawled out of the hole and stood up in plain sight. "Hey!" he called out to the zombies. "You hungry, you ugly bags of shit? Come and get it, you Bieber lovers!"

Back inside the trench, Blaze raised an eyebrow and turned to Scrubs. "Bieber lovers?"

Scrubs shrugged. "Bones isn't a big Justin fan. Swears he'd kill him if the Bieb ever ended up here. Told him not to keep his hopes up. That punk's going straight to hell as far as I'm concerned."

Blaze didn't have a clue who Scrubs was talking about, but this Bieber guy must have committed some seriously heinous acts. He returned his attention to Bones.

"Here they come, guys! Get ready!"

Scrubs turned to him and winked. "Don't get bitten. If any of these sons of bitches so much as give you a hickey, you're as good as dead."

Blaze watched him wrap a bandana around the lower half of his face. He looked like a bandit from an old spaghetti Western. "Same thing happens if you get blood in your mouth, so givin' one a blowjob is out of the question."

Swell.

"Heads up!" Bones called out as he jumped over the trench and landed on the opposite side.

Scrubs and Blaze ducked and stayed low, waiting. Then, one by one, each of the zombies leapt over the trench in pursuit. Dust and gravel rained on them. When the last zombie landed, Scrubs yelled, "Now!"

They emerged from their hiding place and gave chase. The four zombies were too focused on Bones to notice them. It was this flaw that Scrubs and Blaze would soon exploit.

The thing about zombies is that no two are exactly alike. While it may be true that all zombies are savage, flesh-eating creatures driven by hunger, that's where the similarity ends. Each one is in a different state of decay. That means that some zombies are stronger than others. It also means some are weaker and slower.

Scrubs drew first blood; he raised a fist-sized rock that he'd been carrying and struck the last zombie at the base of its neck. There was a sickening crunch, and the creature went down hard. Scrubs skidded to a halt, whooped in delight, and brought down the rock again, smashing its face. Blaze continued pursuing their quarry.

His heart raced, which confused him. If he were already dead, then why could he feel his heart against his chest? He pushed back the questions in his head. There would be time to address them later.

Blaze sped up, closing the gap between him and the next zombie. The creature was still oblivious to his presence. When he was finally close enough to smell the rotten flesh and pluck maggots off the fucker's ass, he swept the zombie's legs. It tripped and did some sort of gravity-defying, flip somersault that would have made any Olympic gymnast proud. It couldn't nail the landing though, and the monster's head ploughed through the soil as if the zombie believed the land was filled with gold and couldn't wait to strike it rich.

Now only two remained.

Without warning, Blaze felt a jolt of energy surge within him as his body drained the zombie's life force. He almost stumbled, barely managing to keep his grasp on the knife as the air around him buzzed and popped like static electricity.

Twenty yards ahead, zombie number three turned to Blaze. Seemed its brother's impression of a Russian gymnast had drawn its attention. It snarled and attacked, kicking up puffs of grey dust.

Without realizing what he was doing, Blaze took a step forward, raised his knife, and flung it. The blade sailed through the air like an arrow shot from a bow. The knife caught the zombie in its right eye, and the sound was like a ripe melon striking concrete pavement. The creature's head snapped back. The zombie did a macabre pirouette and fell.

Another wave of energy washed through Blaze. It almost tickled. He chuckled.

"Feels great, doesn't it?"

Blaze spun around.

Scrubs had taken off his bandana. The former doctor smiled. "Almost like a drug. Like it or not, Blaze, we're all junkies in this place, and killing is the only way to get a fix."

Blaze could only grunt in agreement.

Scrubs stared over Blaze's shoulder. "Ah, here comes Bones. Looks like we aren't the only ones who got lucky."

Blaze turned around and saw Bones approaching, looking like a juvenile who had just scored his first blowjob. "Told you guys it would work," he said, beaming proudly.

"It was a stupid plan," Blaze said.

"The end justifies the means," Bones countered.

"Quit waxing poetic," Scrubs said. "Blaze is right. The plan could have easily gone south, and we've never tried the tactic with a group of zombies that big."

Bones waved off his friend's comments. "Fine, you ungrateful bastards. You geniuses can come up with the next plan."

Scrubs chuckled and winked at Blaze.

"So, how many did you get?" Bones asked.

"Just one," the doc said. He put his arm around Blaze. "But this guy here killed two of them. You should have seen him, man." Scrubs pointed at the zombie lying face-up on the ground. "He got that one with a Jet Li knife throw. It was fucking awesome."

Blaze bent over and retrieved the blade. He wiped off the blood on his pants. "It was a lucky throw."

"Right, and I'm the Virgin Mary. I wish I could do something like that; I'd be out of this shithole in no time. I don't know what you were or what you did before you ended up here, Blaze, but you must have been one bad-ass motherfucker."

Bones laughed out loud, and although Blaze smiled, deep inside he wondered if what Scrubs had said were true.

***

He was on the rooftop of a building. At least, that's what it felt like. He looked up. The sky was a blue satin sheet, marred only by the occasional passing cloud.

24

Below, traffic was light. He didn't know why, but that was a good thing.

Where am I?

He realized he was carrying something heavy. He looked down and stared at the rifle.

What the fuck?

He hefted the weapon—it weighed a little over six pounds—and stepped toward the edge of the building.

He had done this before.

The rifle was fitted with a scope. He braced the butt on his shoulder and surveyed the street below until he acquired his target—a homeless man lying on a bed of newspaper in an alley.

What the hell . . . ?

He adjusted his aim until the nameless man was dead center in the scope's crosshairs. He felt his finger on the trigger.

Wait! What are you doing? No! No, you bastard!

***

Blaze woke up with a whimper. Sweat covered his forehead and ran down his neck. His chest heaved as his starved lungs sucked in air.

"Trouble sleeping?" Bones asked. He stood outside the trench, staring down at Blaze, looking like a gravedigger who was ready to fill an open grave. Blaze felt claustrophobic. "The first nights are the hardest," Bones continued, scratching his armpit. "You'll get used to it. Give it time."

Blaze sat up and rested his back against the wall of dirt. Nearby, Scrubs snored softly.

"I was not a good person," Blaze said, remembering his dream.

Bones roared in laughter. "No shit! You're just

figuring that out? If you were one of the good guys, you wouldn't be stuck here with the rest of us."

"Yeah, but why here? If this is some sort of Purgatory, a halfway point between heaven and hell, why am I here? Shouldn't I be in hell?"

Bones swatted a mosquito. "Ah. Self-pity. Might as well get that out of the way, eh? Fact is no one knows why we end up here. At least no one I've met. Though I don't exactly have what one would call a large circle of friends. All I've got is the doc. I mean, he's a pal, but sometimes I wish I'd been stuck with someone like Jennifer Aniston or Charlize Theron."

Scrubs scratched his balls and grinned in his sleep. Maybe he was having a good dream.

Bones continued. "No one knows who picks us. God? The devil? Space aliens? Does it matter? We're already here. Just be thankful you aren't getting your nut sack deep fried in hell."

Scrubs stirred, and his eyelids fluttered open. His eyes were bloodshot. "What are you guys talking about?"

"Nothing," Bones answered.

"Is it my watch yet?"

"Not yet. I'll let you know when it is."

"Okay." Scrubs yawned and closed his eyes. Within a few short seconds, he was snoring again.

Blaze thought about what Bones had said.

No one knows who picks us. Does it matter? We're already here.

He had a point.

***

Some days were longer than others, maybe because the definition of a day was arbitrary. The sky maintained

26

its hematoma-like quality, and it was impossible to tell day from night. None of them had watches. As a result, a day was determined by sleep cycles.

One day, Blaze asked Bones how long he and Scrubs had been trapped in Purgatory. Bones didn't know. He used to count the days, later, they decided it wasn't worth the effort remembering.

They hunted zombies as a group, never straying far from the trench that had become their home. Blaze longed for a hot shower and a soft bed, but whatever entity created this place wasn't big on comfort, and didn't give a divine ass if you smelled like shit.

Sometimes, there were zombies. Sometimes, there were none.

They had to devise ways to entertain themselves. It wasn't like they had a deck of cards or a wide screen TV. No episodes of *The Walking Dead* or *Breaking Bad*. Entertainment came mainly in the form of practical jokes and pranks like tying one guy's shoelaces while he slept and screaming *"Zombie!"*

One time, Bones built a grey sandcastle. It even had a moat which he filled with piss. Bones proclaimed it the best man-made structure, second only to Castle Grayskull. Blaze tried telling him that Castle Grayskull wasn't even real, and Bones called him a liar.

***

"What's that?" Blaze asked, pointing at the horizon.

Scrubs squinted and looked where he was pointing. "It's a mountain."

"Thank you, Captain Obvious. What's on it?"

The doc shrugged. "Who cares?"

"You've never been there?"

Scrubs looked at Blaze as if the former hitman had found some dog crap, placed some of it on his head, and decided to call it a hat. "Do we look like a couple of mountaineers to you? No, we haven't been there."

"Why not?"

"Because it's too dangerous," Bones cut in. "It's too far, and we don't know what's out there. We could be up to our asses in zombies."

"I think we should at least check it out," Blaze said.

Bones shook his head. "Forget it. You want to stick a flag on that mountain, go right ahead, but I'm not risking my life just because you had the sudden urge to go sightseeing."

Scrubs patted Blaze on the back. "Let it go, man. Could be zombie city there, for all you know."

Blaze took one last look at the mountain but said nothing.

***

The same dream. He could feel a breeze against his skin as he took aim. In the distance, he heard a dog barking. In one of the apartments below, a woman was screaming at her husband. Something about lipstick stains on his shirt.

Back on the street, the homeless guy slept soundly. Blaze found it amusing. The way the guy slept, you'd think he'd checked into the Marriott.

The slumbering man clutched a half-empty bottle of cheap whiskey against his chest like it was the Holy Grail, completely unaware of the danger perched two hundred yards away. Through the scope, Blaze made out the features of the stranger's face as if he were standing right next to him. The scar on the right side of his forehead was probably the product of a childhood squabble, but the bruised lip was likely the result of a more recent one.

Blaze didn't know his name; that detail was irrelevant.

At least it should have been.

On that particular day however, up on that rooftop, that bit of information felt important. He didn't know why it mattered; until a few days ago, he hadn't even known the guy existed.

Blaze took a deep breath and exhaled slowly to clear his mind.

His hands began to tremble. He couldn't bring himself to pull the trigger.

A bead of sweat traced the side of his cheek.

Blaze lowered the rifle.

"Damn it!" he cursed between clenched teeth.

***

"Wake up, Sleeping Beauty," Scrubs said.

Blaze's eyes opened. "Huh?"

"Your turn on guard duty."

Blaze blinked and got up slowly. Working out the knots in his muscles and shaking the cobwebs from his head, he climbed out of the trench and stood in front of Scrubs. He covered his mouth with a hand and yawned.

The doctor eyed him with suspicion. "Hey, shake it off."

"I'm awake," Blaze countered.

"You better be. I don't want any half-decomposed zombie snuggling against me while I'm getting my beauty sleep."

Blaze smiled. "You'd better get to sleep then, if it's beauty sleep you're after, you're gonna need a whole lot of it."

Scrubs flipped him the bird. "Har-har. You and Bones think you're such comedians." He crawled back inside the ditch. "You want to know what my idea of hell is, Blaze?"

"What?"

Scrubs stretched out on the ground, both hands behind his head. "An eternity stuck with you two, that's what."

***

It was the first time Bones and Scrubs had asked him to keep watch over them. It was time to pull his weight.

Blaze scanned the terrain. A novice artist could not have painted a duller landscape. Everything was grey, or a shade of it. The land, the trees, the rock formation fifty yards from his location, the mountain, the shitty sandcastle Bones had built . . . even the air had an ashen appearance.

Grey, fucking grey. It reminded him of a book he hadn't bothered to read when he was still alive.

Something buzzed in his ear. Without thinking, Blaze slapped his cheek a bit too hard. He winced. That did it. If he wasn't truly awake then, he was now. He held out his hand. There was a red stain on his fingers.

Damn mosquitoes. Figures that there'd be a million of them out here. What better way to torment the wretched souls of the damned?

He stared at the blood in his palm.

Blaze looked up at the bruised sky, as if he could see the creator of this cursed place.

Well played, you bastard. Well played.

***

"Maybe you were a soldier," Scrubs suggested. "Ranger? Seal? Explains the skills you have."

It was the first time he brought up the dreams he'd been having. They sat on a rock, facing the horizon while Bones took a dump in the distance but still within sight.

They weren't eating, weren't drinking, but their bodies still retained their functions. Scrubs, the only one of them with a medical degree, had called it *strange as fuck*.

Blaze swatted a mosquito and missed. "That can't be right. I may not remember everything yet, but I don't think I have the discipline to be a soldier."

"Martial arts instructor?"

"Wouldn't explain the rifle in the dream."

"S.W.A.T.?" the doctor offered.

Blaze shook his head. "Same discipline issue."

"No one said you were a great officer. Maybe you just gave blowjobs to the right people."

"Now who's the comedian?"

Bones joined them. Their companion looked pissed. "God, I'd kill for a roll of toilet paper." He looked back and forth at Blaze and Scrubs. "What are you guys talking about?"

"Blaze is going through the whole Who-am-I phase. I told him he might have been S.W.A.T, but he thinks he isn't disciplined enough to have made the cut."

Bones thought about it, and after a long pause, said, "Maybe he sucked the boss' dick."

***

This time, the dream was different. He was in an apartment, smoking a cigarette when his cellphone rang. The number was unregistered. He picked up on the fifth ring.

"Yeah?" he answered.

"Got a job for you," the caller at the end of the line said.

Straight to business. No small talk, no beating 'round the bush. Fine with him. Wasn't like he wanted to compare zodiac signs.

"When do you need it done?"

"Soon. If you're as good as they say you are it'll be easy. A piece of cake."

"I'll decide for myself what's easy and what's not."

"Of course," the man said. "But this job will be . . . different."

"Just send me the details. You know my fee?"

"Yes, my friend mentioned it. About that . . . It's pretty steep, don't you think?"

These assholes always wanted a discount, like they were buying produce in a wet market.

"It's non-negotiable. You want a lower fee, hire someone else. Better yet, buy a gun, and handle the problem yourself."

"Wait." There was a hint of panic in the caller's voice. "I'm sorry if I've upset you. I'll pay your fee."

He smiled. It was like taking candy from a baby. In the end, this guy, and all the other rich fucktards like him were too chicken shit to handle their own business. "Wise choice. Wire me the cash. Half now, then the other half when the job is done."

"I'll be in touch. Thank you."

He hung up, tossed his phone on the couch, and lit another cigarette.

***

Hitman. Gun for hire. Assassin. Blaze finally knew. That's what he was.

32

"Holy shit!" Scrubs said, all excited. "I knew it!"

"That's bull, man," Bones said. "You said he was S.W.A.T."

"I know I did, but they're kind of the same, right?"

Bones gave his companion a funny look. "*The same*? Seriously? Man, it amazes me how you managed to finish medical school."

"Hey, fuck you, Bones. Fuck you and your fucking sandcastle. What pimp school did you graduate from?"

Blaze turned to Bones. "You were a pimp?" he asked. This was the first he'd heard of it.

Bones balled his large hands into fists. He looked like he was ready to stomp Scrubs into the ground, but it had already been said. The cat was out of the bag, and there was nothing he could do. He sighed. "Yeah. I'm not too proud of it, but the money was good." He looked at Scrubs with contempt. "We can't all be doctors."

Scrubs scoffed. "Bones here was on the pussy express. Screw that. He wasn't just on it; he was driving the damn thing." The doc yanked an imaginary chain and made a *choo-choo* sound.

Bones shot him a look that shut him up. "It wasn't anything like that, man. I never forced women to have sex with anyone. I just provided protection. I took them to the places where they'd bang their clients and made sure nothing happened to them. That's how I earned my name. I swore to the clients if they ever hurt the girls, I'd bust them up and break their bones."

"And did you?" Blaze asked.

"Did I what?"

"Ever break their bones?"

Bones flashed a large smile. "Oh, one or two of

them might have accidentally run into a brick wall or fallen down a flight of steps."

"Sounds mighty clumsy of them."

"So how many people have you killed, Blaze?" Scrubs asked, redirecting the conversation back to Blaze.

He hadn't thought about it. Since the latest dream and its revelation, he hadn't had time.

"I . . . I don't know."

"Oh, come on. A dozen? Twenty?"

"Damn it, Scrubs!" Bones said. "The man already said he doesn't know."

"Well, excuse me for being curious. Would you rather I ask how many guys you've thrown down the stairs?"

"You're pretty lucky there isn't a flight of stairs here right now."

***

Blaze stared into the distance. The blade of his knife glinted in the wan light. Behind him, Bones and Scrubs slept.

He studied his bare hands. How many people had he killed? How many men had he sent to their graves? He closed his eyes and concentrated, but the answer eluded him.

Why can't I remember? The fact he could kill someone and just forget about it frightened him. *Jesus, what kind of monster was I?*

His eyes snapped open.

Something was wrong. The air suddenly reeked of decay. The stench was so overpowering, Blaze gagged. He covered his nose with his arm and dropped to a crouch. He swallowed and fought back the rising bile in his stomach.

Something was heading their way.

***

It was a procession of the dead. Blaze counted fifteen, twenty zombies. Maybe more.

Alarms blared inside his head. He quickly jumped back inside the hole and almost landed on Bones.

"What the fuck, Blaze?!"

"Shhh. We've got zombies."

Bones pulled out his knife. "What's the count?"

Blaze shook his head. "Too damn many. They've got an army out there."

Scrubs woke up. "What's going on?"

"Zombies," Blaze repeated.

Bones stuck his head out of the trench and quickly ducked back inside. "There's got to be at least thirty of them out there!"

"What do we do?" Scrubs whimpered. The fear in the doctor's voice was almost tangible.

Bones turned to Blaze and whispered, "Did they see you?"

"I don't think so," he whispered back. "As far as I can tell, they're just milling around topside."

"We should make a run for it," Scrubs said.

Blaze shook his head. "There's no way we can outrun all of them. They'd wear us down. They'd catch up eventually, and by that time, we'd be too exhausted to fight."

"Blaze is right," said Bones. "Cutting and running would be suicide."

"So would staying put," the doctor said.

"Maybe not," Blaze interrupted, risking another look. "They're closer, but none of their movements indicate they know where we are. Just be ready to haul ass."

"That's reassuring," Scrubs said sarcastically.

He was starting to get on Blaze's nerves.

Suddenly, there was an inhuman roar unlike anything any of them had ever heard.

"What the fuck was that?" Bones asked.

Blaze glanced at him unbelievingly. "You're asking *me*?"

"It sounded huge," Scrubs said, on the verge of panic.

They exchanged glances in silence, but no one spoke. They pressed themselves against the trench wall and carefully stuck out their heads. If anyone looked in their direction from ground level, he'd see their heads popping out of the ground like overgrown Brussel sprouts.

Out of nowhere, a horned creature the size of a small bus leapt out of the shadows and fell upon the zombie horde. The creature was nothing like nature could have intended. It looked like something out of an issue of Fangoria, something a drunken silverback gorilla, a giant anaconda, and a rhino would have after some freakish orgy.

A handful of zombies scattered. Blaze could not be certain, but he thought he recognized fear in their faces. Previously, the only emotions he'd ever seen them display were hunger and rage.

The monster made short work of them. With one swipe of its bear-like paws, two, three zombies fell. Another zombie lost its footing and stumbled. The beast brought its massive foot down, and the zombie's head exploded, splattering chunks of brain matter and maggots in every direction. More of the undead met their demise as the hellish monstrosity impaled them with its enormous tusk.

After ten minutes, all that remained of the zombie army was a pile of rotting bodies with entrails, decapitated heads, and torn limbs strewn everywhere. The stench was almost too much to bear. Blaze breathed through his mouth. He could almost taste the rot and violence in the air.

Finally, the killer beast loped away, as if it had realized it had something better to do. Or more zombies to kill.

Blaze exhaled. His hands shook, and there was not a damned thing in the world he could do about it.

***

"I vote we get the hell out of here," Scrubs wailed.

"And go where?" asked Bones.

Scrubs blinked at his friend. "Does it matter? Jesus, man. You saw what that thing did, right?" He pointed. "It went that way. It doesn't take a genius to figure out that we should head the opposite direction."

"Oh, really? We don't even know what's out there," Bones argued.

"Yeah, but we know what's here, don't we?"

"I'll have to agree with Scrubs this time," said Blaze.

The doctor threw his hands in the air. "Finally, some common sense. Thank you."

"We got lucky," Blaze continued. "If King Kong and Godzilla's lovechild comes back, we're dead."

"We're already dead," Bones pointed out.

"True. But there's dead, and there's the *dead* kind of dead. We stick together and stay under the radar. If our luck hasn't run out, we might find shelter somewhere."

Bones thought about it, his brows furrowing as he

weighed their options. He looked back at the pile of dead zombies. Finally, he sighed and wiped a hand over his weary face. "Okay, but I don't like it."

"We don't have to like it," Blaze answered bluntly. "We just have to stay alive."

***

Like three wraiths, they marched across the grey terrain, occasionally glancing back to check if the monstrous beast had returned for seconds.

"What do you suppose it was?" Scrubs asked.

"Don't ask me," Blaze answered. "You two have been here longer than I have."

"It's something new," said Bones. "At least, as far as I can tell. Have any of you two noticed anything strange?"

Blaze scoffed. "That thing back there not strange enough for you?"

"Not that. Look around."

Scrubs was the first to notice. "Where is everyone?"

"Exactly," Bones said. "I thought it was nothing at first, but we should have run into someone by now. A zombie, a hunter . . . someone."

"What are you saying?" Blaze asked. "You think that monster wiped them out?"

Bones sighed. "Maybe some of them. I don't know. Or maybe those in control are bored and want to have a little fun with us. That *thing* back there, maybe it's their curve ball. A wildcard."

Scrubs raised an eyebrow and snorted. "Those in control? You've read too many Ludlum novels."

They carried on, occasionally coming across whatever it was that passed as vegetation in this place. The bushes and trees were completely bare, branches thrusting out at odd angles without so much as a single leaf to their claim. One tree looked like the skeletal remains of a man who had been buried alive, limbs reaching out of the ground like arms, as if the dying man believed someone would mercifully reach down and pull him out.

Apparently, no one did.

***

Hours passed. At least, that's what it felt like; there was no sure way to tell. Sometimes, one of them would stumble. Sweat drenched their shirts. Despite already being dead, the exhaustion and fatigue were very real. Finally, when they could go no further, they stopped.

"That's it!" Scrubs wheezed. "I can't take another step. If I'm dying today, you can just kill me right now and get it over with."

Blaze scanned the area. There wasn't any form of shelter. No trench, no cave, not even a rock formation that offered them some degree of concealment.

They were exposed.

His calf muscles burned. The blood vessels in his temples throbbed, and he felt a headache coming on. He needed to rest.

"I hate to say this, but I think we should stay here for the night. I can take first watch."

"No argument here," Scrubs announced and proceeded to lie down on the ground. Dust and sand clung to his wet shirt.

Bones went up to Blaze. "You sure you don't want me to take first watch? You look tired."

The hitman almost laughed. "We all are. I'll be fine. You can take the next one."

Bones nodded. "All right. Wake me up after an hour. Well . . . whatever feels like an hour to you."

"Thanks. Go get some rest."

"Excuse me?" Scrubs said. "A little consideration, please. Some of us are trying to sleep here."

"Asshole," Bones chuckled. He turned to Blaze. "Maybe we should have taken his offer and killed him."

Despite their current situation, Blaze smiled. "You're probably right."

***

They'd left their home, if you could call a hole in the ground that.

This region was different, if only slightly. Bones' sandcastle was nowhere in sight.

The mosquitoes stayed with them though. Perhaps these bugs were different, too. Or maybe they were relatives of the ones they'd left behind.

Blaze slapped his arm.

Fucking mosquitoes.

Sleep beckoned, taunting him like a sidewalk hooker promising the time of his life.

He paced back and forth, and when that didn't work, he hummed songs he could remember. He also tried to recall all the women he'd ever slept with. The fact he couldn't remember a fifth of their names was embarrassing.

Finally, he crouched next to Bones and nudged him on the shoulder.

The former pimp rolled over and slowly opened his eyes. "Mhhmm?"

Blaze smiled. "Hour's up."

Bones pushed himself to a sitting position. "All right."

Scrubs snored. Blaze glanced at him and shook his head. "I don't know how the doc does it. He could probably sleep through a zombie apocalypse."

Bones scoffed. "I'd believe it." He got up, rolled his shoulders, and stretched his arms. Finally, he spat on the dirt.

"No sign of zombies or that thing," Blaze reported.

"Thank God for small miracles, huh?"

"Do you still believe in God after all you've been through?"

"Actually, it's what I've been through that strengthens my belief."

"Really?"

Bones reached in his shirt and pulled out a small crucifix attached to a small, silver chain. "Mama raised me to be a Christian. I may have made some bad decisions in my life, but I never stopped believing."

"If that's true, you shouldn't be here."

Bones smiled, but it was a sad smile. "One has to do more than just talk the talk. He has to walk the walk as well." He stared up at the sky. "We should be burning in hell right now, Blaze. By all means, we should be. But we're not. You hear what I'm trying to say?"

Blaze nodded. "I think I do."

"We've been given a second chance. That's another blessing we should be thankful for." Bones caught himself and grinned like a Cheshire cat. He looked at Blaze. "Bet you never thought you'd get religious insights from a pimp, huh?"

Blaze laughed. "I never did."

They were silent for a moment. Then Bones raised his chin. "Look."

Blaze turned and saw the mountain. It was much closer now.

"Maybe you'll get to plant that flag after all."

***

He was driving down Jalandoni Street, weaving through traffic, when the cellphone rang. Blaze answered the call and placed it on speaker phone.

"Is it done?" the man asked.

"No."

A pause. "We had an agreement."

He looked in the rear view mirror. No one was tailing him. "I'll wire back the money you paid me."

"We had an agreement," the caller repeated.

"Fuck you and the agreement. I don't kill homeless people."

Another pause. "I don't recall forcing you to take the job. I told you it would be different, but that didn't seem to bother you. What was it you said? Half the payment before the hit, and the other half when it was done? The job—*your* job—isn't done."

He gripped the steering wheel until his knuckles turned white. "I'll give you back your damn money."

"I'm afraid it's too late for that. Goodbye."

The man hung up, and the line went dead.

***

Scrubs farted and scratched his balls.

He would have given anything for a cold beer and a pack of smokes.

Admittedly, he missed being a surgeon—the Stat procedures, saving patients' lives, service to mankind. He didn't know how good he had it then. Maybe if he'd taken his practice more seriously, remembered why he became a doctor in the first place, he wouldn't be here.

Perhaps money *was* the root of all evil. It was certainly true in his case.

A lot of good all that money did him.

He was born Matthew Fulbright, the only child of the world-renowned neurosurgeon Dr. Chandler Fulbright, so Scrubs had some big-ass shoes to fill. Sometimes, he thought that his entire existence—the private schools he attended, pre-med to med school, his entire career—had been prepped even before his birth like one of his father's carefully planned surgeries.

When he arrived in this God-forsaken place after accidentally downing a lethal cocktail of pain killers and Jack Daniels, his mind could not grasp the idea of Purgatory. His eventual encounter with Bones led to an alliance that was awkward, at best. It was an unlikely partnership, but Scrubs and the pimp realized that there was safety in numbers. Two wasn't much of a number, but it sure as hell was a lot better than one.

Unlike Bones however, Scrubs wasn't as quick to accept the idea of a limbo between heaven and hell. Eventually though, when you ruled out every possibility and factored in the walking dead that wanted to tear him limb from limb, then the impossible had to be the explanation.

His eyelids grew heavy. He still hadn't recovered from their trek. Nearby, Blaze rested on his side, eyes closed. Bones lay on his back with an arm over his face. After taking one last look around, Scrubs stretched out on his back and looked up at the starless sky. Where were the stars? Their absence made him feel more alone than ever.

He closed his eyes and dreamt he was back at Saint

Dominic Hospital, the big shot doctor, saving lives and hitting on cute nurses.

***

For the first time in weeks, he slept soundly. No dreams of jobs or assignments, and no more phone calls from his angry client.

Then the screaming started.

Instinctively, Blaze rolled and rose from the ground, bringing up his fists in a defensive boxer's stance.

His senses were on full alert, a fight or flight reflex, and he immediately recognized the source of the commotion.

It was Scrubs.

A mere fraction of a moment passed before Blaze realized what had caused the doctor to cry out. A bloated zombie in a jumpsuit had seized Scrubs' leg and dragged him away.

The doc must have dozed off while on guard duty. That was the only way the zombie could have snuck up on him.

The former doctor was on his belly, floundering and clawing the soil as the fat zombie pulled him farther away.

Shit!

Blaze reached for his knife tucked under his belt but changed his mind. His target was too far away for a knife throw, and he didn't want to spend half an hour searching for his weapon if he missed.

Crouching, he picked up a stone the size of a tennis ball. Plenty of those lying around.

Gauging the distance, he curled up like a pitcher and flung the rock. The stone bounced off the shoulder of Scrubs' attacker. The zombie dropped the doctor's leg and howled in pain. Their eyes met, and the monster's agony transformed into undiluted rage. It growled. Yellow saliva dripped from its mouth, completely forgetting about Scrubs. Then the zombie roared, and charged at Blaze.

With a battle cry of his own, Blaze rushed to meet the undead attacker. The distance between them closed fast. When it was down to the last few yards, Blaze drew his knife. As the enraged zombie reached out to claw at his face, Blaze ducked under its arm and slashed the blade across its belly. The zombie's entrails poured out like strings of rotten sausages, and Blaze felt himself draw the creature's life force.

"Damn it!" Bones cursed behind Blaze. "That was too close." He watched Scrubs sit up and brush sand and dirt from his belly. "You okay, Scrubs?" he yelled.

Scrubs got up and gave them a thumbs up.

"He was on guard duty," Blaze whispered.

"I know," Bones said.

"I think he must've fallen asleep."

Scrubs jogged up to them. "Hey, Blaze, thanks. I thought I was a goner for sure."

"You mind telling us how a zombie got the jump on you?" Bones demanded.

At the sound of Bones' tone, Scrubs took a step back. "I . . . I don't know."

"Bullshit!" Bones spat.

Scrubs looked from Bones to Blaze. "I must've dozed off for a second, all right? I was exhausted, man."

Bones looked like he was about to explode. "And

we're not? Jesus, man. You're lucky Blaze was here to save your lazy ass, you fuck. You could've gotten us killed."

"Hey, back off, Bones," Scrubs answered back. "I don't recall electing you president."

Blaze glanced around. "Keep it down you two, or it's going to get crowded here really fast."

That seemed to calm Bones down a bit. He froze and backed away from Scrubs. He pointed at the doc's leg. "You're bleeding."

Scrubs glanced down and saw the blood on his left leg. His face paled.

"Christ, Scrubs," Blaze said, taking a step back. "Did you get bit?"

Bones drew out his knife.

Scrubs saw it and panicked. "What? You're crazy, man."

Bones gripped the knife handle. "Answer the question, Scrubs," he demanded.

"No! I don't . . . I must have scraped my leg getting dragged out there. Blaze, come on. You saw what happened."

"I didn't see much of anything, Scrubs," Blaze confessed. "When I woke up, you were already halfway to Manila. For all we know, that could be—"

Bones struck before he could finish. Blaze glimpsed a flash of metal. The next thing he knew, the knife was buried in Scrubs' neck.

Blaze shouted. "What the fuck?"

Scrubs staggered back, eyes wide with surprise. He fell to his knees, pawing at the knife handle. Blood foamed from his mouth, guzzled from his neck. His lips opened and closed like a fish gasping for breath.

Finally, his eyes rolled back, and the doctor's lifeless body collapsed to the ground.

And just like that, Scrubs was gone.

Blaze held out his knife at Bones and backed away.

Bones raised his hands in front of him. "Take it easy, Blaze."

"You fucking murderer. He was your friend."

"He was infected," Bones said matter-of-factly. "And that's cute. A hitman accusing me of murder."

Blaze snarled. "I should slit your throat right now."

"Check his leg," Bones said calmly. Scrubs' body lay face down on the ground. "Go ahead," challenged Bones. "Check it." He moved back, giving Blaze room.

Without taking his eyes off the pimp, Blaze got down on one knee. Carefully, he raised Scrubs' pants leg. Three deep, parallel cuts ran across the doctor's shin. After examining them, Blaze was positive that the wounds would match the nails of the zombie he'd just killed.

He got up and replaced his knife under his belt. "You were right," he said, lowering his voice. "There's an injury on his leg. That's where the bleeding came from. Zombie must have done it."

Bones breathed a sigh of relief. "See? I told you. Within a few hours, Scrubs would have turned into one of those things."

Blaze looked down at the body, and then, something occurred to him. "Where were you when Scrubs was attacked?"

"What are you talking about?" Bones asked. "I was right behind you."

"Right. You were *behind* me."

"What's your point, Blaze? What are you getting at?"

Their eyes met. "My point is, even I couldn't tell that Scrubs had been bitten or scratched. How is it you were so sure?"

The silence drowned out the wind and the buzzing mosquitoes. Finally, Bones sighed and ran a hand through his hair. "I wasn't. I just couldn't take that chance."

Blaze stared at his friend, speechless.

Bones looked right, then left, surveying the land. He turned to Blaze. "We should get moving. What happened here is bound to stir up more trouble."

***

Only the strong survive.
To the victor go the spoils.
Nice guys finish last.
You snooze, you lose.

There are about a hundred other sayings and quotes, but they all mean the same thing: Man up or get fucked up. In the office, during a game of tennis, whether you're studying to be at the top of your class, running a marathon, or avoiding being someone's bitch in prison, the sayings all apply.

Bones showed no remorse over the murder of Scrubs. Perhaps he'd embraced the philosophy.

The pimp led the way, and Blaze followed. Blaze didn't say anything, but he didn't want to take point. He didn't like the idea of his back turned to Bones.

Was it murder? Scrubs had been injured in his scuffle with the zombie. He'd been infected and was as good as dead anyway. Did killing him constitute as murder?

Scrubs.

They'd left their friend's body.

"Shouldn't we at least bury him?" Blaze had asked.

"There's no time," said Bones. "He's dead." They walked farther until finally, they reached the base of the mountain. "I've never been this far before," Bones said, panting.

"Do we turn back?"

Bones shook his head. "No. I say we keep going. We've come this far. Maybe there's a cave up there, some place less exposed."

Blaze looked up. The climb was steep. There were large outcroppings of boulders but no zombies as far as he could tell. The mountain would give them a better vantage point over the land, and the boulders offered concealment. The thought of shelter and a chance to rest was like a wet dream.

Bones studied him, waiting. "Well?"

"All right," Blaze said. "Lead the way."

***

Halfway up the mountain, lightning flashed, occasionally illuminating their surroundings. Shadows pounced and shifted, disorienting them.

They pressed on, Blaze fueled by the zombie he had killed and Bones, by the life force that had once belonged to Scrubs.

Another flash of lightning revealed a small opening on the face of the mountain. At first, Blaze thought he was seeing things, but another strobe-like flash confirmed it.

Fate had finally smiled down on them. It was about time, too. The crazy bitch had been holding out long enough.

It was a cave.

They'd finally found shelter.

***

They paused at the mouth of the cave.

It was dark inside there, and even the occasional lightning did little to penetrate the gloom.

When Blaze was a child, his father—a lazy, unemployed bastard who thought knocking up Blaze's mom earned him the right to be called a dad—had locked him inside a broom closet for an entire night.

Blaze couldn't remember what he'd done to anger his father. Maybe it wasn't so much something he did. Maybe his dad was just a sadistic psycho.

That closet terrified him and was by far the darkest place he'd ever known.

Until now.

As they stood outside the entrance of the cave, Bones whispered, "What're you thinking?" It was as if he believed raising his voice might awaken something horrible inside.

"Should I stay, or should I go?" Blaze answered, quoting the song by The Clash.

"It's messed up, I know, but what other choice do we have?"

"We could keep going," Blaze offered.

"And go where? The weather here is crazy. You want to get struck by lightning and turn into a crispy critter? Besides, we might not find another place like this."

Blaze tried to peer into the darkness. "I wouldn't exactly call that a bad thing."

"Point taken," Bones said. "I'm just saying we were looking for shelter, and we found it. You weren't seriously expecting a five-star hotel, were you?"

Inside, sinister shapes skulked and hissed. A dozen eyes blinked menacingly in the dark. Instinct told Blaze that death awaited them inside the cave.

Something roared. It didn't come from within the cavern but at the foot of the mountain. In unison, Blaze and Bones turned.

Bones cursed like a drunken truck driver having a bad day.

Steadily climbing up the mountain was the gigantic beast. The only thing slowing the creature down was the loose rocks on the soil which caused it to slip.

Bones' face contorted with fear. He grabbed Blaze's shoulder and shoved him up the mountain. "Run!"

Blaze didn't need to be told twice. He hurried up the slope, no longer caring if he was behind or in front of Bones. They had a bigger problem than petty trust issues, and that problem was steadily making its ugly way up the mountain, showing no signs of slowing down.

A quick ascent was treacherous. It was dark, and the loose soil and gravel shifted under their weight. A slight misstep could lead to a fracture or more serious injuries. Rather than taking the direct route, Blaze zigzagged up the slope, reducing the risk of an accident. Bones followed suit, repeating the word *shit* like some sort of Buddhist chant.

Below them, Blaze could hear the monstrosity snort and growl. It was closing in.

"Move your ass, Blaze!" Bones shouted.

They had to devise a plan. Blaze knew there was no way they could outrun the hellish beast. Nevertheless, he quickened his pace. Twenty yards to the left, then twenty to the right. A jagged bolt of lightning ripped the sky, painting their ghost-like faces in its phosphorescent wake before plunging them back into darkness. Thunder echoed like a thousand tumbling bowling pins.

They rounded a boulder the size of a New York cab. Blaze felt his heart against his ribcage like a fist pounding on a wall. He could hear his racing pulse in his head. He looked back and saw that Bones had stopped. Bones rested a shaky hand on the boulder's surface. He breathed heavily and coughed. He stared at Blaze.

"What the hell are you stopping for?" Bones said above the rumble of thunder. "Move! I'm right behind you." He pushed himself off the boulder.

Blaze nodded and continued on their path, breaking left. He breathed through his mouth, supplying his starving lungs with much-needed air.

A miscalculated step caused Bones to slip. Pebbles rained down the side of the mountain. Bones screamed.

Blaze hurried back to his friend's side and inspected the damage. Bones had accidentally stepped into a fissure on the ground. Working fast, Blaze freed the leg and helped his friend up. Bones took a step and crashed back on the ground. He writhed in pain. "Motherfucker!"

Bones stared at his leg, touching it gingerly. He hissed in pain. He looked up at Blaze, anger in his eyes and fear in his voice. "It's broken. Just leave me." Blaze didn't know how to respond. "Damn it, Blaze. Snap out of it."

"I'm not leaving you," Blaze said.

"Don't be stupid."

"I'm not." Given the gravity of the situation, it felt childish to resort to name calling.

"Just stubborn."

Sticks and stones.

In the distance, the beast roared as if agreeing with Bones' assessment.

"Look," Bones said, sounding urgent, "I'll only slow you down. If that ugly fuck comes for me, you might actually have a chance of getting away." He pulled out his knife. He grinned, and there was a hint of madness in his eyes. "Besides, I don't intend to go down easily."

Blaze knelt beside Bones and tried to lift him, but his friend shoved him back.

"What's wrong with you?" the former pimp fumed. "Didn't you hear? Get out of here, you son of a bitch."

"I already told you I'm not leaving."

Bones held out his knife and pointed it at him. "Then I'll kill you myself."

"And then what?" Blaze asked. "The way I see it, you can either let me help you, or we can both die here." Precious seconds ticked by. "So what's it gonna be?"

"Fine," Bones relented. "Damn it, Blaze. You are one stubborn son of a bitch."

Blaze grinned. "Yeah, you said that already."

He repositioned himself and got down on one knee. Bones draped his left arm around the hitman's shoulder, and Blaze wrapped an arm around his waist.

"On three," Blaze said.

Bones nodded, his lips pressed together to form a straight line.

"One . . . two . . . three!"

Bones managed to get his good leg under him, and

pushed himself to a standing position. He leaned against Blaze, steadying himself. Sweat dripped from his chin.

"Ready?" Blaze asked.

"About as ready as any guy with a broken leg."

A roar erupted in the inky darkness. It was too close for comfort.

Blaze and Bones exchanged glances.

"Guess that'll have to do."

***

In the wild, Mother Nature equips all her children. The lion has strength, teeth, and claws; but the gazelle has the gift of speed. The crocodile has stealth, an armored hide, and powerful jaws; but the migrating wildebeest travel in great numbers.

Hence, the playing fields are always even.

Not today, though, for Mother Nature did not lend a hand in the creation of this ferocious beast whose sole purpose was to kill any creature it encountered.

Bones leaned against Blaze. He kept the weight off his broken leg but still grimaced with every step. Each step felt like a hundred; every yard felt like a mile. Blaze supported him, but the exertion was slowly taking its toll.

Finally, they collapsed on the ground, so exhausted, Bones hardly cried out in pain.

"It's hopeless," the former pimp murmured.

"We still have the high ground," Blaze pointed out. "That should be worth something."

Bones laughed. His voice teetered on the edge of madness. "I'll tell you what it's worth. It gives us a courtside view of our deaths, that's what."

Blaze ignored him and quickly scanned the area.

"Maybe there's something here. Something we can use to defend ourselves."

"Not unless there's a bazooka lying around, I'd say we're fucked. We've got two knives, and that's it. They're little more than toothpicks against that thing."

Blaze kept searching, his eyes panning back and forth. There had to be something he'd missed. A stick he could fashion into a spear . . . Anything!

Bones tossed Blaze his knife. "Take it. You'll need all the help you can get."

Blaze stared at the blade but made no move to take it.

His friend lay down on the ground, sprawled on his back. Tears welled in his eyes. "I'm sorry about Scrubs. He was my friend, too."

"It wasn't your fault he was hurt."

"But I didn't know that," Bones sobbed. "Didn't know for sure, but I killed him anyway."

Blaze finally picked up the knife and slipped it under his belt. "Maybe he's in a better place," he offered Bones. "Maybe killing him set him free."

Bones sniffed and wiped his eyes with the back of his hand. "God, I hope so." He smiled as he pictured Scrubs in his mind. "Maybe he's living it up right this moment. Maybe the guy's watching us right now and laughing his ass off."

"That sounds like Scrubs all right."

"You still have a chance to get out of here, Blaze."

Blaze shook his head. "I already told you I'm not leaving you."

Bones nodded, knowing there was nothing he could say to change his friend's mind.

Something moved. Something big. The time was almost upon them.

"You know what this reminds me of?" Bones asked.

"What?" Blaze took out his knife and steadied his breathing. They weren't dead yet.

"The story of David and Goliath. When I was a kid, my mom read me that story every night before I went to bed." He chuckled. "Too bad we don't have a slingshot and a couple of stones, huh?"

"I'd much prefer a shotgun or a sniper rifle."

The gears inside Blaze's head began to turn as if a switch had been flicked. "Wait here," he said and ran off.

"*What?*" Bones asked, but Blaze was gone.

A silhouette appeared, towering over Bones. Two large, menacing eyes glowed like torches. The air reeked of death. Whimpering, Bones rolled over on his belly and crawled away. He felt warmth spread to his legs and realized he'd lost control of his bladder. He called out for Blaze, but his cries went unanswered. He was alone, helpless, with nothing to protect himself.

"Though I walk through the valley of the shadow of death, I fear no evil."

Even as he spoke the words, Bones knew it was a lie. He feared evil. He feared it big time. Hell, he'd pissed on himself. If that wasn't fear, he didn't know what was.

His chest and belly hurt like a bitch, so he rolled onto his back, propelled himself with his good leg, until he backed himself against the wall of a cliff.

There was no way he could scale the wall.

End of the line.

The beast was covered in grey scales, giving it a reptilian quality. Its single tusk, located at the bridge of its nose was the size of a roadside emergency cone. Eyes burned like pools of molten steel.

The feature that stood out the most, however, was its mouth. The serrated teeth were large and uneven, each one easily capable of severing a limb or munching on a human skull.

The nightmarish thing lumbered toward him casually as if it knew Bones had nowhere to go. It sniffed the air and licked its lips with a large, slimy, purplish tongue that seemed too large for its mouth.

Bones spotted some cracks on the cliff face and used them to pull himself to a standing position. If he was going to get slaughtered today, by God, it would be on his feet, not on the ground like some broken, two-bit punk. He leaned against the wall and faced the granddaddy of all nightmares.

Unconsciously, his hand clutched the crucifix around his neck. "Though I walk through the valley of the shadow of death, I fear no evil," he recited.

The beast made a strange, guttural sound. Bones thought it was impossible, but he could swear it was laughing.

"I fear no evil," Bones repeated, his conviction growing stronger. "I fear no evil."

Laughter.

"Do you hear me, you butt-ugly motherfucker?" Bones screamed in a final act of defiance. "I fear no evil!"

Evil roared, and the beast charged.

Bones closed his eyes but stood his ground.

Pebbles rained on the creature's head. The beast shook its head, blinking sand and grit from its eyes. Bones held out his hand, shielding himself against the dust.

Without warning a large, fridge-sized boulder

crashed on the behemoth's skull. The creature's skull caved in. The sound reminded Bones of the time when he was a kid and lightning had struck the large oak tree in old man Bloch's backyard and split it in two.

The hellish monster tipped on its side, and gravity did the rest. The beast collapsed, sending up a huge cloud of dust in its wake.

Bones coughed and fanned the dust away.

"Hey!" someone called from above.

Bones looked up, but couldn't see past the haze. "Blaze? You crazy bastard, is that you?"

"Yeah," Blaze answered. "I'm glad I didn't kill you. I'll be right down."

Bones had never been so happy to see someone. Blaze returned wearing a huge smile on his face.

"I thought you'd left me for sure," Bones said.

Blaze approached his friend. "The notion crossed my mind."

"Your little stunt could have killed me, you know."

Blaze chuckled. "Another thought that crossed my mind. You're lucky I didn't miss. It's not like I had a lot of boulders to go around." He looked at the fallen beast. "Those sons of bitches are heavy."

Bones shook his head, smiling. "I'll bet. Thanks."

Blood seeped out of the creature's cranium, but its chest continued to rise and fall.

"It's still alive," Blaze said.

Bones patted him on the back. "Kill it. The life force from a monster like that's sure to get you out of here. You make sure to tell Scrubs I said hi when you see him."

Blaze nodded. He took a step toward the beast, imagining what it would be like to finally leave this forsaken place. His body trembled in anticipation. He stopped. He turned and stared at his friend's broken leg.

Bones sensed his hesitation. "What's wrong?"

Blaze pulled out one of his knives and handed it to the former pimp.

His friend's brows furrowed as he stared at the blade. "What's this?"

"You do it," Blaze said. "Cut it across the throat. The flesh is softer there, and it'll bleed out faster."

Bones' eyes grew wide. "You're shitting me."

"Don't worry about me. I'll catch the next trip."

"Bullshit, man. This is your kill."

"You know, I never pegged you for a whiny bitch."

Bones laughed, and tears of joy welled in his eyes. "Still trying to be the good guy, huh?"

Blaze grinned. "I gotta walk the walk. Now go on before I change my mind."

Knife in hand, Bones hop-stepped toward the giant monster and found the area Blaze described—the throat. He took one last glance at the hitman.

Blaze nodded.

Bones turned back to the creature. He raised the knife high, and with all his remaining strength, plunged the blade into beast.

***

Three zombies—one female and two males—wandered the desolate land in search of food. Pus trickled from their noses and mouths. Neither the dreary landscape nor the mosquitoes bothered them.

A figure that had gone unnoticed emerged from the ground.

One of the male zombies was the first to spot him. It growled, drawing the attention of its companions.

The second male zombie, the hungriest of the three, charged, the other two close behind.

The figure stood his ground and made no attempt to flee. At the last minute, he pulled out a pair of sharpened knives.

The blades gleamed in the pale silvery light, slashing, cutting, and stabbing into undead flesh.

In this wretched land, the man fought like he was possessed. He attacked like a demon.

A demon destined for a far better place.

ANOTHER WAY OUT

TONIA BROWN

SLEEP WAS IMPOSSIBLE. As much as Blaze tried, he couldn't find rest—not in any real sense of the word. The best he could do was close his eyes and let his mind wander. This managed to refresh his worn and hungry body, though not by much. Just another terrible aspect of this brave new world, he supposed.

Blaze thought about this as he curled into a tighter ball under the shelter of the bush.

Where was he, anyways? What kind of place encouraged the kind of wholesale destruction Scrubs and Bones were talking about? Kill the zombies or kill the people. Either way you looked at it, killing was the only way out. Blaze knew it all to be true, too. It was the only thing he was sure of since awakening in this place.

Kill or be killed. That was the only way to leave here . . . wherever here was.

No way was this heaven, yet it didn't seem like hell. Not exactly. At least, not like any hell Blaze could ever remember hearing tale of.

He supposed—given the wide gulf of human culture that existed and all the possible myths within—

that there were a whole bunch of hells all over the world that he knew diddly squat about. Which one ended up being this real hell then? Maybe this was something from Oriental mythology, or Native American. Perhaps it was some kind of otherworldly playground for hell bound souls.

Actually, this place seemed more alien than anything else.

Alien.

The notion of this got Blaze wondering about those things that carted him out of the cavern and into the empty, endless night. The ones Bones called the Gatherers. Beasts in robes, with the red eyes and cold skeletal hands. They were obviously in charge. Or were they? Perhaps that was just another façade. Like the faint promise of release. The ever present sense of a storm that he knew would never come.

"Hey, Scrubs," Blaze said.

"What?" Scrubs said.

"Can you two keep it down?" Bones asked, raising his head. "I'm trying to sleep here."

"You know you ain't gonna sleep, moron."

"Won't stop me from trying." Bones settled back down and fell quiet.

"What is it, Blaze?" Scrubs said. "You made up your mind already?"

"I just wanted to know if anyone's ever talked to a Gatherer."

Bones laughed aloud at the question. Scrubs joined in, chuckling away.

"I'm serious," Blaze said. "Has anyone ever gone up to one and asked where we are? What in the hell this is all about? I don't mean attack them. I just mean, you know, talk to them."

Bones laughed louder, but Scrubs scolded the man into silence.

"Brother's got a question and you laugh at the man," Scrubs said. "Give him a break, he don't know any better."

"If he goes walkin' up to one of those things," Bones said, "and tries to have a conversation with it, he'll know better. He'll know better for about ten seconds before they rip his skin off in one piece." Bones settled down again, leaving Scrubs to explain it to Blaze.

"Man," Scrubs said. "You gotta understand, those things aren't like us. They practically ignore the zombies and the zombies seem all to glad to steer clear of them. But give those Gatherers a human, and that's a different story. They prey on us like we are here for their amusement, which we probably are."

"What if we aren't?" Blaze scooted out from under his bush and sat up. "What if they are trapped here, just like us? What if they have to follow the same rules we do? Maybe that's why they kill humans."

"What does it matter? They don't just kill people . . . they torture the fuck out of them until that person is dead, dead, dead. Those bastards hate us and show it every chance they get."

"But what if we got them on our side?"

Scrubs sat up and looked across the gully at Blaze. "You're out of your fucking mind, you know that? Get them on our side. What are you smoking?"

"I just think it's worth a try." Blaze returned to his place beside the bush, curling up on his side as he scooted under it again. "That's all I'm saying."

"Look," Scrubs said as he lay down. "You haven't been here as long as Bones and me. So let me give you a little piece of advice. Don't fuck with the Gatherers. The end. Got it?"

"Got it," Blaze said as he closed his eyes and began to plan just how he was going to that very thing.

***

The next morning—or rather 'morningish'; it was hard to tell considering the sky never featured more than the phosphorescent clouds and distant lightning—Blaze decided to cut his new friends free. It was obvious from their conversation the previous night that the guys had no intention of helping him in his quest to discover more about their apparent dictators. He didn't want to kill or harm the Gatherers. He just wanted to know where they came from, who they were, and why they were here.

And then maybe kill them.

Blaze had given it a lot of thought over the last few hours, and decided the best place to start would be at one of those communities the guys told him about. He needed to find someone who had been here for a long time, much longer than either Scrubs or Bones, someone on the verge of succumbing to the change, but not quite there yet. Anyone that had lived here for that long was bound to know far more than a pair of thugs trying to buy their way out of hell, one zombie kill at a time.

He didn't want to travel all the way to The Commons, or reveal his plan to the people that lived there. He reckoned a place as large, surviving for so long, was privy to some kind of special treatment from the Gatherers—if the beasts were really the ones in charge. Best to avoid it, he decided. No, instead he would head for the nearest small village.

Before he said his farewell, Scrubs told Blaze there was a small community named Tempest not ten miles east of where they spent the night. Should the path remain clear, Blaze supposed he could make it there in just a few hours.

"Is there anything I should know?" Blaze asked. "Anything else you haven't told me?"

"The zombies are fairly easy to kill," Scrubs said. "The people, not so much. Just keep in mind that any human you run into was sent here for a reason; a bad reason. Once upon a time, most of them were killers, which mean they probably still are. That's why they are so eager to kill again, because they know how."

"Just get a zee right between the eyes," Bones said, jabbing a twig in the air for emphasis, "and that should drop 'em."

"Between the eyes?" Blaze said.

"Yeah," Scrubs said. "Any damage to the skull will drop a zee. A blow with a blunt object will do it, if you hit them hard enough. But piercing their skull between the eyes seems to drop them like that." Scrubs snapped his fingers. "And don't worry about the bone getting in the way. They start to decay pretty rapidly, so a full on zee will be soft enough in the head to punch your blade through with ease."

"All right then," Blaze said. "Between the eyes."

They three men fell quiet for a moment.

"I guess this is goodbye then," Scrubs said.

"I guess so," Blaze said.

"Bye," Bones said. He almost looked happy that Blaze was leaving.

Scrubs held out his hand, "Take care of yourself."

Blaze shook the offered hand. "You too. Both of you. Thanks for helping me out."

"No problem. Sorry we can't help you more. I'd give you stuff to take with you, if we had any stuff."

"Damn it, Scrubs," Bones said. "He's got his knife, ain't that enough?"

"It'll have to be," Blaze said.

With nothing but the knife in his hand, the clothes on his back and the stolen shoes on his feet, Blaze set out for Tempest.

***

The trip was dull. Hours of endless walking with nothing more than the occasional dried bush to look at. Of course, all travel was dull as far as he was concerned. Regardless of spending twenty years on the force, and most of that roving all over the world, he always found travel a bore.

Blaze stopped in his tracks as he was struck by the sudden, clear memory.

He grinned as happiness overcame him for a golden moment. To remember something so vividly made him feel more human, less like an empty shell. He was a police officer? Of course he was. That explained the highly trained reflexes and combat knowledge. Maybe it also explained his thirst for answers, this burning need to investigate.

It didn't, however, explain why he was here.

Blaze tried to push the thoughts away as he trudged onward. Dwelling on whatever mortal sin landed him in this place was the last thing he wanted to do. Frankly, it was the only thing about this place that truly terrified him. What in God's name had he done to end up here?

Rape. Murder. Pedophilia. Torture.

No.

He couldn't waste time speculating on his sins. When they came back . . . if they came back, he would deal with it. Not until then.

Focusing on the joy of his recently returned memory, Blaze rolled the idea around in his mind. He was a police officer, no wait, that wasn't quite right. He was with some kind of Special Forces. Maybe FBI? CIA. Yeah. The title of Special Agent felt vaguely familiar. He was more than just a hometown badge kind of guy. Otherwise the idea of travel would've seemed like a grand thing, but to him it seemed mundane. Like something he used to do all of the time.

"Well, then, Special Agent Blaze," he said to the shrub beside of him. "Welcome to hell."

***

He made it two hours without interruption. According to his earlier conversation with Scrubs and Bones, that kind of thing was rare. One didn't just walk about and not get attacked. Blaze figured maybe the thugs roaming the landscape could tell he wasn't a man to be fucked with.

Maybe he just got lucky.

Either way, his luck eventually ran out.

At first he thought it was just the wind; a light groaning breeze traveling down from the distant mountains to his side. After a few minutes, the groaning grew louder and stronger, and he realized it wasn't coming from the mountains. The sound came from somewhere behind him. Blaze turned about to see a pair of shambling, grey bodies making their way toward him.

Zombies.

They didn't move like people, or at least like the other people he had seen here. The guys said the zombies were slow and clumsy. These two sure looked it.

Easy enough.

Blaze hefted the blade in his palm, measuring their approach, distance, and sizes. The smaller one on the left staggered a clean three paces behind its larger brother. That would give Blaze a few seconds to kill the first one before the second could get at him.

No problem.

Blaze stood, swaying from foot to foot, steadying his nerves as he waited to see which way the first zee would lunge.

It took a full five minutes before they caught up with him, thanks to their slow stagger and poor sense of balance.

Just as the first one reached out for him, Blaze stepped forward, meeting the lunge halfway. He shoved the tip of the blade in between the zombie's eyes. It slid in and slipped out as easy as a hot knife through warm butter. For a moment, Blaze doubted it did anything at all, but sure enough, the zee stopped, shuddered all over and fell to the ground.

The second zombie shuffled right into the fallen one and tumbled to the ground as well, reaching out for Blaze on the way down. Not expecting this, Blaze was dragged to the dirt along with the zee. It didn't take long for him to get his bearings again and he was on his feet in a matter of moments. Blaze flipped the blade over in his palm, grabbing it underhanded. He then jabbed it between the last zee's eyes. Again the blade went in and out with little resistance, dropping the zee with ease.

Blaze stepped back from the fallen pair and waited a few heartbeats to make sure they weren't going to get back up again. With a soft pop, the first corpse fell apart in a cascade of gray ash. The other followed in seconds. Blaze shuddered as a double rush of energy coursed through him from the kills. It wasn't nearly as much power he got from killing people, but it was enough.

"I don't think I will ever get used to that," Blaze said.

"Sure you will," someone said.

Brandishing his knife, Blaze turned about to confront this new enemy. To his surprise, he found a beautiful woman standing approximately ten feet from him. Blonde and tall, pale and shapely, she wore a dark and dusty robe cinched tightly about her curvy waist. A rucksack hung from one shoulder, while a curved blade was tucked into her belt. She peered at him with curiosity, her blue eyes sparkling in the phosphorescent of the sickly sky.

"Where did you come from?" he said, trying not to let her beauty keep him from losing focus.

"I was here the whole time," the stranger said. "It's hard to keep an eye on everything, isn't it? Especially when you're fighting zombies."

"No," Blaze said. He pointed his blade to the distance behind her. "I had my eyes on the prize the whole time. You weren't here ten seconds ago."

The stranger shrugged, the long sleeves of her robe fluttering with her movements. "Ten seconds. Ten minutes. What does it matter? I am here now. What are you going to do about it, young man?"

"Young man?" Blaze snorted. He had at least ten years on the chick. "Who do you think you are?"

"Wrong question, ask again."

He narrowed his eyes at her. "What are you doing here?"

"Nope. Try again."

Blaze stared hard at her now. What kind of game was this? He didn't have time to fool around with some woman in the middle of nowhere. He was too busy looking for someone who had been here for a long . . . oh . . .

"How long have you been here?" he said. "I mean in this place."

She smiled. "Very good. As near as I can recall, I've been here about a year."

"A year? Is that all?"

"It's long enough. I've been here long enough to know more than I should, but not long enough to change into one of those undead things, thank goodness."

Blaze snorted again. "Goodness? It's a little late to thank goodness for anything, isn't it?"

"Why? Do you believe everyone here is beyond redemption? That we are all irredeemable sinners, destined for something worse than even this?" She waved her free hand, motioning to the dead and barren landscape around them.

"Aren't we?"

"What do you think? And I don't mean what someone told you already. I mean what do you think?"

He looked down at the knife in his hand, and thought about the two men he killed without hesitation. About the power he gained with their final deaths. About how weak the zombies were by comparison. "I don't know."

"Good. Admitting you're stupid is the first step." With that, she turned and walked away from Blaze, heading toward the mountains in the distance.

It only took Blaze a few steps to catch up with her. "I never said I was stupid."

"You didn't have to say it. It was inferred."

Coming to a dead stop, Blaze's mouth hung open in surprise at this jab. He snapped his mouth closed as he caught up with her once more. "I don't think I like you very much."

"Good. Liking folks here will get you killed. Everyone knows that."

"Everyone just knows that, eh? Well, what do you think? And not just what someone told you."

The woman stopped in her slow shuffle and glance up to Blaze. He stood an easy foot and a half over her. She nodded to him. "All right then. Now we are getting somewhere. I'm Elena Balan." She held out her hand.

Blaze took her hand and shook it slowly. Something stirred deep inside, something that once upon a time might have been passion or lust. No sooner had it started when it stopped, leaving him feeling nothing toward the woman. Just another side effect of this place, he supposed. "Blaze."

"Nice to meet you, Blaze. I take it that's not your real name?"

"No." He released her hand and ran his over his red hair. "But you know your name? All of it?"

"Yup. Stay here long enough and all kinds of stuff come back to you." She looked to the ground and gave a sad sigh. "All kinds of awful stuff. Don't worry, though, your name will come back to you in time. As will . . . other things."

"You mean I'll remember why I am here."

"I do, and you will." She began to walk again.

"Where are you going?" he said, falling into step beside of her.

"Same place as you."

"I wasn't headed this way. I was heading east."

"East? What do you want to go that way for? Nothing out there but death."

"I was looking for a village called Tempest."

"Tempest is gone. Got overrun by those gray bastards about three days ago."

Blaze stopped walking and let the woman pass him on by. "Oh."

"Yeah. Like I said; nothing out that way but death. But if you want to make your way out of here on the back of zombie kills, that might be your best bet. It's an all-out zombie buffet that way. Don't let me stop you."

Blaze laughed as he caught up with her. "You know, you're all right for a broad." He winced at the slang.

"Broad? You're from the USA?"

He scratched his head. "I think so."

"I am from Romania, around the Dobrogea area. Don't think too hard about it, I guarantee you have never heard of it."

"You speak excellent English. I would've never guessed you were foreign."

She chuckled. "I was about to say the same thing. Your Romanian is perfect."

"But I'm not speaking . . . ah, I get it." Blaze snapped his fingers as it settled on him. "We're talking different languages but we can understand each other. Must be a side effect of this place."

"Good. You're quick. I like that."

"What else do you remember?" Blaze asked, eager to hear how much of her memories she got back. He considered it a possible glimpse to his own eventual recovery.

"I remember the vast sunflower fields of my homeland." She walked along at a maddening slow pace, with not a care in the world. "I didn't stay there long, but I always remembered the flowers. It was the first thing to come back to me when I got here."

"Ah," Blaze said, but he could tell she was just reminiscing.

"When I was old enough, I got out of there and got myself an education. This was something women in my village didn't do. Then I travelled a lot, all over the world. Lived an interesting life, from what I can remember. I eventually ended up in Germany. I taught at the university. Something else women of my time didn't do."

"What do you mean your time?"

She ignored him and pressed on with her story. "I also remember the bombs. I remember the screaming and the crying. I remember the soldiers marching. Always marching. The horrors. The denials. The deaths. I even remember my own death. How the fire consumed me. I shouldn't have ever gone to Dresden. I should've never left Romania. My father was right. I should've stayed home."

Blaze furrowed his brow. Dresden? Why did that sound familiar?

"I said don't think about it too hard," she said. "You

recognize the name because it's history for you. What's my present was your past."

"I don't think I understand you."

"I died in 1945."

Blaze's mouth was open before he realized he was gaping at her. "That's impossible."

"How so?"

"You said you've only been here for a year."

"And?"

"Well, how can you be here for a year if you died in 1945 because I died in . . . " Blaze's words trailed off as it all came back. His death. His final moments alive. He closed his eyes, letting the memory of it flood his very being.

"Yes? When?"

"2014," he whispered as a violent and bloody film played behind his eyes. "I remember because we just celebrated New Years the week before. I was working a case overseas, drugs and guns. Lots of each. We were tracking a cocaine operation in the . . . I think it was a jungle. I was beat to death with my own machinegun." He winced as a clearer, more painful image came into focus. "No, wait, I was beaten first, then they started cutting off bits of me, starting with my toes and working their way up to my—"

"Ugh, spare me the details, please."

Blaze opened his eyes and blinked a few times, trying to clear the tears away. The woman stood a few scant steps away, watching with worry.

"Sorry," he said. "I don't usually cry. At least, I think I don't."

"No worries," she said. "It's a traumatic experience to remember such a thing. And congratulations. Most people don't remember their own death for a good, long while."

"But you do. You remember a lot."

"Quite a bit, but not all of it."

"Do you remember what you did to end up—" Blaze started, but cut his question short when he realized how rude it was to ask.

"Yes," she said, guessing the question anyways, and returning to her slow and steady walk.

She said nothing else on the matter, and Blaze couldn't fault her. A short quiet period of time passed as they walked along in silence. Blaze was just wondering where they were headed, but before he could ask, she spoke again.

"You know there are two ways out of here, right?" she said.

"That's what I was told," he said.

"But you knew it already. Instinctively, and inexplicably, you knew the minute you woke up. Better than you know your own name, your own death, your own sins. You know how to escape from here but you don't even know who you are. We all know. We are reborn here with that knowledge. It is the tie that binds. Aside from our evil nature, of course."

"Is that what you think? That we are all evil?"

"Don't fool yourself. If you and I were saints, we wouldn't be here." Her mood soured as she swallowed hard. "I remember why I am here, and it is no prettier than my own death, I assure you. It is also the reason I abstain from participating in any more killing."

Any more killing? Blaze supposed she could be every bit the killer as everyone else around here.

"Once I remembered what I was here for," she

continued, "once that terrible truth returned to me, I made a solemn vow. No humans. No zombies. I will just remain here, wandering eternally, until I either die a final death or become one of the undead."

"Then what is the blade for?" Blaze said.

She touched the curved blade at her belt. "I keep it just in case, but I don't have to use it often. Otherwise I stay on the move and keep out of sight as best I can. It's strange to say this, but protection seems to find me."

"How?"

"You, for instance. If you hadn't wandered into my path, those zombies would've caught up with me for sure." She smiled at him, as if his presence pleased her in some way. "So Mr. Blaze, what's your plan? Zombies or humans?"

He chewed his lip for a moment, "Neither."

The woman raised a thin eyebrow. "Neither? I didn't take you for an abstainer."

"I'm not. I have a theory."

"Oh, this I have to hear."

"You know those Gatherer things, the ones in charge?"

"Yes?"

Blaze took a few minutes to tell her about his experience in the caves, how he woke up before they were done carting him outside. "I think those caves hold the answer. I think they are the real way out of here."

Elena nodded and rubbed at her chin. "Interesting. You know, I like you. You remind me of my brother. What I can remember of him, at least. Count me in."

Cocking his head, Blaze glared at her. "What do you mean, count you in?"

"I am coming with you."

Blaze kept his eyes on her as she moved ahead of him. "I'm sorry to say this, but no, you're not."

"Why, because I am feminine and fragile?"

"Well, yeah."

"Ah, I am, true. But I also know where the Gatherers gather."

He trotted up to her side. "What?"

"You think you know where you want to go? You're wrong. You think the Gatherers just hang around the catacombs waiting for a new body to appear? Hell no, young man. They have got far better things to do with their time. I know where they go after they deliver a new body here."

"They go back into the caves."

"Really? Did you see that with your own eyes? Or did someone just tell you that?"

He thought back to the moment he arrived here. He remembered hearing those beasts shuffle away but he didn't actually see where they went. She was right. He didn't know where he was going. "You know where they go?"

"I do."

"Tell me."

"I'll do you one better. I'll take you there."

"I can't let you do that."

"I don't remember asking permission, Blaze."

Blaze fell quiet as he realized he was stuck with the woman.

Whether he wanted her or not.

***

Her slow pace made the journey far longer than Blaze would've liked. He tried prompting her into a quicker stroll, but she insisted on taking her time.

77

"No need to rush," she said. "Those things will be there tomorrow and the next day and the next day."

"Yeah," Blaze said. "But I don't want to be here tomorrow, or the next day or the next day."

"I hate to burst your bubble, but I have no desire to rush into the arms of death. Slow and steady is fine for me."

"You let me worry about the Gatherers. I have a plan when it comes to them."

"Oh, ho, ho. A plan? Well, as much as it would humor me to hear how you plan on dealing with those near gods, I feel compelled to inform you I am not speaking of the Gatherers. I am talking about the Furnace."

"Furnace?" Blaze groaned. What fresh hell was this?

"That's right. I forget you don't know everything, do you?" The woman walked along at her maddeningly slow pace, but said no more.

Blaze wished he had a gun right at that moment. Not so he could shoot her. No. He wanted to put himself out of his own misery. "Okay. Tell me. What is the Furnace?"

Elena grinned, knowing she had gotten the best of him. "There is a strip of territory that has become an arena of sorts. Folks who want to die, go there to die. Folks who want to kill, go there to kill. But mostly, folks go there to test their mettle. The whole place is a foot deep with the ash of the dead. It's such a hotbed of death, that folks have dubbed it the—"

"Furnace," Blaze said over her. "I get it. So I take it we are heading right into this territory?"

"Correct."

"Where people go to die?"

"And fight."

"And you expect me to protect you?"

"Of course."

"How big is this Furnace?"

"A few miles wide."

Blaze slumped. "A few miles?"

"Just a few. Could be worse."

"How could it possibly be worse?"

"Could be a few more miles."

Blaze groaned again. "How far are we from the Furnace?"

"A day's journey." She chuckled to herself. "Could be worse."

Blaze ignored her bait, letting it rest at that.

They walked a long time with little discussion, only meeting up with the occasional zombie, which he put down without much effort. To his surprise, they ran into no other humans. It was as if they were the only two humans left on the face of this God forsaken plain.

"Where is everyone?" he said after a bit of silence.

"Most folks avoid this area," she said. "Wouldn't you?"

"Because of the Furnace?"

"Because of the Gatherers. The Furnace is just in the way. But you wish to see the ones in charge? I will take you to them."

"Yeah, I guess so."

"You remind me of a young Jew eager to meet the death squad."

"That's right. You were alive during all of that." Blaze knew he should just let it go, but his curiosity got the best of him. "So, what was it like, you know, the whole World War II thing?"

Elena grunted. "You mean the whole Holocaust thing?"

"Yeah. Sorry."

"So am I. It was horrible. So much death and dismay. So much fear. The air was thick with the screams of the damned and the smell of the charnel houses. It was much like this place, only sunnier."

"Were you, um, are you Jewish?"

"I was and am."

"Did you end up in one of those places? Those camps?"

"Me?" She sighed. "No. I witnessed their rise, but I never ended up on the other side of the bars. I was blessed with beauty . . . some say curse: Blonde hair and blue eyes. I was a stranger to my own community, but I was still a Jew at heart. I just didn't look like one. This gained me pity, as long as I lied about my faith and my past."

"And you did?"

She stopped and whipped about to face him, tears standing in her eyes. "I did what I had to do to survive. I tried to help, but those were difficult times. We all did things we don't want to talk about."

Blaze looked away rather than face her sorrow. "I'm sorry. I didn't mean to upset you."

She softened at his guilt. "I do not mean to yell. It was . . . it was a terrible time. I tried to help out. I worked with the underground. I passed information so others could escape."

"I'm sure you did what you could," Blaze said. "Let's not talk about it anymore."

"Agreed." She turned away from him to face the looming mountains once more, lifting her shaking finger as she said, "Besides, the outskirts of the Furnace is just over that rise."

Blaze was surprised by the sudden announcement. He looked up to the slight incline. It was just steep enough to hide what lay beyond. "Really? So close?"

"I suggest we camp by those bushes over there." She motioned behind her to a pair of desiccated bushes at the base of the rise, resting in a small depression. "We should be safe enough tonight. Like I said, no one comes around here because of the Furnace and the Gatherers. Those that do aren't interested in easy prey like us. In the morning we can strike out again."

"Sounds good." Blaze followed her to the bushes, glad to get off his feet for a few hours, if nothing else.

Elena made herself as comfortable as she could under one bush, while Blaze gravitated toward the other. The pair of small shrubs lay no more than a few feet from one another.

He studied the dried out branches, snapping off a thin twig as he dropped onto his backside. "What do you supposed happened to his place?"

"What makes you think something happened here?" she asked.

"It looks like things used to grow. I mean these bushes and the occasional tree. I've even seen some tough clumps of grass here and there. Things must've used to grow here. Something happened to change that."

"Interesting theory. You remain here long enough, and you could become a philosopher."

"Like you?"

"I am no philosopher, by any stretch of the definition." She relaxed under her dismal canopy and turned to look at Blaze. "Who were you?"

"I don't know."

"You do. You seemed to take to the idea of stalking thieves in the jungle with a certain finesse. I am sure you were prepared for such a thing."

"Is that so?"

"It is." She looked to the heavens as she added, "That and I can spot a liar at twenty paces."

Blaze lay back as well, looking up between the dried branches, into the strange, shifting clouds. "They were drug runners, not thieves. And I never said I was okay with it."

"You didn't have to, it was—"

"Inferred. You sure you weren't a shrink in your other life?"

"A what?"

"Never mind." Blaze put his hands behind his head and drew a deep breath, steadying his nerves as he pulled up the courage to share his recently returned memories. "I was, I think, a lawman of some kind. Either CIA or FBI. A Special Agent of some sort."

"A lawman?" Elena pushed herself up on one elbow to eye him. "If you were supposed to be on the right side of the law, then what in the world are you doing here?"

"I don't know. I guess I wasn't a very good officer. Maybe I was on the take. Or maybe I was overzealous about deadly force. No way to tell until it comes back to me."

"Won't be the first time. I met a judge a few days before we joined up."

"A benchwarmer, huh? Did he say what he was here for?"

She returned to her reclined position. "Apparently he had a penchant for young girls. The younger the better."

"Scumbag."

"Indeed. It was a pleasure to watch him die."

Blaze didn't ask for the particulars about that. Instead he closed his eyes and tried to get a little rest.

Little being the operative word.

***

"Blaze," Elena whispered. She touched his shoulder, shaking him lightly.

"What is it?" he said. Surely it wasn't time to get moving already? It was then that he realized she was lying beside of him, spooning him close enough to feel the heat of her body through his clothes.

Wow. When the hell did that happen? And how did he miss it?

"Someone's here," she whispered. Blaze attempted to sit upright, but Elena pushed on his chest, keeping him flat on his back as she continued to cradle against him. "Keep down," she said softly. "They will pass us by."

He held still, her hand against his chest, just inches from his thumping heart. She lowered her head to his shoulder, all but folding herself against his side, as if she were trying to vanish. The sound of footsteps in the dry dirt sounded around them. A few came close, but not enough to find them. Eventually, the footsteps faded into the distance. Elena patted Blaze on his chest as she lifted her head again.

"You can get up now," she said.

"I thought you said we were safe here," he said as he jerked upright. His heart continued thumping loud enough to fill his ears.

"I did, and we are."

"Then who the hell was that?"

"Does it matter? They didn't find us." She grabbed her bag and made herself comfortable under the brush again. "Trust me, nothing else is as important as going unseen. As long as they don't find you, you survive one more day."

Blaze couldn't ignore her authority on the subject. "I suppose you would know."

"What is that supposed to mean?" she asked, her voice snippy with attitude.

"I just meant because of the whole Nazi thing. Hiding out and stuff. Must've been hard."

"Ah, yes, of course." She rolled away from him, flashing a bare, pale thigh as she settled back down. "Get some more rest. We have a ways to go."

"I'll try."

Blaze tried not to fall into such deep thought this time, lest she sneak up on him again. Or, God forbid, someone else sneak up on him.

***

"Are you ready?" Elena asked as they gathered their meager things and headed out once more.

"Ready as I will ever be," Blaze said. "You sure this is the only way."

"I never said it was the only way, just the shortest."

"Then we don't have to go through the Furnace?"

"No. We could go around."

He thought about this a moment. "I take it the other way is much, much longer."

"At least ten times as long. The Furnace might only be a scant few miles wide, but it stretches as far as the eye can see, then farther. It would take a long time to go around."

"I see. I guess this is the only way then."

"The only direct way." She cocked her pretty head at him. "Unless you want to go around? Like I said, I am not eager to rush into death. I just supposed this was what you would desire most."

"It is. I don't want to go all the way around. If I have to fight a few folks for a few miles, then so be it."

Elena started toward the rise before them. "Have you killed anyone so far?"

"No," he lied. He wasn't sure why he did. Perhaps he didn't want her to think of him as that kind of killer. Zombies were one thing, but killing people seemed wrong. At least, now that he was here it did. "Just the zombies."

"Good. Try not to kill too many in here."

"Why not?"

She glanced to him with a look that said he had asked the stupidest question he could've possibly ever asked in the history of ever. "Do you want to speak with the Gatherers or not?"

"Yes, of course."

"Well then, if you kill twenty men before you get there you won't make it."

"Ah," Blaze said, the rules of this sick game coming back to him. "I almost forgot."

"It's a good thing I am here to remind you then."

"Yes, it is. I like you being here." He smiled, unsure what he meant by that.

"And I like you, but we don't have time for that

right now. Welcome to the Furnace." Elena held out her hand to the ashen gray landscape.

Blaze had noticed that the greenery—dead as it was—seemed to be getting thicker the closer they got to the Furnace, but now that they were over the crest of the place, Blaze could truly appreciate what that meant. He almost couldn't believe the difference between the barren desert behind him and the veritable forest ahead.

Trees and bushes and patches of grass and other shrubbery almost covered the ground. Half dead vegetation grew thick enough to create plenty of cover for anyone looking to hide. It almost surely held plenty of people in hiding already. And here Blaze and Elena just wandered up, out in the open, for everyone to see.

"We need to get out of sight," Blaze said.

"I was hoping you would say that," Elena said. She allowed Blaze to take the lead, following him as he made for the thin line of trees to their right.

"Get those motherfuckers!" someone cried, and three men jumped up from the clumps of tall, brown grass to Blaze's left.

Blaze fell into action, pulling his blade and setting upon the threats with practiced ease. The first one went down with a simple snick across the throat. Blaze pushed him aside as the man clawed at his open windpipe. The second attacker, a fat fucker with piggy little eyes, came at Blaze with a screeching holler. Blaze stepped back and gauged the man's onrush, leaping to one side just as the guy was almost upon Blaze. The attacker's momentum drove him to his hands and knees as he stumbled into the dirt. A quick handful of hair and a blade across the throat ended the second menace.

Blaze basked in the glow of the kill, the sudden rush of power it gave him. He also took this moment to turn his attention to the third and possibly most genuine threat of the crew. This man had to be at least a foot taller than Blaze, as well as a foot or two wider. He made his way toward Blaze with a slow and calculated pace. No rushing into danger here. This man knew what he was doing. He had that look of deadly experience all over him.

Blaze flicked the blade toward himself. "Come on, fucker, let's dance."

"Only if I can lead, little girl," the man said, then lunged for Blaze.

Blaze twisted out of the way, hoping to repeat the same trick as he did for the second attacker. The much bigger man anticipated this, and reached out in the very direction Blaze moved toward. Blaze tried to feign a jerk to the other side, but it was too late, the larger man had Blaze in a tight bear hug.

"What was that about dancing?" the man said, then laughed. He squeezes Blaze tightly.

Blaze wheezed. It took everything he had to hang onto his blade. The man squeezed again. Blaze just about shit himself with the effort of holding up against the powerful grip. His legs dangled in the air as the big man lifted him from the ground. When the man prepared to squeeze a third time, the first attacker finally stopped clawing at his throat and keeled over, sending a surge of energy into Blaze. Blaze put it to good use, by kicking out as hard as he could. Luckily, his right foot connected with something soft and tender.

The man howled while his eyes bulged from their

sockets. He dropped Blaze and immediately covered his own groin with both hands. Blaze didn't waste a moment gloating, instead he rammed the blade into each of the big man's eyes. Snick. Snick. As quick as a cobra strike. Blaze stepped back as the monster of a man fell to his side and writhed in pain.

"Finish him," Elena said.

Blaze looked over to find her cowering against a dead tree, the back of her hand hovering over her mouth in horror.

"Please," she said. "I can't stand it."

He nodded, and freed the man from the pain with a quick swipe of the blade. The body fell into ash, sending another jolt of energy into Blaze. He breathed deep, inhaling the power with each breath.

"Feel better?" she asked.

"I do," he said.

"Good, because here come some more." She nodded to the trees behind him.

Blaze turned about to face this new menace with grin.

This was sort of fun.

***

"How many does that make?" Elena said.

"Dead or dropped?" Blaze said.

"Dead."

"Aside from the two dozen we fought off, there is, oh . . . " Blaze counted back as best he could. "Five at the border and six near the dried up watering hole. Another four by that burnt out building, whatever in the hell that used to be. Then these two, brings it to—"

"Seventeen," she said over him. "You should try to

slow down a bit. Three more and you'll go to the great beyond."

Blaze nodded his understanding. He tried to ignore the surge of seventeen dead men coursing through his veins as he patted down the ash from his shirt and pants. At first it was hard, fighting and killing like that, but once the power of the other men ripped through him, well that was all she wrote. It was all Blaze could do not to kill. The last two were a matter of smashing skulls together, simple as that.

Somehow, during all of this, Elena managed to keep her hands out of dealing death. She coached him, led him, but never once lifted a finger to take a life.

"Where do you suppose people go after this?" he said.

"Who knows?" she said. "Hopefully somewhere better."

"Hopefully. How much farther?"

"Just another mile or so. Are you ready for this?"

"I'm not sure."

"What are you going to do, if you don't mind my asking?"

"I had a lot of ideas at first, but now that I am here, I don't really know."

Elena chuckled. "I figured as much. You aren't rethinking your strategy are you?"

"What do you mean?"

"Three more men and you could be out of here."

One more would send him on, actually, but she didn't need to know that. With the two men he killed when he first arrived, and the last seventeen, he topped at nineteen. One more and he was gone. "No. I don't want to go that way. I only defended myself. I didn't come here seeking to kill those men. Understand?"

"I understand."

"I want you to know I am not like that. I didn't want to kill those men."

"Like I said, we all do what we must to survive." She turned away and began walking toward the nearing mountain range.

Blaze fell into step behind her again. "I've never seen people so bloodthirsty. I mean, this place is overrun with zombies, and they're so placid. If we all helped each other instead of fighting each other, we could set up a corral and take turns just slaughtering them wholesale."

"I wished I knew what drove them," she said.

"I suppose people just fall back on what they know."

"What do you mean by that?"

"A lot of those men bore prison tattoos and scaring. They're probably murderers, every single one. They died in the chair or whatever, and woke up here? Of course they're gonna take the kill or be killed option. It's all they know."

"That's a very astute observation."

They went quiet again as they neared the mountains, the terrain changing from nearly dead grassland to gravel and rock and stone. Blaze peered to the foot of the mountains, seeking whatever cave or opening Elena was leading him to.

She held out her hand, warning him to stop. "Hold still." She looked back and forth, across the rocky landscape. "Over there. That rock. Get behind it. Now!" She pushed him along, forcing him behind a large boulder to their right.

Blaze ducked behind the boulder with her, wondering what was going on now. He thought he was keeping an eye open for danger, but obviously she sensed something he didn't. Or couldn't.

Elena pushed him against the rock with one hand and peered around the edge of the rock with the other. "Damn it. Too soon."

"What is it?" he said.

"They are here."

"They? How many?"

"Enough." She turned to look at him, something akin to pity rising to her blue eyes. "They must've seen us coming. I'm so sorry. I thought we would have more time."

"Don't be sorry. This is what I am here for."

"I wished they would've waited. I really enjoyed talking with you. I almost regret bringing you along."

Blaze chuckled. "Bring me along?" He laughed again. "What are you talking about? I brought . . . you . . . along . . . " his words faded as he watched her shaking her head. A sensation crept over him, one that said he had been played for a fool by a pretty lady. Even without his memories, he knew this wasn't the first time. "What have you done?"

She stared hard at him, all trace of emotions draining from her face. "You were right when you said we fall back on what we know."

"What?" he whispered, more confused than ever.

"You were right. We do what we know. What we remember. Do you know what I remember?"

"No."

"I remember how many extra rations I got for every Jew I turned over."

He shook his head at her. "Rations? What are you talking about?"

"Do you know how many days of extra life a whole family would buy you? How much freedom a rabbi won you?"

Blaze understood then. She was talking about her past life, but what kind of life did she lead? Blaze had spent the last few hours wondering what horrible thing she had done to land here, but all at once he didn't want to know. His stomach twisted as she pressed on with her confession.

"And it was easy," she said, a smile finally tracing her lips. "So simple. They were so trusting. Of me. Of anyone. All you had to do was tell them you were going to help them. You got them all in one place, and then called the authorities. That was it."

"You turned over your own people?" he asked.

She ignored him, standing tall as she backed away from him. "They called us Greifers behind our backs. Catchers. But I called myself smart. I did what I had to do. I survived. I always survive." By this time she was well out of the boulder's cover, standing out in the open. She raised her finger, pointing to him. "There he is. Be careful, he is dangerous."

Blaze furrowed his brow, wondering for a half second who she was talking to. When a pair of robed figures eased into his peripheral vision, it dawned on him what was really happening here. She turned over her own people to the Nazis, and now she was doing the same to him. Elena hadn't brought him here to confront the Gatherers. She brought Blaze here to sacrifice him to them.

"This was a setup?" he said, mostly to himself.

"Are you just now figuring that out?" she said.

"How can you do this?"

"Easy. I get people to trust me. Get them in one place. Call the authorities. Easy as that. Just like before."

Blaze held out his blade, waving it at the robed beasts approaching from both sides. "Keep back. I'm warning you."

This wasn't right. This wasn't what Blaze wanted. He was supposed to sneak up on them, not the other way around. He was supposed to get inside, supposed to find out the truth, supposed to win his own way out of here on his own terms. Not to die screaming under the torturous blades of the enemy.

Again.

"It's no use," Elena said. "You can't kill them. You can't even hurt them. If you put up a fight, you'll just make it worse on yourself. And it's going to be pretty bad as it is already. Don't make it harder."

In the echo of her warning, Blaze found a shining gem of hope. He couldn't kill the Gatherers, but he could kill her. One more kill would make twenty, and twenty would get him out of here. Again, it wasn't what he wanted, but right now it would do. Anything that didn't involve letting those bastards get their hands on him would do. The death of the other nineteen men surged through him. He drew up this fresh power, and focused it on his new target.

Blaze sneered at Elena. "You bitch."

"I might be a bitch," she said, "but I've only got three more suckers to turn over and they say they will let me free from here. You, though. You will suffer beyond torment. You will wish you let those other men kill you before this is done. You will—"

"Bitch!" Blaze shouted as he pushed against the boulder, leaping toward Elena.

The act took her and the Gatherers by total surprise. Blaze streaked past them and straight onto his new prey. He landed square on her, knocking the pair of them to the ground. He plunged the blade into her chest, over and over, relishing in the spray of blood and wild screams of the cold hearted woman underneath him. It was a matter of moments before the Gatherer's swooped in and pulled him off of her, yet the deed was done. Even if he hadn't killed her, he got his licks in, and that's all he cared about.

Elena groaned and rolled around in the dirt. "You bastard! You god damned bastard!"

"I suppose you would know," he said, and laughed aloud.

"It won't matter. You will still suffer."

Blaze's skin tingled with that familiar rush of oncoming stolen life. "I don't think so. You see, you aren't the only one that lied. I killed two men before we met. That makes nineteen. Not seventeen. You make twenty. Thanks for that."

The woman gave one last groan and fell still, her body disintegrating to a pile of ash just as Blaze's very being all but burned with the power of her death. His hands began to shine, turning from flesh to white light. This effect ran up the length of his arms, to his elbows and shoulders. The Gatherers dropped him and backed away, shielding their hooded faces and shrieking at the bright light.

Blaze closed his eyes and prayed to whatever

goodness there was left in the universe. As the light consumed him, his memories flooded back to his tired mind, all at once, and with it he finally knew what he had done to deserve a visit to this place.

And he had deserved it. No doubt about that. He didn't know where he was headed, but he hoped he would end up somewhere he could atone for his mistakes, now that he understood exactly what they were.

THE BATTLE AGAINST OURSELVES

ALEX LAYBOURNE

BLAZE'S FIRST NIGHT in the new world was not one he cared to relive.

The temperature plummeted and as the phosphorous atmosphere lit the barren landscape, the ground sparkled with frost.

They had made a fire. Bones and Scrubs had tried hard to persuade Blaze into foregoing the exhausting task of creating the flames, but he was persistent. After a long discussion, he relented.

Blaze sat on the cold ground, the knife firmly clenched in his fist. He shivered and pulled his knees up to his chest. Now he understood why his companions had been so against the idea. He could feel none of the fire's warmth. Seeing the flames, and knowing the absence of heat, only served to heighten the bone aching cold. Not forgetting that the exertion of creating the flames had produced a hunger and thirst—which he'd been assured, would only be quenched through dealing out death. Then, his companions had clearly explained one kill was never enough.

The sky was clear; black as onyx and filled with stars. More stars than Blaze thought possible. They shone in every color imaginable and held various shapes. It was as if they had been embedded into the surface of reality.

Beside him, Bones and Scrubs lay still. Blaze could not tell if they were asleep, but it mattered little to him. This was his world now, and he would have to find a way to survive.

They had explained to him what it took to survive. Kill the undead, the same monsters he would become if he didn't find a way out soon enough. He could also kill the living. That would be the quickest exit, if his conscience could handle it. Twisting the knife in his hands, seeing the flames reflect on the steel blade, he thought he could. Then there were the Gatherer's—fire breathing demons that controlled the lands. Kill one of them and your passage was as good as guaranteed. Passage to what . . . nobody knew. It was just an assumption, and logic. There needed to be a way out.

It didn't matter either way. Blaze knew what the real fight was.

It was against time.

He could not remember much about his life, but he felt sure that fighting was part of it. He tightened his grip on the knife and felt confidence surge through him.

A gust of wind rolled across the flat prairie, and Blaze was sure he could hear the screams of those trapped in the mountains.

It was not the disembodied screams that kept Blaze awake that night, but sounds much closer to home. He jumped at everything, nervous that some Purgatory-produced Hellhound would emerge from the shadows and eat them.

Something growled to his right.

Blaze turned around, knife held out before him. His hands shook. The source of the growl moved. It was behind him now. They were surrounded. Blaze sat upright. He would be ready when they came.

Nothing came.

Blaze had been with Bones and Scrubs half of the day, and all of the night, but he had no idea how long he had been dead before the Gatherers had dumped him there. He forced himself to think back, to pull some strand of memory from his mind, but there was nothing.

Shifting, Blaze sought a more comfortable position on the hard ground, but there was none to be found.

***

Blaze woke stiff and still tired. The cold had seeped into his bones and the process of rising to his feet elicited a series of creaks and groans from his body.

"How was the first night?" Bones asked as he sat up. Stretching, every joint in his body seemed to give a satisfying pop.

"I didn't sleep a wink," Blaze answered.

Bones laughed. "You'll get used to it." He smiled and spat a thick ball of phlegm into the dying fire. The embers gave an angry hiss and sent a cloud of glowing ash into the air in protest. Beside them, Scrubs rose and went through a similar morning ritual.

"So, what's the plan for today?" Bones asked. Blaze was thrown by how relaxed the two men seemed to be with everything. They approached the world as if they were merely gearing up and heading to work.

"Well, we need to get this guy caught up." Scrubs pointed at Blaze. "At least get him his first couple of kills." He smiled at Blaze and gave him a wink.

"All right then. Let's find me a fresh face to kill." Blaze didn't recognize the words that came out of his mouth. The way the violence rolled from his tongue made him shiver. The willingness should have scared him.

His hand tightened around the blade and he felt a change beginning to sweep through his body. It started in his voice. In the words he spoke. Soon it became something much more. A hunger, a desire.

"I think we should learn to walk before we run." Bones laughed, clapping Scrubs on the shoulder. "Bambi here thinks he's ready for the big game."

"That's a sure fire way to get yourself killed. Especially out here." Scrubs walked up to Blaze and clapped him on the shoulder. "Let's find you a couple of zombies first. Easy kills, get yourself worked into it." Scrubs smiled, while Blaze merely offered a stern look in response.

"I did well enough yesterday." Blaze offered.

"Ah yes, and I am sure you will be way better at this than we are, but you've been here a day now. The rules change. The body stiffens. Let's just warm you up today and see where things take us." Scrubs began to walk, kicking out what remained of the fire.

At first Blaze didn't move. He felt rage building up inside him. The two friends had laughed at him. The sound of their entertainment echoed in his head, increasing with every reverberation until it was deafening. Blaze gripped the knife until his hand cramped. It wasn't until Scrubs' hand fell onto his shoulder that he was brought back into the present.

"Come on, man, we're just pulling your leg." Scrubs led Blaze away from the camp. "Who knows, maybe you were some kind of serial killer in the real word. All I know is that things are different over here. Everything feels different. So let's take down a couple of zeds and see where we stand." There was a calm air to the words Scrubs spoke, and it was easy to imagine him as a doctor. They joined Bones, who was waiting for them.

"You're part of the team now, Blaze." Bones smiled. "We need to get you caught up in the numbers, and then we can all get out of here at the same time." He raised his arm and pointed to the west. "I think I see the perfect target." The shuffling figure was a few hundred meters away and appeared to be moving with no real direction or purpose.

"Great, let's get going." Scrubs clapped Blaze on the back and they set off.

The creature became more aggressive as they drew closer. In life, it had been a woman. Her once large breasts hung low against her body, empty skin sacks that reached her navel. Her skin had a grey pallor. Her body was covered in blisters and lacerations, while the stench she emitted was truly the worst thing Blaze had ever encountered.

"She's all yours, buddy." The two men smiled at Blaze. "Remember, go for the head."

Blaze followed their orders, eventually. By the time the blade was driven through the woman's skull, it had been used to pierce her flesh close to the thirty times. A fury had settled over Blaze's mind; red mist clouded his vision, and all Blaze wanted to do was get it out. Purge his system.

When the bloody mess of a body fell to the ground, Blaze felt a sudden calm wash over him. This was followed by a second sensation, one he could not place. It left a foul taste in his mouth.

Blaze's companions stood with looks of surprise and even a little fear on their faces. They must have seen the change in his demeanor, however, as Bones soon spoke up. "They don't taste too good, but they will keep you going." His voice had lost the friendly tones it had before the kill.

Blaze stood panting, exhausted. His muscles tingled on the slight high from the zombie woman´s essence. It rolled through him like a slow shiver.

"Well, I'll be eating fresher meat soon." Blaze answered.

His lips pulled back into a smile and he felt the red mist descend once more. He waited as it enveloped him. Blaze welcomed it, like an old friend coming home.

"Lighten up, dude." Scrubs moved forward. "It's heavy the first time, but it gets easier." Scrubs faced Blaze, his arms forward, hands open.

"I bet it does." Blaze sneered. His words came out as a growl. He lunged before either man had heard his response.

Scrubs was the first to fall. The blade swept through the air and sliced the skin of his throat, splitting the flesh across the full available width. There was a moment, a brief second when there was no blood. The gaping wound across Scrubs' throat was clean, the wet meat exposed. A look of shock froze on his face. Then the blood came. It came in a flood that jettisoned from the wound. A burst hit Blaze in the face. It was strange because the warmth of the blood seemed to scald his skin.

Bones had hardly seen what happened, or rather, it was unclear to him. By the time Scrubs fell to his knees, gasping for air, it was too late.

Blaze drove the blade into Bone's gut. However, the large man was not going to be finished that easily. Bones cried out in pain and pushed Blaze away. The power surprised Blaze, who stumbled backwards, leaving his knife buried in his companion's gut.

"Why?" Bones asked as he stumbled forward. His death was inevitable, yet he refused to meet his end on his knees.

"You said it yourself. You have to make tough decisions if you want to survive." Blaze smiled; his rage held firm. "I guess I'm just not much of a team player." Blaze moved forward and feigned a punch. When Bones flinched, Blaze adjusted his balance and threw a palm heel strike into the bridge of Bones' nose. The bone crunched and the big man staggered backwards, falling to his knees.

Blood covered Bones' face and pain blinded him. Blaze crouched down and pulled the blade free, twisting it slightly as he did.

"It's nothing personal, Bones. I'm getting out of here, and you two . . . well, you were just in the wrong place at the wrong time." Blaze drew the knife over Bones' throat and hushed him as the final moments of his life ticked by.

Blaze sat with the two bodies for a while, positioned between both men. He closed their eyes and made sure they were comfortable.

The sensation of absorbing the two men's essence

was far more intense than after killing the zombie. It was a powerful, full-body experience that lasted for a few seconds, during which time Blaze was held immobile.

Blaze moved on, making sure he stole Bones' shoes. They were a little too big for him, but much better suited to wander the barren landscape.

The day was hot, and as Blaze moved he found himself wondering where he was heading. His two dead companions had explained the general layout of the land, but the exact geography of the world had been skipped.

There was no shortage of zombies for Blaze to kill, but it soon became apparent that there were plenty of other creatures in the world that were more than willing to kill the undead. The largest of which were creatures with the appearance of wolves, only larger and thicker. They had wide, powerful shoulders, and thick muscular legs. They would charge at their prey and remove limbs in a single swipe. With unbroken strides, they charged through small groups of people and zombies alike. The human victims of these creatures screamed as they were attacked, but had no time to even consider mounting an offense.

Blaze had set his eyes on them, three easy kills. The mist had formed in his mind's eye, but then he had seen the creatures making their move.

He had no idea where they came from, charging toward the group.

It wasn't even a fight.

The new additions to the world didn't stand a chance.

Blaze took shelter behind a rocky outcrop, waiting

for the creatures to leave so that he could continue his journey.

The presence of the wolves, a pack no less, did allow Blaze the chance to get an approximation of his location. Bones and Scrubs had told him of a forest. A zombie filled forest, chockfull of death. Nobody in their right mind would go there.

Even in a world such as this, Blaze assumed that the wolves would stick close to the trees. This thought allowed him to place the forest away to his left, the vague direction he had been heading in. Until then, Blaze had moved with no set objective; a plan was yet to formulate in his mind, but trees meant many things. Amongst them, shelter and food.

The terrain became rockier and more challenging as the day wore on. Thirst parched Blaze's throat as the sweat continued to stream from his every pore. Travelling alone felt natural to Blaze, almost as natural as killing. The only problem was that as Blaze grew tired, he found himself drifting off.

His mind lost in thought.

He still couldn't piece his past together.

Blaze discovered that Purgatory was a dangerous place to lose focus when a zombie stepped out from behind a large rock. It would not have been so bad had Blaze not walked straight into its hungry arms.

The dead creature embraced him, and growled as its teeth snapped hungrily—searching for sustenance.

Blaze's mind focused in an instant. He thrust his head forward, not thinking about the gnashing teeth or the consequences of being bitten. Flesh and bone collided, and only one man would come out the victor. The zombie stumbled backwards, giving Blaze enough time to reach for the knife. Once he had the blade in his hand, the result was inevitable. He stabbed at the creature until his arm burned from the effort.

He had opened a wound in the creature's belly that allowed a rotten sea of indistinguishable offal to spill to the ground. Still the zombie snapped and grabbed at Blaze.

Blaze stepped back half a yard, staring at the creature. The wound seemed to cause the creature no ill effect. Its movements were slowed by the dripping organs, but its advance was unhindered.

"I won't become you," Blaze whispered as he pushed the blade through the creature's skull.

Blaze promised himself that he would remain alert; he would not be caught off guard again.

The terrain continued to become harder to cross as the day wore on. When night fell, or what felt like night, Blaze found himself on the edge of a small cliff. In the distance he saw the forest.

It was too risky to chance scaling the cliff. He was exhausted from his travel. The passage of time was impossible to gauge, the light faded and rose again with no discernable pattern. Blaze decided that it would be best to settle down for the night, rest up and head out early in the morning. A plan was formulating in his head, and depending on the size of the forest, he believed he would be out of this Purgatory land within three days.

Blaze had only come across three zombies in the later stages of the day, the ground proving too difficult for creatures of their limited means. He felt safe to settle down and rest.

As darkness fell, Blaze watched from his lofty

position as small orange balls began to appear in the black void spread out before him. Fires started by those new to the world, or those too stubborn to accept the reality of their situation. One such ball appeared at the base of the cliff. Blaze didn't care, but what he found strange was the way the first simply disappeared a few moments later, blinking out of existence in an instant.

Nestled between two rocks, Blaze lay back and waited for sleep to come. He was exhausted, but the howl of the wolves kept sleep from him.

His stomach growled and his head ached from thirst. His lips were dry and cracked, but Blaze forced it all away, deep into the back of his mind. Finally, after a long wait, sleep arrived and took him away.

The slumber was not deep, nor was it easy, but somehow it still managed to be restful. The phosphorous world was still dim when Blaze woke.

It didn't take long for Blaze to realize he was not alone.

Jumping to his feet, adrenaline pumping through his body, Blaze went for the knife, sure that it had been taken from him as he slept. His hand found the handle. That same rage-induced calm swept through him.

"Oh please, Blaze, you won't need that knife," a female voice said. The tone was familiar, spoken as if they were old friends.

"Who's there?" Blaze asked, looking around. He turned full circle but didn't see anybody. "At least come out and show yourself."

"All in good time, my dear. You need to earn it first." A breath of warm air caressed Blaze's neck, sending shivers down his spine.

Turning once more, Blaze swiped out with the knife. Rage continued to consume him. All he wanted to do was see blood spilled. It was as if the voice added to his anger, driving his thirst for blood through the roof.

Blaze's heart raced, and as he returned the blade to his belt, he felt it slow down, and a laugh escaped his throat. It was a dream. That was why the voice sounded familiar. It was the same woman who had been calling his name in his dream.

Chiding himself for being so stupid, Blaze settled down and took another look at the world. Nothing had changed. The forest stood in the distance, while the mountains rose to his left, tall and imposing. At least the world was stable. Blaze stood a chance at making it out.

Blaze's body ached. He needed something to stave off the hunger; he needed to kill. A zombie would do, but a human would be best. A good breakfast and all that. The zombies had tasted foul, but the essence of Blaze and Scrubs had filled him with an exuberance that was as satisfying as any meal could be. It stood to reason, in Blaze's mind, that an even fresher kill would taste even better.

Blaze was halfway down the cliff face when the dim light began to brighten. It was a subtle change, but Blaze was exposed while he climbed down, and any change in light increased the change of him being spotted. It was an easy descent, and the light of a new day made the task that much simpler. Blaze saw no signs of life, but he remembered the campfire from the night before. He drew his knife. He was getting close.

Once on the ground, Blaze felt better. He had lost

the advantage of height, but at the same time he had more room to maneuver.

Blaze tried hard to move as silently as possible, but stealth, it appeared, was not his strong suit.

There was no sign of any camp, or fire at the point where he had expected it. It didn´t make any sense to Blaze. He was sure this was the spot where their fire had been, yet the ground was unblemished. He refused to waste his time searching. The world was filled with people. He would just push on and have a late breakfast. He had an end game now, though, and nothing would keep him from it.

The stretch of land that separated Blaze from the trees was large and flat. There were few places to hide, should the need arise. It also meant that he could be attacked from any direction. He would need to stay alert. Steeling himself, Blaze moved off.

It didn't take long before he met his first zombie.

It didn't pose much of a threat, however. Somebody, presumable the wolves, had ripped the creature's legs off. It crawled along the floor, inching its way along. Blaze didn't even stop to kill it, striking out with his boot as he walked past. The skull burst like a piece of over-ripened fruit.

"They won't all be that easy, you know that right?" the female voice whispered in his ear. It sounded as if she stood beside him, her words were so close. Another chill ran down his spine.

"Show yourself," Blaze demanded. Anger surged through him. It seemed as if the voice was another automatic trigger for his rage.

"When the time is right, Blaze. Always so impatient." She sounded disappointed in him.

"How do you know me?" he asked, pointlessly searching.

"It will all come to you when you are ready for it," she assured him. "Now, watch out." Her warning was fair, but delivered too late.

Something heavy clubbed Blaze on the back of his head, and he fell, face first. His head bounced on the hard surface and the world changed into a spinning star-filled existence. Blaze tried to get to his feet, but a booted foot connected with his head, and he was absorbed by the darkness.

When Blaze came to, the first thing he realized was that he was tied up. His shoulders burned with cramps. His arms were tied behind his back and attached to something high. He assumed a tree branch. The second thing that dawned on Blaze was that his head hurt . . . a lot. He could feel the hair stuck to his skull, and could smell blood.

"You're awake," a voice spoke. The muffled sound came from Blaze's left side.

Blaze jumped. He twisted toward the voice. He wasn't sure how he felt when he realized it was merely a man: A prisoner, like him.

"Where are we?" Blaze asked. He was afraid and confused, and his voice did nothing to cover the fact.

"I don't know. This is their camp," the voice answered. Blaze hoped he did not sound as weak as his new friend.

"Whose camp?" Blaze looked around. He saw the remains of a fire; the circle of stones told him that the camp site was a long term fixture.

"I don't know. There's a group of them. Three men and two women, as far as I can tell." He spoke quickly, hurrying to get the words out.

"Where are they now?" Blaze saw a pile of clothes and shoes on the floor. The ground around them was flattened.

"Hunting."

That single word froze the blood in Blaze's veins. He looked at the man and saw the same thing he felt reflected back.

The man was smaller than Blaze, but at close to six feet six, that didn't say much. He had a shaved head with a goatee, which looked much darker against his pale skin than the light brown shade it was.

"Hunting?" Blaze asked, his head fuzzy from the blow it had received.

"Yeah. They hunt for fun. They get off on it." The stranger answered.

Blaze shivered. "So they just kill for fun?" He started to form a picture of the group in his mind. "They don't want to escape or anything?"

"I don't know. They caught me a few days ago. They aren't like any other people I have met here." He stopped, his breathing taking on a wheezy quality.

Blaze's head was pounding and the world was fading in and out. He knew that if he wanted to remain conscious, he would need to keep talking. "What's your name?" he asked.

"Jerry," the man answered. He looked weak. His body had a sickly pallor to it. Blaze wondered how he could have survived at all in this world.

"They call me Blaze," he answered. His words were hard and to the point. He needed to talk, but wasn't looking to make friends.

"Blaze . . . you a firebug or something?" Jerry gave a tired laugh.

"Firebug . . . Oh no. I got this name here. These two guys gave it to me," Blaze said, pausing. "They saved me," he added after a while.

"Where are they now?" Jerry asked.

"Dead."

"Oh. Better that way." Jerry's eyes widened and his voice trailed off. His body tensed and a look of great pain set onto his face. He gave a grunt.

"You all right?" Blaze asked, his concern genuine.

"Yeah, I'm fine. I've got this thing with my kidneys. Always have. You get used to it after a while. I'm lucky, I guess, that I got to live as long as I did." Jerry smiled, before he erupted in a coughing fit that shook his whole body. When he calmed, his lips were red with blood.

"What do you mean?" Blaze stared at the blood on the man's lips, and thought how different he had felt the last time he had seen the substance shed. He wished he had his knife.

"The people I was with. They'd all brought something with them when they died. We had one guy who was like some sorta ninja, and another who was in the military. He died in a roadside bombing in Afghanistan. He would just start screaming at random moments. Crying out orders to us, like we were his soldiers. Then he would start crying. He died first."

Blaze thought about everybody he had met. They could all remember their past. "So they all brought something, and you came through with medical problems?" Blaze was pleased his voice did not sound as condescending as the words suggested.

"It was the constant in my life. Don't feel sorry for me. I had a great life. I worked, I played, I fucked . . . a lot. It was all good." Jerry smiled, but Blaze did not reciprocate.

"What about you?"

"I don't remember anything." Blaze hung his head, staring at his feet. He wanted to sleep.

"It'll come to you, when the time is right. I think you remember when you're ready, once you've earned it, or something. It's what this place is about." It was a logic that Blaze hadn't considered. "Can you remember anything at all?" Jerry pushed.

"I'm good with knives," Blaze answered.

"That's good. Maybe you were a chef."

"Not like that." Blaze looked at Jerry, his face stern.

"Oh."

Movement caught Blaze's attention. Looking up, Blaze saw a woman. She was a distance away from the camp, but did not have the look of a zombie, or that of a human threat. She was observing them.

Their gazes met, and pain erupted in his head: He was alive, he was with that woman. They were running together. She was a short distance ahead of him. It was evening, the sun setting, casting them in a golden glow.

The vision cleared, and Blaze was back in captivity.

"They're coming," he said as his gaze rose, searching for the woman, but there was no sign of her.

"And they brought us some new friends," Jerry added, looking in the opposite direction. Turning in his bands, Blaze stared as the group appeared. Between them they dragged a kicking and screaming couple. The men led the way with the women close behind. Blaze stared, squinting to get a clearer look. Neither of the women looked like the one from his previous life.

They were dressed in rags, and the women wore considerably less than the men. Blaze looked away as they approached, hanging his head as if he were still unconscious.

"What do they want from us?" he whispered to Jerry.

"To die." Jerry's answer was cold. "Don't worry. I'll go first." Blaze was not sure if that was supposed to comfort him or not. "Now keep quiet. Just play like you're still passed out. They don't like it when we talk." Jerry didn't need to be any more descriptive. Blaze knew what he meant, and lowered his head.

The gang arrived and proceeded to string up the two new arrivals in a similar fashion to Blaze and Jerry.

"He's still out. Are you sure you didn't hit him too hard?" One woman asked in a hoarse voice. Blaze fought the urge to raise his head, to let them know he was still alive and they had not won. He focused on the ground by his feet, his eyes all but closed.

"I'd feel it if I had, wouldn't I," one man growled roughly.

"Maybe he's not dead. Just a vegetable or something," the other woman spoke. In contrast to her female counterpart, her voice was light and airy.

"Why the hell is this damned bimbo still with us?" The first women asked. This was followed by a cry of pain, probably from being struck the blonde.

"Because she's with me," a new voice growled. "If she goes, I go, and then you wouldn't stand a chance."

"Don't make me laugh." The hoarse voiced woman coughed. "It's a miracle you can stand her. Then again, she's not often standing is she? The little slut figured out how to survive here, didn't she?"

"Hey!" the blonde yelled, and then cried out when another shot was delivered.

"Cut it out, all of yous," the third man spoke. His voice had a tone of seniority to it. Deep and gravelly, it was a smoker's voice. "I'm sick and tired of your arguments. She´s a slut, you're a slut, and we know and appreciate it.

"Fuck you, Ben," the woman replied, spitting the words out between a fit of rasping coughs.

The group of hunters quieted down, but it soon became clear that they had no real concept of the lay of the land. They found each other along the way, and decided to work as a team in order to survive. They killed, but not out of necessity.

They showed no inclination to add to their numbers, and so Blaze kept his head down and his mouth shut. He channeled his focus on twisting his hands to slowly loosen the bonds that held him.

Time ticked by and Blaze became lost to the knots locking him into place. It was hypnotic. He floated away to a place in his mind. He could feel the progress, and that only served to drive his fingers even harder.

He only became aware of the world again when he saw the foot enter his field of vision.

"Wake him up," the leader of the group spoke.

Before Blaze had the chance to open his eyes himself, he was manhandled with unnecessary force, until he opened his eyes. A ball of warm phlegm was spat into his face, before Blaze could say a word.

"Rise and shine, sleeping beauty," the authoritative voice growled at him.. He was old, his face twisted in an inhuman way. Whatever had happened to him in life, Blaze had no desire to learn. Cold eyes stared at him, and a toothless smile broke his face into a gaping maw. A thick beard worked hard to obscure the lower portion of his face, but it was not enough to improve his looks.

"We don't want you to miss this," the deep voiced woman laughed.

Blaze looked at her. She was tall and athletic, her body screaming sexuality. She wore only her underwear, showing off skin blackened with dust and sweat. Her deep auburn-coloured hair hung loose over her shoulders, untamed, just as she appeared to be.

Blaze lusted after her immediately.

She giggled, and then pulled a roughly fashioned knife from behind her back. The flirty laugh died, but a vicious smile remained.

Only then did Blaze understand how dangerous she was, and who was truly in charge . . .

Without pause, she walked over to Jerry and grabbed him by the head. He looked paler still, and his eyes had a strange unfocused look to them. His body was slick with sweat, but it did little to deter the blade as it was drawn across his throat. Blood spurted from the wound. The woman squealed with delight.

Blaze's stomach churned at the sight of all the blood cascading down the torso of the thrashing man. A cold sweat ran down his back as he stared at the crimson flood. He could almost feel the thrill of the kill surge through him. Yet it was not his life to claim. In that moment, Blaze's desire for the knife outweighed any other longing thoughts in his brain. He needed to spill blood. He craved the sensation of its warm flow over his flesh.

The woman dropped the knife to the floor, before

she rubbed her hands over her body. Aroused by the blood, the scent of death, she groaned and gave in to her primal urges.

The blonde walked over, grabbed her by the hair and they started to kiss. The three men cheered.

Anger filled Blaze, consuming him. He felt his strength return, the knowledge of him being the next victim spurring him on.

The grip on his hair disappeared, but Blaze did not allow his head to fall.

He watched as the group joined together. Clothes were shed and blows exchanged; a violent orgy developing in front of the remaining three prisoners.

"You will need that knife down there," a voice echoed inside his head. .

"Who . . . ? What . . . ?" Blaze looked around. He found the same woman he'd seen earlier, standing on the edge of the camp again.

"You are almost free. Hurry up and get the knife. You know how that makes you feel." She laughed and disappeared.

Blaze twisted his wrists. With a series of sharp, increasingly painful movements he managed to pull his arms free. The sudden change in his center of gravity made Blaze fall to the ground. The blood rushed back into his arms. It felt as if they were on fire. The knife was within reach, but he could not get his limbs to obey his commands.

"Hey, he's loose," the auburn haired woman groaned. She was unable to move due to her precarious position. The men, unfazed by Blaze's escape just watched him for a moment, before continuing their ritual. The blonde's nose bled, her eye swollen shut from the force of their union, but she fucked them with an intensity that could not be stopped. It would not stop for anything.

Blaze's fingers closed on the handle of the blade, and their fate was sealed.

Genitals flapped in all directions, a cacophony of grunts and moans filled the air. Blaze realized he had never seen anything so disgusting. The ugliness of it all made him feel so much better about killing. At least killing was a natural human condition. This display, however, couldn't be described as anything other than demonic.

Blaze charged the orgy, knife in hand, and drove the blade into the blonde's stomach. She didn't die immediately from the wound, but Blaze almost lost his grip on the knife. It didn't matter. Blaze drove his elbow into the chest of the man, still ramming into the dying blonde. It drove him back a few steps. Blaze reached out, grabbing the flailing man's arm. Twisting it around, he pulled until the shoulder popped out of the socket. A single step later and Blaze was behind the man. His arm slid beneath his chin, and with a sharp twist Blaze snapped the man's neck, and let his body fall to the dirt. The red mist finally descended.

Screams rang out from the still fucking threesome, their dead friend disappearing into the ball of slick sweat, and God knows what else.

They came simultaneously as the realization of their fate hit them.

Blaze pulled the knife out of the blonde. Her wound was fatal, but her death would be the last.

Blaze was on the others before their tangled bodies could free themselves. He slit the woman's throat, and drove the knife through the toothless man's skull.

Blaze allowed the last man the chance to get to his feet, and allowed him to run a few paces before he launched the knife through the air. He hit the ground, and the first burst of absorbed death hit Blaze. Once again, he was held immobile while the essence of death flowed through his body.

Wiping the blade clean, Blaze became aware of a presence standing beside him.

"That must feel better." There was a melodic quality to her voice. "If you keep taking them down like that, you will surely be out of here in no time." She smiled. "But what about them? You can't leave them here." She pointed to the two new arrivals. They had stopped struggling, and now wept uncontrollably. Their bladders and bowels had emptied having witnessed the carnage that Blaze had created.

"Oh Christ, I forgot. I'll let them go, but they are not coming with us." Blaze retrieved his knife and walked back toward the pair.

As he walked past the woman, she leaned in close and whispered, "Are you sure that's the right thing to do?"

"Yes. I won't be responsible for them," Blaze answered. He approached the pair, eyeing their bonds. He reached into his belt and pulled out the knife. The moment Blaze's fingers wrapped around the blade's handle, he felt that familiar change within him. Red mist descended over his vision, and all he could imagine was the feel of their blood being spilled. Gripping the blade he stepped forward, and slid it across the man's abdomen. He screamed as Blaze twisted the knife, opening a black hole just above the navel. Blood gushed from the wound like liquor from a punctured cask.

Blaze felt a moment of disgust at what he had done. A brief moment where his brain saw through the haze. Then the scent of warm gore filled his senses and he was once again lost to it.

The woman screamed, begging for him to leave her alone.

"I promise, I won't tell anybody." She coughed and spluttered as tears and snot streaming down her face.

Blaze ignored her cries. He raised the knife to his face and peered at her over the blade. Power surged through him, and a smile spread across his lips. Advancing on his prey, Blaze laughed.

He swiped out playfully, slicing a deep gash in the woman's flank.

"Please, please, no. I don't deserve this. I shouldn't be here," she cried, her voice faltering as the second pass of the knife carved a lump of meat from her upper leg. The skin pulled back, rolling away from her body, tearing an even longer wound.

The woman's voice caught in her throat, and all she could manage was a spluttered gasp for air.

"Shhh, it's all going to be alright now," Blaze whispered, kissing her on the cheek and ear as he drew the blade across her throat. That rush of air and blood made him shudder. Power filled him as the life force of his victims poured into him. His hand tightened on the knife, and he groaned in pleasure. A few seconds after that, a nauseating wave hit him. His body shook and a momentary lapse in consciousness saw him fall. It was over in a second Blaze had been able to steady himself against the bodies.

He stood, allowing his composure to return. His hand brushed the blade again, and the feelings disappeared. Taking a deep breath, Blaze turned around, and walked away.

The camp was long behind him by the time Blaze began to come down from his murderous high.

"So, where are we heading? You must have a plan," the woman asked. She walked a few paces behind him. Blaze kept his pace fast in an attempt to keep conversation to a minimum. His head ached with thirst. His throat was dry and his lips sore, yet his body buzzed from the power he had absorbed. Even with the knife tucked away in his belt, he could still feel the rage and the anger bubbling beneath the surface.

"I'm stronger now, so I am heading toward the forest," Blaze answered. "There is a camp on the other side, or maybe this side, I don't know. They call it The Commons."

The woman matched his stride now, and continued her tirade of questions. "Do you really think you can kill your way out of here?" She looked at him, surprise etched into her expression.

"The way I´ve heard it, you either stay here and die, or fight back and earn your escape." Blaze stopped walking and looked at her. "You've seen the things that wander around here. You must have seen what happens to you, if you stay too long." Blaze swung his arm out, as if the world around them needed to be highlighted.

"Those people back there were not like those creatures," the woman said.

"That was your idea," Blaze snapped.

"No, you came up with it all on your own. But hey, I guess killing really has become your thing now." She quickened her pace a little so that she now led. "This place is like a puzzle. It knows us all, and I think escape is different for everyone. I don't think it's about how many you kill, but how much you learn, that counts."

"You do it your way and I'll do it mine. We'll see who is laughing on the other side. We may have known each other before, but out here, it's a whole new world." Blaze put on a burst of speed, and left the woman behind.

"You remember," she stammered. The revelation was unexpected, and Blaze couldn't help but smile at the look of shock on the woman's face.

He said nothing, but started walking again. The woman followed, but her pace was slow. In the distance, Blaze saw one of the zombie creatures staggering in their direction. Before he knew what he was doing, he found himself charging at the creature. The knife was in his hand before half of the distance between them had been covered. The creature seemed to sense Blaze's approach. It began to snarl and growl long before their bodies collided. Blaze tackled the creature to the floor, pinning it beneath him. Holding the blade in a double-handed grip, he plunged downward, stabbing the creature in the gut. The blade withdrew with a wet sucking sound. Blaze raised the weapon and stabbed down again, and again. Each time the blade pierced the thin, rotting flesh, he gave a triumphant cry. His body was splattered with fetid, black blood. The stench was atrocious, but in that moment, Blaze didn't care.

Blaze knew he would regret his actions later, but he felt better than he had in hours. The rage that had built in him had subsided.

His hand shook as he replaced the knife into the

band of his trousers. He was walking again before his female counterpart caught up with him.

"You didn't kill it you know," the woman said. Behind them, the creature flopped on the floor.

"I'm not bothered by them," Blaze answered. "It's only the fresh meat I want," he growled, turning to stare at the woman.

"Oh, you big frightening man, you." She smiled away his threat, ignoring the way Blaze held the knife in his hand. "Watch yourself." She pointed as two more zombies appeared from between two large rocks. One was old, its body a bloated bag of liquefied innards, while the other was new, fresher. It had an air of humanity still clinging to it.

Blaze killed them both with a series of powerful blows, even managing to decapitate the older, softer creature.

"We must be getting close," Blaze told her. "The forest is teeming with these bad boys. You really need to start killing. I'm not always going to be there to protect you." Two more zombies appeared, and suffered the same fate as the rest. Blaze was breathing heavy by the time he finished them both.

"I don't need your help."

Blaze wondered why he kept her around. Why not just kill her like he had done the others? Something stayed his hand. Something he didn't understand. "Have it your way," he grunted.

The forest came into view the moment they made it beyond the rocks which had formed most of the terrain since their meeting. They encountered several more zombies as they moved. Blaze didn't care to count. Some he killed, some he left. They were nothing but roaches in the new world.

The day wore on, and a gloom settled in. It was what passed for twilight in the sunless world. They needed to find a place to camp, but there was nothing ahead of them that looked to offer much in the way of shelter, and Blaze refused to go back even a short way. A dry wind kicked up, and drifts of dust and dried earth fell like an abrasive rain.

Blaze looked at the trees. They would provide the shelter he needed, but it was clear that the zombies would be unstoppable.

Scrubs was right, Blaze thought to himself. *It would be madness to wander through the forest, let alone make camp within its borders.*

Turning left, Blaze headed parallel to the trees, toward the mountains that now rose taller than ever on the horizon.

"Do you really expect violence to free you from this place?" she asked. They had not encountered more than half a dozen zombies since they had changed course, and it was clear that the living also avoided getting too close. "We need to rest." The woman called a while later. Her pace had slowed, and Blaze had pulled ahead of her. "Hey, I need to rest. We both do." She hurried her steps and drew level with Blaze, who did not so much as glance at her. His pace continued, only slowing when she pulled on his arm. She gave a loud sigh, and continued to walk, when Blaze stopped. He pointed to a set of rocks that rose out of the ground like a clenched fist. "What, you want us to camp there? I don't know what you are thinking, but I don't understand your random pointing." Her reply was curt, but Blaze once again offered no reaction to her.

"We can rest up there," he finally answered.

"That doesn't look like much of a campsite," the woman bit. Her voice was beginning to grate more and more with every word she uttered.

Blaze sighed. "It's high ground, and that is all we can ask for out here." He dropped to one knee and offered the lady a boost.

"It gets cold—" she began, but Blaze gave her a shove that propelled her onto the rocks.

"Fires don't work out here," he said as he sat on the uneven surface. "Besides, it's not the dead—fresh or not—that worries me. It's the wolves, and whatever else lives in those trees." As if on cue, a howl took flight in the night air. An uncomfortable silence fell over them. The woman had her back to Blaze, and stood on the edge of the rocks. She showed no sign of wanting to sit. She stared into the dark in silence, seeming to find comfort in it. "Who are you?" Blaze asked.

For a while the woman offered no answer.

"I am here to help you," she answered. The confliction was clear in her voice. "Once you remember, all will become clear, but it's not my place to tell you. Now, get some sleep," she ordered.

It was clear that there would be no further conversation until the morning, so Blaze settled down onto the rocks and fell into a light sleep. He lay with his hands on his chest, the knife clutched between two closed fists.

***

Blaze was back in the same dream, running. Only now the woman was closer to him. There was something frantic about her pace. She wasn't jogging. She was running. Fleeing. The look in her eyes when she glanced over her shoulder was not happy or flirtatious. It was panic and terror.

In his dream, Blaze raised his hands to reach out to her. His feet pounded the pavement, his heart racing. His body was alive on the current of adrenaline.

"Come here," he called, breathless.

That was when he saw it: The blood, the knife in his hand. It glistened in the moonlight. His arms soaked in crimson.

Blaze stopped running and looked down at himself. He was naked, every inch of his flesh slick with blood. His heart stopped in his chest. *This is how I died.* Blaze looked at the standard kitchen knife.

Turning around, Blaze saw the house he had just come from. All the lights were burning and the front door was open. Abandoning his pursuit he returned to the building.

Two sets of clothes were strewn through the entrance way, leading up the stairs, telling the common tale of uncontrolled passion. Blaze followed them to the hallway where they stopped and were replaced by something else: Bloody footprints running the other way.

Entering the bedroom, a large pool of blood and smears lead to the closet. He opened the door, his heart thundering in his chest. A flurry of memories hit him as the doors opened and the scent of lust and flesh filled his nostrils.

The naked body of a young woman lay curled on the floor among the clothes she had pulled from the hangers.

Outside, the sound of approaching sirens were followed by the screech of tires. Voices shouted, but were soon drowned out by the sound of gunfire. Three shots.

In the house, Blaze's body jerked and three small black holes appeared on his flesh. He fell backwards onto the bed, as the final moments of his life returned to his mind. Blaze lay back, closed his eyes . . . and woke up.

Blaze startled awake, jumped to his feet, knife raised. He grabbed the woman from behind and pressed the blade against her throat, applying enough pressure to dent the skin, but not break it.

"You remember." She was calm, and seemed unsurprised at the situation.

"Tell me what happened!" Blaze roared.

The woman didn't answer. She made no attempt to fight. Instead, she raised her hand, placed two fingers on the tip of the blade, and effortlessly pushed it away. "Don't be a fool Blaze." She turned to face him. "You must understand now. The knife, the way it makes you feel. Rage . . . it consumes you." They stood face to face on the edge of the rocks.

"Who are you?" Blaze asked, the knife trembling in his loose grip.

"I was your wife, Blaze." The words hit him like a snowball to the side of the head. Blaze went numb, and the knife fell from his hand. It bounced on the rocks and landed on the ground beneath them.

"Then who . . . " Blaze began, but he already understood.

"She was the neighbor's daughter. She was eighteen years old, and I caught the two of you in our bed." The woman's body had gone stiff, rage flushed her cheeks. Turning them first red, and then an even darker shade. It was the color of thunder, the sky before a summer storm. Her words began calm, but soon became a screeched roar, the likes of which can only be achieved by a woman scorned.

"So you killed her?" Blaze asked. He knew it wasn't true, but the question was automatic.

The woman gave an explosive laugh. "No Blaze. *You* killed her. We argued, moving through the house. She was by your side, crying and clawing at you like a lovesick puppy. You grabbed a knife from the kitchen rack and threatened me. She tried to calm you down, and you stabbed her, repeatedly. I saw that rage come over you. I'd never seen it before, and so I ran." With that the woman jumped from the rocks to the ground. Blaze followed. "But as always, you chased me," she added, a sigh laced with melancholy following.

Bending down, she picked up the knife. She ran her fingers along the blade, tracing its edge, and suddenly it changed. It became the kitchen knife of Blaze's dream.

"You chased me down, and killed me." She lifted her shirt to reveal an open, but bloodless wound in her chest. "Through the heart . . . Ironic, huh?" She looked forlornly at Blaze. "The police arrived, soon after, but they were too late to save me or the girl. You refused to put down the knife, so they shot you." Tears glistened in her eyes

"So why are you here?" Blaze asked. "What is the point of this place?"

"We need to find our redemption," she answered.

The woman, Keri—Blaze's wife in life—handed the knife back to him. "I guess you want this back." She looked at him, and Blaze knew it was a test. He was being tested.

"Thank you," he answered, reaching out to take the knife. His hands shook, but holding the blade felt right in his mind, and he was powerless to resist the urges.

"Be careful, Blaze. That's all I want to say. Think about this." She looked at him, the rage slowly being replaced with disappointment.

"If you were my wife, why do you still call me Blaze? He asked as he returned the knife to its rightful place by his side.

"Because you are not the man I married, and I would sooner call you this false name, than admit to who you really are." Those words were cold, and her hurt was reflected in them.

They moved off together, Blaze no longer consumed with the conflicting sense of emotions surrounding his wife and the end of his life. The forest continued to their right, and the groan of the dead that filled the eternal shadows echoed.

"The Commons should be just around the back of the trees there," Blaze spoke as the forest thinned.

"What is there?" Keri asked.

"People."

Keri stopped walking, the realization dawning on her. "You mean to kill them all, don't you?"

"That's how we get out of this place." Blaze's words were cold, emotionless. The blade turned over and over in his hand, twisting the air. "Killing sets you free," he added, thinking back to everything Bones and Scrubs had told him.

"What happened to you? Listen to yourself, Blaze. This isn't you. You died angry, but don't let it define who you become for eternity."

"I will not stay in this place. If I need to kill to

survive, then I will kill. I died, and this place will not be my eternity," Blaze bellowed in response. The rage boiled beneath his surface.

"Fine. If that is what you want. Okay. I am your wife, and I will support you." There was resignation in her voice, but also something else. Some deeper tone, but Blaze could not pinpoint what it was. The next thing Keri saw was the blade arcing through the air toward her. She had no time to react. The blade met flesh with a wet slap and the zombie which had crept up behind her, fell to the ground. "You saved me," Keri stuttered.

"I killed a zombie. One step closer to freedom." Blaze shuddered as the taste of the dead filled his mouth.

They walked in silence, a fiery heat beating down upon them. Blaze's body was cramped from thirst, his throat raw on the inside.

***

Keri allowed Blaze to take the lead, falling back a step or two. She winced as Blaze dispatched another zombie. Every time he cut or stabbed in this world, she felt it. That was her punishment, and therein lay her atonement. Tears filled her eyes as the blade decapitated another old creature that had stumbled into his path. His disinterest in killing the undead seemed to have left as he neared his goal.

The forest was coming to an end and they had altered their direction, slowly drawing closer to the trees, cutting corners, as it were. The mountains also loomed large over them, and both were keen to keep their distance from that place. They knew what dwelled there. Over that point, no discussion was needed.

"The Commons is right there," Blaze whispered. They were crouched behind a tree on the edge of the forest. The Commons was smaller than Blaze had anticipated, but the sight of the walled community made his body tremble in anticipation.

The main gate was pulled open upon their arrival. The Commons' outer perimeter was rudimentary in its construction, but served its purpose well. Through the open gate, Blaze made out the basic shelters.

As they watched, a group left the camp. Five people walked, dragging three bodies between them.

"What are they doing?" Keri asked.

"Bringing out their dead."

Keri shivered at the thought, but Blaze paid it no mind. He was focused. "Don't you see, Blaze? These people didn't find their redemption, and so they are made to suffer. They die and live here forever." Keri stared as the group dumped the bodies on the ground at the edge of the trees, and turned away.

"No, they are people who won't fight. Who just give up and let this place consume them. They are quitters, spineless fools and I will not join them." Blaze stared at the people as they disappeared among the shelters.

"So they deserve to die?"

"If I survive, and they don't want to try, then yes. They deserve what they get." Blaze was not in the mood for further discussion, but Keri wasn't done.

Keri moved away from her husband, disgusted. The final revelation of his new character was too much for her. She was washing her hands of the man who had taken both her heart, and her life. "You are a monster. That knife controls you. It has consumed you and you don't seem to care about it." Tears streaked her face.

Around them, the wind had kicked up, swirling dust and dry dirt into the air.

"I will do whatever it takes to survive," Blaze roared, shaking his knife, wielding a fist in the air. "I am not going to just stand there and wait for things to fall apart. I'm not a coward."

"But you are, Blaze. You always were. You were the kindest, sweetest man I had ever met. You hated fighting, and you hated confrontation. It made you sick. Don´t let one moment of violence change who you are. I know you better than that." Keri was close to falling onto her knees in an attempt to get through to her husband.

"That man is dead. I don't remember him. I have been reborn, and stand a chance of escaping this place." Blaze stepped out from behind the tree, and made to move toward The Commons.

The wind continued to rise, and the sand billowed around them. In seconds the world was greyed out.

***

Blaze could not see his own hand, the storm was so thick. He tried to keep moving forward, but the wind was so strong he was unable to tell if he was moving at all, let alone in the intended direction.

The wind howled and Blaze thought he could hear the mournful cry of the wolves. *Are they coming for me?*

The wind reached its peak and began to settle. The swirling dust calmed and fell away.

When the world came back into focus, everything was gone: The Commons, the forest, everything.

Blaze and Keri stood side by side. It was then that Blaze noticed what was there, rather than that what

132

had been removed. He and Keri were surrounded, trapped in a circle of large hooded figures. Blaze could not see their faces, but felt their eyes boring into him.

Keri gasped, but Blaze refused to respond. The wind seemed to swirl around them, as if it was their pet, waiting for the next set of orders to come through. Their capes fluttered in the breeze, but Blaze felt nothing.

In unison, the figures raised their right arms. Long decaying fingers extended from beneath the robes. The bones were yellowed with age, but clumps of rotting skin still clung to their unfurling talons.

Blaze turned to Keri. "Sorry, honey, looks like my ticket to freedom just arrived." He smiled at her . . . just before a burning sensation exploded inside him. It consumed him with its white hot agony.

"What . . . ?" he managed to call out. "What's happening?" The pain soon became too much. Blaze body began to shut down.

In an instant, the group had closed around him. Keri was gone, lost on the outside of their closed circle. Blaze was pinned between them. Their stench was so great it managed to cut through everything he knew. There was pain, and the stench of rot—a wet rot, the kind that reeked of ancient times.

"You have failed to atone for your ways. Rage and anger destroyed you, and this is what has continued to control you." The voices wailed in a chorus of sorrow.

"Wait . . . I didn't know!" Blaze protested, but it was too late. Reaching arms found his skin. Their touch burned with a cold so intense it felt as if Blaze was on fire. His body was forced away, pushed, carried and thrown. He was helpless, unable to offer even a cry of resistance.

Blaze was aware of where they were taking him, but he had no concept of how long or how far their journey lasted. The creatures moved as a single organism, and he was the prey, trapped within their midst. Even as the mouth of the cave loomed above him, and the force of their attack subsided, it took all of his strength to utter a single plea. "Help me."

There was no need for the hooded figures to enter the cave, nor to push Blaze over the threshold. The pull of the darkness was strong enough to consume him. Shadows formed around him, and as the light disappeared, so did the world. The blackness inside the cave was more than darkness, it was absence.

In a surge of heat, flames burst from his mouth like dragon's breath.

His skin dried and cracked like a riverbed in drought. The cracks were black, but soon began to glow. The pain increased until molten blood flowed from the opened wounds.

"I'm sorry. I will do better," Blaze cried, but there was now only black. Black, black, and that was when the pain set in.

Blaze opened his eyes to a world of fire. Twisted faces formed around him. Demons clawed at his flesh, all eager to taste fresh meat.

LAKE OF FIRE

JOE MYNHARDT

And Satan, who is the beast, was thrown into the lake of fire, which is the second death. It is the beast who gathers the kings of the earth, and their armies, to prepare for war against God.

BLAZE'S EYES FLASHED open to the purple, starless night gazing down on him. He was unsure whether he'd fallen asleep, but screams of tortured souls now travelled from the encircling mountains, hollow and eerie. He wondered how far the screams were from him—a miserable attempt to distract himself from the real, terrible thought: *Why* were they screaming?

Blaze closed his eyes to block out his surroundings along with the hunger pangs emanating from his stomach, but every time he drifted to the brink of sleep he'd startle awake, certain someone would hear his snoring and come kill him.

He rolled onto his side, facing the dark mound of sand bordering their little hollow. Trying to fall asleep was futile. It would take him a long time to get used to this place.

If you live that long.

Finally on the brink of sleep and lost in thought of his earthly origin, he registered the voices of his companions behind him.

"Don't do it. Not yet." Bones' piteous voice said.

Blaze realized it wasn't a dream and cradled the handle of his new best friend—the knife nestled against his chest.

The voices stopped.

Someone crept closer.

Blaze did his best not to move or alter his breathing pattern while the possible attacker inched closer, pebbles crunching beneath ruined boots, each step trying to be softer than the last.

Knees creaked, hunching down beside him.

Blaze snapped his eyes open and turned his head, staring at Scrubs' widened gaze. Before Scrubs could utter a swift vindication, the knife flashed through the air and with unnatural ease slipped into Scrubs' neck.

The man sat motionless on his knees as a river of blood flowed silently into the dry ground. His eyes blinked several times in frozen shock.

Blaze moved into a crouch, his breath fast yet controlled, not knowing why or how he'd dealt a death blow without any thought behind it. He had no solid proof that Scrubs was coming in for the kill.

He stared at Scrubs, whose mouth hung wider than his fading blue eyes.

The thought of apologizing crossed his mind, but then a smile wriggled across his face. Except for the evident power he had gained from the kill, he didn't know why he was smiling. 'Rather him than me' seemed reason enough.

With a gurgle Scrubs dropped a large rock from his hand and toppled to the side, tiny blood bubbles popping at the corner of his mouth as he continued to breathe.

Blaze jumped to his feet and turned to the last remaining companion. "You bastards!"

Bones raised his hands in innocence, his quivering lips incapable of finding the correct words. His gaze, filled with hurt and sheer hopelessness, moved rapidly between Blaze and his dying companion. "I told him . . . not to."

Scrubs' death gurgle grew louder, a dark red liquid oozing through the clenched fingers covering his neck. His legs kicked out and he rolled from side to side, fighting to stay alive.

Blaze hesitated but took a deliberate step closer to analyze Bones' motive.

Bones remained still.

Blaze knew he'd never be able to trust the man—or anyone else in this godless place. He taunted him again.

Nothing.

The inexperience inside Blaze yearned to ask 'Why?' while the warrior inside him itched to take another kill. He spat toward Bones, "Run, or I'll have no choice but to kill you, too."

Uncertainty veiled Bones' expression. One moment he appeared inches from charging, and then certain to flee. He glanced at his friend, sighed, and left.

Blaze turned to the now motionless body of his kill. He relished in the diminished hunger and renewed strength that accompanied such a kill. Poor guy was only doing what he needed to get out of this place, like so many more desperate men and women Blaze was bound to meet.

Could *any* of them be trusted?

And how long would Bones survive without his friend? *They* had managed not to kill each other, somehow.

For an instant Blaze thought he could hear something soaring through the air before it hit him against the head. It smacked his head forward, sending Blaze reeling. In his dazed stupor the knife began to slip from his hand, yet his thumb and middle finger managed to pull it back.

He swung around, fighting to keep his balance. The world was lost in a blurry haze, yet he was ready to defend himself—one hand on the knife, the other holding back the flow of blood from his head.

Bones and a dozen zombies he'd lured slowly came into focus. Bones picked up another rock. "All you had to do was lay still," he said shaking his head. "That's all."

For a moment Bones seemed to have forgotten about the zombies, and the look of anger seeped from his eyes as some of the zombies turned toward him. Most of them still lurched past, toward the body beside Blaze, overwhelmed by the scent of fresh blood.

Bones was clearly not thinking straight anymore, and if Blaze didn't act fast, he'd lose a kill to the zombies. "Motherfucker!" Blaze screamed as he charged forward, determined to cut Bones down and distance himself from the zombies.

Bones raised the rock and charged, both men

pushing their way through the zombies. Bones swung the rock toward Blaze's head.

Blaze sidestepped the assault, skillfully cutting a deep gash in Bones' forearm, followed by cuts to the back of Bones' knees and a final blow to the back of his neck.

Bones stumbled two feet forward and crumpled to his knees while Blaze grabbed hold of him before he could collapse to the dirt.

"Where's The Commons?" Blaze asked, hoping to get the answer before Bones faded; the cut to the arm was deep enough to bring forth a river of thick, dark blood, and his head hung limp, threatening to tear from his neck.

Blaze surveyed the approaching zombies—seconds away. "Tell me, damn it!"

Bones vomited a mouth full of blood and spit at Blaze's face. Red-stained teeth tainted his smile.

"Damn you," Blaze whispered as the first zombie started to raise its hands toward him. Now he'd have to find his own way to The Commons.

Bones was dead long before he hit the ground, the blade piercing his spinal column with surgical accuracy.

A dry corpse-hand grasped Blaze's shoulder.

Blaze spun, pulling the blade out of his latest kill and plunging it into a zombie's stomach in one swift movement. The zombie hardly registered any sensation as it continued to push forward, intent on piercing its next meal with those crooked teeth.

Don't let them bite you.

Blaze tried to pull away, but the weight of the zombie pushed them both to the ground. Dust swirled around Blaze's head.

The others were mere feet away, enclosing him in an even more suffocating darkness.

Blaze raised the zombie's head and slit its throat. Decayed and chunk-ridden blood oozed from the wound and into his mouth. He spat out the foul fluid and rolled the zombie off him.

Blaze jumped up. He slammed his hands against the chest of the nearest zombie, then dashed through the gap and jumped over the bodies of Bones and Scrubs toward relative freedom.

A couple steps farther and a few deep breaths calmed his senses.

He turned around. The zombie had settled on the two other men, pulling and tearing at limbs and intestines, lapping at pools of blood.

The fellowship of Bones and Scrubs was no more.

In the gloomy distance Blaze noticed more zombies meandering toward the fresh battlefield, yet he hardly noticed any significant increase in power or health from his latest kills. His head still ached. Dabbing his fingertips to the wound, he saw that it still bled.

Perhaps one more kill was all he needed. He decided to take on a single straggler as an experiment—to find out its weaknesses and possible benefits.

Blaze treaded carefully so he wouldn't be surrounded again, and approached a lone straggler.

The zombie raised its head, loose flesh dangling from its cheek like someone had bitten down in an attempt to tear it from his skull. With outstretched arms it turned toward the source of fresh meat.

Blaze pivoted his back foot in the dirt to strengthen his base and thundered a powerful kick to the zombie's chest. Its sternum snapped and a cloud of dust puffed out of its body like an old carpet taking a beating.

The zombie fell on its back. Its head barely slammed down before it struggled to push itself back up again.

Blaze rushed closer and stood over the zombie. He plunged the knife into the zombie's neck. Still it continued to claw at his arms, snapping its jaw toward him, feasting on the foul air.

Piercing the heart proved even less effective, the blade extracting with barely a drop of blood on it. Left with little other choice, but scared the blade would snap, Blaze thrust the blade into its brain, and the zombie's eyes flipped over before its body fell limp. The skull was a lot softer than he'd anticipated.

The pain in the back of Blaze's head decreased marginally, barely enough to register. At least he wasn't feeling dizzy anymore. Although zombie kills did not offer the same reward as human kills, they seemed to at least help a bit. He'd have to kill at least a thousand zombies to get out of this place.

If only killing a human was as easy, both physically as well as ethically.

Sure, the people of the plain had a lot more experience than him. If he was going to make it here, he had to learn everything about the place—and of his life before.

Perhaps he was hasty in his decision to never trust again. He had to survive long enough to remember what had happened to him. Why he was here.

But who would he trust?

He needed true survivors, people with knowledge who would benefit from his talents.

Blaze freed his knife from the skull of the zombie, careful not to snap the blade. He surveyed the area and silently moved away from the slaughter, hoping he was moving in the direction Scrubs had mentioned The Commons were situated.

The mountains surrounded him like an arena of spectators, unseen eyes following his every move—judging his performance.

Blaze was barely out of sight of the feeding zombies when a scream echoed across the plains. Several hunters had descended upon the zombies. He turned back to the renewed battle and crept closer. The hunters swiftly took care of the brain-dead wanderers with blades and spears to the head. Blaze couldn't tell if they were working together, until two hunters scrambled for the last zombie before turning their blades on one another.

The rest of the hunters eyed their competition and skulked back into the dark, content on not endangering their lives more than necessary.

The two men continued to fight to a draw, then withdrew, weak and bleeding. They'd be lucky to survive much longer, a soft target to other hunters waiting in the flanks.

That was all it took for Blaze to make up his mind about the hunters. He didn't belong among such vultures. At least he didn't *want* to.

Certain he was making the correct decision on finding The Commons, Blaze turned his back on them. He needed to find a group strong enough to survive, yet weak enough not to overpower him. A group with answers, at least until he remembered more. Knowledge was key to survival in this world.

Blaze stared at the distant fires, seeking the widest gap to sneak through. The fewer people that saw him, the better.

He snuck across the plain. Hopefully he wouldn't run into any more hunters or zombie hordes. He was a great fighter, how he still couldn't recall, but he just couldn't take on so many of them.

The risk, and the threat they posed, was too great.

He wiped the viscera from his blade and set off. A thick suspense accompanied him on his journey, not knowing what to expect, always wondering if someone would jump from behind the next crooked tree.

They'll fail, he told himself in an attempt to build his own confidence and to force himself to stay focused on the dangers surrounding him.

As time went on Blaze's pace quickly turned to a shamble as the remaining energy seeped from his body. He shuffled on, tiny dust clouds swirling in the wake of his boots. Except for the distant screams every few minutes, the land was quiet, waiting for something to happen. He felt like a cowboy, a lawman walking across the dusty plain toward the setting sun—only difference being he had no gun, there was no sun here, and he was fighting off zombies and demons and hunters. Not to mention . . . he was no longer among the living . . . sort of.

It was strange how he could recall cowboys and other stuff that didn't exist in this world, but he couldn't remember his own damn name, or what kind of man he'd been.

Dirt crunched under a boot somewhere to his right.

Blaze kept walking, his senses instinctively sharpening.

A soft footstep followed, barely audible.

His fists yearned to clench, but he'd wait until the stalker revealed himself, then crouch down and strike straight for the groin.

A twig snapped, this time from the left and back, the figures staying out of his peripheral vision. These were no mere opponents, these were predators hunting together—their prey in sight.

Blaze could wait no more. He swung around and crouched slightly, in case they were already in mid swing. The hunters, mere shadows floating in the darkness, one to his left and the other two to the right, sprinted toward him.

He could barely see another one coming straight at him.

Too many.

His choices were simple: flee or die.

Blaze retreated two steps and flung himself around and forward. Trying his best not to trip, he pivoted over rocks and dashed past thorny bushes and under low hanging branches.

They were closing in.

He could hear their ever-increasing breaths over his shoulder. It wouldn't be long before he'd have to turn and face them.

The distant fires grew closer. Perhaps he'd find safety in numbers with one of the groups, if they could be trusted. At the very least, the hunters might withdraw or pick a new, softer target.

But for some reason it felt like they were after him for a very specific reason.

Blaze saw his escape, a pitch black section in the middle where no fires burnt. He quickly realized it was not a wall but a little forest of dense trees, hundreds of bamboo standing erect.

The hunters were close, his energy on the brink of depletion, his throat burning with thirst.

Blaze was only a few meters away from safety when a hissing sound closed in from behind in. A sharp pain cut into his back sent him sprawling forward. He could still feel it inside his flesh.

He turned back to see the hunters as he stumbled and crawled backwards into the dense bamboo, barely able to clutch the blade.

"Fuck!" one of the hunters shouted.

Blaze collapsed to his knees, but continued to crawl deeper into the bamboo forest. The maze of bamboo constricted his movement, broken pieces cutting into his flesh.

"I ain't going in there," another voice spoke.

"'Course not. He's probably dead already."

Blaze sat in silence and listened. The footsteps of his attackers faded into the distance. He reached around to grip the knife sticking out of his back but couldn't find the hilt. Streaks of pain pulsed from the wound like a heartbeat. With no other choice, he pushed his back against a cluster of reeds and rubbed it to and fro, clinching against the pain as the blade slowly wiggled from side to side until it dislodged.

It was a small blade without a handle, a perfectly balanced throwing knife. And although he sighed with relief, he hoped the nightmare would finally end.

I need food. I have to sleep!

Once the initial pain slightly subsided, Blaze tucked the blade into his boot and weighed his options: Leave the grove as quickly as possible and risk the attention of hunters—and whoever gathered around those fires—or carefully maneuver his way through the dense bamboo, risking the unknown force that scared off the hunters.

Each choice carried its own risks. While the bamboo offered cover, it also restricted his movement. Then again, he seemed to be pretty well adapted to fighting in close-quarters. Not that combat was something he'd be able to partake in anymore, not in his current condition. Travelling close to the fires was a gamble he couldn't take.

He pushed himself up and slipped into the wooded area, turning his body sideways as he glided quietly past each bamboo.

It didn't take long for the bamboo, standing longer and wider the deeper he went, to swallow him whole. He could no longer see the mountain marker he'd travelled toward upon entering. It grew so dark he had to feel his way around, reaching out into the unknown, begging not to lose a finger to a snapping jaw. His limbs kept getting stuck, as though the bamboo stalks were trying to grab hold of his feet.

A growl rumbled from his right . . . no, behind him. Next to him.

Blaze fumbled to raise his knife.

Another growl reverberated through the bamboo. More growls followed—each reacting to the one before. Were they communicating, telling each other that someone had entered their grove?

Blaze stopped to listen.

Where are they?

The more he turned, listening to his surroundings, the more paranoid and directionless he became.

They could certainly smell him.

Perhaps even hear his heartbeat, their skinny bodies surely gliding through the thicket with ease.

With a deep breath he gathered his senses and moved toward what sounded like a less inhabited area. He had to find his way out, and fast.

Their growls followed him through the dark.

He tried to be quiet, but the bamboo kept crunching and snapping in his wake.

A hand grabbed Blaze's shoulder, a bony digit moving under his collar like a worm seeking a dark hole.

Blaze reacted on instinct and fear, grabbing the zombie's fingers, crunching and twisting them at the same time. He ducked down and curled the zombie's arm behind its back, anything to keep its rotten teeth away from his flesh.

He plunged the knife into the darkness at a raised angle toward the zombie, hacking away several times. Each time, he aimed his blade slightly higher until it could slip through the spinal column and into the brain.

The zombie shook, and fell.

Blaze turned, trying his best to move quickly but quietly.

The surrounding growls grew more intense. Angry.

A zombie crashed headfirst into Blaze. All he could do was arch back, away from its teeth. The zombie grabbed onto his arm but lacked the space to dig its teeth into any fresh meat.

With his free hand, Blaze pushed against the zombie's chest. Teeth clacked inches from his arm.

In that brief moment Blaze had to decide his next

move, he wondered if the zombie had known the blade was something to fear and had deliberately grabbed that arm. Had it somehow remembered what a knife was?

It couldn't, because that would also mean . . .

Fuck! They can see in the dark.

Blaze quickly pulled his hand away from the dead man's chest, pushing his open hand toward what he hoped was the zombie's throat and not his teeth.

A wet slosh proved his strike landed on target.

The zombie gargled and staggered back, releasing Blaze's arm.

A quick stab in the dark pierced the zombie once more, but before Blaze could remove his blade another zombie grabbed his shoulders from behind. He ducked straight down, knowing the zombie's clenching jaw would only be a second behind.

His fingers clutched for the handle of the knife, which slipped from his grasp as the first zombie collapsed.

Blaze turned to face his new attacker. He thrust several short elbow strikes to its head, each shot sinking deeper and deeper into its rotten skull until it also dropped.

"Asshole," Blaze whispered. He knelt down to search for his blade, and after his fingers curled around its familiar hilt, he quickly moved away.

By the time the growls grew distant, Blaze had no idea where he was, yet each stepped was greeted by more and space and light from above. Warm blood ran down his back and legs; the bamboo seemed to have struck out at him. He wondered if the zombies used this bamboo grove as a resting place . . . or were they as lost as he was?

Forever wandering.

A dim light drew his attention off to the side.

He noticed the red and orange glow of fire reflecting off the bamboo. The gaps between the wickers grew wider until the plain opened up before him. He'd never thought the barren plain, with its scattered fires, mountainous barricades and purple sky, could look so welcoming. Never again would he dwell within forests, unless a Gatherer was after him, of course. He walked on, and the dark figures around the fires grew larger, their shadowed bodies reflecting in the firelight.

Other than reentering the forest, Blaze had little choice but to sneak closer to a small group. It was the only way he'd get past and move ahead to the dark grounds and The Commons ahead. It bothered him that no one cared to live in the area closer to the mountain. Why risk spending the night so close to each other?

Most groups seemed to consist of three or four men, one person keeping an eye out for zombies and hunters while the others slept.

Blaze spotted a few women here and there. Although he was certain they'd be capable of taking care of themselves—anyone who ended up in this place had to have been a tough SOB at some point in their lives—he knew they stood no chance against the hunters he'd seen.

The groups didn't look or act like killers, not when they lived this close to each other. Sinners? Of course. But nothing more, he hoped. It seemed the people in these small groups only wanted to survive.

Easy pickings, sure. Unless that's what they wanted him to believe.

Was he just being gullible? Is that how he got killed in the first place? Trusting humanity?

I need to be more careful.

Blaze ducked behind a shrub, peeking through the barren branches. Three figures lay sleeping, curled up on the ground, while another stood guard.

Blaze twisted his foot for better balance.

One of the men sat up as if he'd heard it. He looked from side to side. This man was either a newbie like Blaze, or there just wasn't getting any proper sleep in this place, ever.

"Everything alright, Jack?" the man asked.

"Not a problem. I'll wake you when it's your turn to stand watch."

Blaze peeked over his shoulder, deliberating if the man hadn't really sensed something approaching. The plain stood behind him like a macabre oil painting, an ocean perhaps, and for the first time since he'd arrived, he felt truly alone.

Who were these people? What did they do to end up here? They were probably even more tired and hungry than he was.

He needed to find a place to sleep.

Fast.

Damn, these people really are a soft target. Like food on a platter.

They *seemed* harmless enough, and he could do with a few more kills before moving on to The Commons. The blow to the head had left him dizzy, stuck with a seemingly permanent headache.

"Shit," Blaze whispered as several hunched figures emerged from the shadows behind the group. The watchman, called Jack by his companions, hadn't noticed them.

Blaze's breathing quickened as he contemplated his next move. Should he warn them? This wasn't even his battle, but why did he feel he had to do something? Did this sudden onslaught of emotions mean he wasn't, and had never been, a killer? Hadn't he, only moments earlier, thought about killing them himself?

Fuck it!

"Watch out!" he called. Blaze jumped up and dashed toward them, more out of instinct than design. "Behind you!"

Jack looked at him but quickly spun around to meet the ambush. His four companions were already on their feet, joining the fight. They weren't bad fighters, but the zombies had caught them unawares, trapped in a limbo between awake and sleep.

"Fuck!" Blaze shouted as he drew his knife from his belt, looking for his first easy target.

One of the men was already on his knees, doing his best to keep a zombie's snapping teeth away from his flesh. Blaze punched the blade through the zombie's forehead, almost beating a hole through its skull.

He double-stepped backward, wary of being knifed by one of the humans; just because he was helping them didn't mean he trusted them.

He checked whether there was another zombie he could take down without putting himself too close to any kind of danger. Behind him, several people screamed, one clearly female.

Blaze couldn't turn around to help, a charging zombie only a few seconds away. He dared a quick glance over his shoulder to see a woman kicking a zombie off the injured man. He turned back and finished the zombie with a blade to the temple and a kick to the chest to free his blade.

He spun around to face two of the men in a standoff.

"What, not even a thank you?" Blaze asked.

No one said a word.

Behind them the woman, who Blaze had earlier mistaken for a man, tried to stop Jack's blood from seeping into the dry earth. It popped and gurgled from this neck and shoulder.

Jack was drowning in the woman's tears. Her ragged clothes, much like all the other clothes he'd seen in this world, were grey and dull.

"Shut up," one of the men ordered without taking his eyes off Blaze, "you're drawing too much attention."

Blaze looked around for any approaching hunters or zombies lured by the smell of fresh blood, then to Jack and his companions. "You're going to take care of him, right?"

The confused look on the man's face answered his question. They knew what to do, but clearly lacked the fortitude to carry it out.

"Please," Jack moaned. "I don't want to turn. Do it now."

"No," the woman cried.

"End it. Please."

The two men hesitated between tending to their friend and keeping a watchful eye on this new outsider.

"I know what you're thinking," Blaze said, "but you'd be dead already if that's what I wanted." He shrugged. "So?"

"We can't just kill him . . . he's our friend."

"Well you can't fucking leave him like this."

Jack's moans turned into screams of agony.

Blaze cleared his throat. "Fuck it. Step back and I'll do it. As in, step way back. I don't trust you either. Nothing personal, of course."

The two men hesitated for a second, nodding to each other before stepping aside to let Blaze through. He kept his eyes on them as best he could, ready for any sneak attacks. If they did attempt an attack, he'd go for the one on the left first, who seemed to be the faster of the two. A quick knife thrust to the throat should send him down, while the heel of his right foot would catch the other one squarely on his chest. The woman certainly didn't seem to have any fight left in her.

Jack lay silent, and as Blaze approached, he wondered if he'd be able to kill a man who wasn't fighting back. Perhaps his pity for this seemingly nice fellow would be enough to get the job done.

He stared into the woman's semi-dead eyes; she'd died a long time ago. She just didn't know it yet. She was so close to being a zombie, it scared Blaze more than the actual zombies. How long had she been trapped in this place? Waiting . . . yearning to die.

She was about to lose the only thing she had worth 'living' for.

She mumbled a few words as Blaze nudged her aside.

Blaze almost fell into the brown eyes of the dying Jack. He kept an ear on the two men behind him, in case they were thinking of attacking. While he wondered if he could truly be ruthless enough to kill an unarmed man, his hands moved without thought and slit the blade across the man's throat in one smooth motion, like he'd done it a thousand times.

The woman sobbed louder and collapsed onto her side, her knees tucked to her chest.

Blaze swallowed hard, shocked and ashamed at what he had done with such ease.

But why does it feel so good?

He turned to the others and stepped back, keeping all three of the survivors in view. He wouldn't attack them now. That opportunity had passed.

One of the men nodded to him. The proper response, of course, would've been a "Thanks," but this was no proper world filled with proper responses from proper people.

Blaze smiled and withdrew, stealing into the shadows the zombies had emerged from. Perhaps he would've killed them if the zombies hadn't showed up, for a killer surely lives inside him. They would never know it, but those zombies probably saved their lives.

He'd barely left them behind when the woman's scream slashed through the air.

Blaze spun around, his eyes searching. A hunter had descended upon the small group and, before Blaze took his first step in their direction, he stopped to watch, crouching behind a boulder.

The hunter, a tall man with dark hair down to his shoulder blades, had already killed one of the men. The second one blocked the hunter's first overhead strike, but he couldn't do anything about the second blade in the hunter's left hand, which thrust so hard into the man's skull his entire body lifted from the ground before crashing down again.

The hunter was stronger and faster than anyone Blaze had ever seen, including himself.

The poor woman hadn't stopped screaming since it began. Blaze's conscience screamed at his feet to move, but he just couldn't. Even with his skill, how would he ever be able to fight such a foe? It was all about self-preservation . . . Right?

Or was it just fear.

The almighty, ever-conquering FEAR.

The hunter walked up to her and stopped for a second, as if contemplating her worth. "Where is he?" he asked, his words traveling far enough for Blaze to hear.

She stopped crying, sat up on her knees and just stared at the hunter, awaiting her fate.

But when he put away his knives and reached with both hands for her neck, she couldn't help but scream—suffocating screams that halted the moment the hunter ripped her head clear off her shoulders.

Holy shit! What the fuck is this guy? Is he looking for me?

Was it possible for anyone to gather enough strength on this plain to do something as inhumane as snapping a backbone in two and ripping a person's head from their torso?

Weren't they supposed to leave this plain once they've killed that much?

The thought of becoming so strong excited him, but the knowledge of what had just happened was too disgusting to contemplate. He should've killed them himself. At least it would've been a bit fairer for everyone involved.

The hunter stared into the darkness, searching, almost sniffing the air.

Blaze slowly retreated as the hunter began searching for footprints, hoping he'd never see that man again, at least not until he himself had gained such powers. It would be a great pleasure to torture this man, and hopefully through that have a one-way ticket out of this hell hole.

***

Blaze hunched down and peered through the skeleton-like branches of a small thorn bush. About 100 yards across a barren piece of land stood The Commons, a makeshift wooden fort equipped with thick timber spikes for outer walls and a two story structure in the center.

Whoever had built it must've been around for a long time. He hadn't expected such a large structure.

Red and orange eyes flickered through the tiny cracks between the spikes, where fires burned from within The Commons. The spikes stood like fingers stripped of flesh, pointing to the heavens.

Heavens? Really?

Watchmen patrolled the walkway beyond the spikes, only their upper torso and heads visible. Spears bobbed up and down before them.

Contemplating his next move, Blaze glanced back and wondered how big the plain was. How long had it taken him to get to The Commons? Time was insubstantial in this place—somehow immeasurable.

That bastard is out there somewhere, as well.

When Blaze had first seen The Commons, he'd been ready to collapse. He'd dragged his weary feet through the dirt, yearning for food and water. Rest!

The center of the plain proved the most treacherous. He'd taken down a few zombies along the way to sustain his energy going forward. The longer Blaze went without a kill the more tired he grew. At times he had to travel out of his way for a quick kill. It made him wonder how the 'peaceful' Commoners dealt with this problem.

There had been one moment where he felt more afraid than ever, when he'd spotted a massive horde of zombies, zombies that never stopped or slowed, never slept. If they weren't feeding, they were searching.

For what?

Him?

Blaze hoped they'd stick to that area and leave him alone. Steer clear of The Commons. No wonder those human groups stayed clear of that part of the plain.

There were no trees in the immediate vicinity of The Commons. In a world like this, builders were limited in their choice of building material, but Blaze knew they wanted to keep the area clear to spot approaching threats. The question, however, was what would they do to an approaching threat?

What bothered and surprised him the most was the location of The Commons. It was too close to the mountains. He'd thought he somehow missed it, but then spotted it in the shadows; the mountains looming over the refuge like a guardian. He could clearly hear the blood-curdling screams coming from the caves up the hill.

How can they live here?

How were they allowed to live here?

Why would they live here?

Wooden walls would hold back the zombies and hunters, but it wouldn't hold back the Gatherers? Not from what he'd heard.

Something was clearly off about this place. He doubted whether he could trust these people, but he hadn't travelled all this way to turn back now.

Blaze stood up to allow everyone to see him. Pulling his knife out, he approached what seemed to be the gate, his arms outstretched and the knife dangling harmlessly from his fingertips. He immediately regretted not checking if the blade he'd pulled from his back was still safely tucked into his shoe.

"Stop right there," one of the guards called after spotting him.

Blaze stopped and the world turned silent, waiting to see what he'd do next.

"You'd best turn back if you value your life."

Blaze kept quiet. He eyed the man shouting orders at him: A stocky red-head with a long wooden spear resting on his shoulder.

"I said, take your little blade and turn around, friend. There's no room for you here."

Blaze wet his throat. "Not much of a life to live out here, you know. Thought I'd make myself useful and help you guys out."

"Fuck off! We have no need for more of your kind."

"What's that supposed to mean."

The men behind the wall laughed. There were now about ten who came to watch, looking healthy and strong—not to mention content. They had clearly found a way around the problem of growing weak without any kills.

Blaze peered over his shoulder, double-checking whether the guards, or that overzealous hunter, weren't sneaking up on him. "At least tell me your name."

The man's smile faded. "And what would you do with that?"

"Thoughts of the man who sent me to my doom will give me something to think about as I die alone. Or . . . if fate so demands, I need to know who you are when I bash your fucking skull in."

The silence accompanying the man's reddened face was only disturbed by one of the men finding himself in a fit of choking coughs.

Blaze slowly approached them. "Since you're clearly too ignorant to lead anyone, I suggest you send word to your leader. Tell him I'm waiting for him, and I'll keep waiting until he hears me out."

"Marcus!" the redhead shouted. "Show this filth what happens to folks with big mouths."

One of the men disappeared behind the wall. Seconds later, two men leaned over the palisade, each pulling on a rope connected to a sliding door. The wooden panel rose up and a zombie stumbled from the gap. Blaze noticed a small cubicle within the wall where the zombie had been standing, waiting for who knows how long to be freed.

Realizing it was their way of testing him, Blaze flipped the knife over and approached the zombie. "Let me put you out of your misery."

The zombie shuffled forward. The faded symbol of an unknown metal band adorned the zombie's torn T-shirt.

Blaze stopped and moved backward, luring the zombie away from the wall. He didn't trust the guards, and the last thing he needed was a spear through his torso. The distance also assured that all the guards would get a good look at his skills.

Blaze thought about a quick kill, but realized putting on a show for these men would be more beneficial. Whatever it took to get inside would be worth the risk. A fancy move or two, which he'd never do in a normal fight, now seemed the suitable option.

These thoughts allowed doubt to creep in, since most of the moves he had done up until then had been reflexes more than calculated efforts.

Blaze widened his stance and straightened his back foot. With the zombie approaching, he waited for the exact moment to torpedo his back foot forward, thrusting a thunderous kick to the zombie's chest.

The creature lifted off the ground and fell, before scrambling to its feet in a mindless effort, only to be met with a roundhouse kick to the temple.

Before it could turn back toward him, Blaze clipped the back of the zombie's knees with another kick. The zombie sat in a praying position and looked up at Blaze just as the blade was thrust into the top of its skull.

What was first mocking laughter from the onlookers now turned to a hush.

Blaze tucked the blade under his armpit and wiped the blood against his shirt. "You didn't really think one little zombie would scare me off, did you?"

Everyone stared, whispers moving from one man to the next.

"Can I see him now?" Blaze winked, not caring whether they saw it or not. He knew he'd made quite the first impression.

The redhead nodded to the others, his face pulsing a shade darker than his hair. All he needed was for smoke to plume from his ears.

A few moments later their leader, a skinny man

appearing to be in his early forties, emerged. He seemed to have been quite fat once, judging from the loose skin dangling from his arms, face and neck.

"Well hello," the man said, way too friendly to be taken seriously. "So, state your business, my friend."

"I need rest. And foo—" Blaze stopped himself, knowing there would be no food, unless his earlier 'saviors' had lied to him.

"Can't help you with food, mate. Sorry 'bout that."

"Please," Blaze said. He didn't plan on begging, but the lack of basic needs had weakened him more than he'd care to acknowledge. "There's not much else to do around here."

The redhead whispered into the leader's ear. Blaze hoped he was telling the man about his soon to be notorious fighting skills.

The leader shook his head, visibly dissatisfied.

"I'm quite handy, if that's what you're thinking."

The leader cleared his throat. "Like I said, we don't have much, but for a man of your apparent talent, we'll be happy to share. If you're prepared to do your part, of course."

The redhead shook his head as he turned away from his leader. "Let him in!"

***

Blaze entered a dark, stuffy room where a small cot covered the length of the farthest wall. He collapsed onto the cot, which seemed to be made from grass and what he hoped was some sort of animal skin.

Animals? Here?

He stared up at the ceiling, which was nothing more than widely spread, interlacing plant fibers. The gaps allowed some light to illuminate the room, but there would be no escape through the roof if things turned sour; he'd surely pull it all down.

He took off his shoes, rubbed his feet and flexed the tension from his toes, relishing the value of good shoes. No wonder men killed each other for a proper fit.

"If there's anything you need," Magdalene said as she peeked inside the room, "you'll have to go without it until morning. The others won't take light of you wandering around on your first night." Magdalene was an older woman who had cleaned Blaze's wounds and led him to his room—chamber, as she called it.

"Of course, I understand." Blaze couldn't help but feel things were too comfortable all of a sudden. Too easy. Then again, perhaps his luck had just turned.

I might just actually belong here.

Magdalene smiled. She was old enough to be Blaze's mother.

Memories pushed their way through the fog: His mother, back when she was a woman far too young to have two kids of her own. His father, whose botched family massacre/suicide had left him, young Jason, an orphan at twelve. He had managed to evade the family slaughter, since he'd already cultivated the habit of sneaking out of the house to visit his friends down the road. His disobedient streak had saved his life that time, but only worsened his life from there on out.

No wonder I ended up here. I'm damaged goods.

"You sure you're alright? You look a bit pale."

Blaze raised his head. "Just remembered some stuff." He smiled. "Damn, I must be quite pale if you can spot it in this gloom."

"Oh, the bad lighting. We only use the candles

while moving through The Commons, not the rooms. It's just too dangerous. But don't worry, you'll get used to it . . . eventually."

That final word stretched from her mouth with uncertainty. Did she know something he didn't? Would he even be around long enough to acquaint himself to the darkness within the fort?

"Thanks again," Blaze said. "Oh and my real name is Jason. That's what I remembered earlier."

More words halted at the edge of Magdalene's lips, yearning to be spoken. Words Blaze could only guess at: "You shouldn't be here" or "Go now, run before it's too late." Or perhaps she'd hug him and tell him how much she'd missed him. Blaze brushed away the odd thoughts of his forgotten mother.

"Goodnight then," she finally spoke.

"And I'll see you in the morning," Blaze said before Magdalene left, the light from her lamp fading away with her every step, darkness filling the gap. Her final glance still lingered within the room. Her lack of a smile in response to his words convinced Blaze he wasn't going to be around anymore by morning, and she knew it.

And now he did, too.

No wonder she didn't ask him his name, or even use it once he'd shared it—it was her way of keeping a distance.

He had indeed made a mistake. He should never have come to the fort. In fact, he hadn't felt safe since entering the fort. Of course, being forced to trust *any* people in his current situation was going to be quite an undertaking.

It had all started when he was required to

relinquish his blade before he could enter. With no other choice, he did what they asked and followed Houston, the redhead who'd set the zombie on him earlier. It didn't take Blaze long to realize Houston was second in command around the fort, while the leader introduced himself as Carl. There was no need for surnames on the plain.

"You'll get the knife back when you win our trust," Carl had said as he accompanied Blaze into the fort.

"I understand."

Blaze noticed Houston following them at a distance. It would take time to win Houston's trust, especially after their introduction. At least Houston hadn't discovered the small blade hidden in Blaze's boot.

The fort looked a lot more organized from this side of the wall—the walls barricaded with thick struts, and the guards heavily armed with spears, wooden shields and sheathed blades at their hips.

"It doesn't look like much," Carl said, a confident smile on his face, "but many a bloodthirsty hunter have thought us a weak target, only to be proven wrong. They think there are enough kills in here for a free pass back to earth."

"Do you also think so, that we'll go back to earth?"

"Back to earth or on to the next world . . . who knows. I just try to make the most of this one while I'm here."

Blaze nodded. "Well I look forward to helping out where I can. Whatever you need."

"I expect nothing less. Weak links put all our lives in danger."

As they walked on the soldiers paid Blaze little

attention, but most of the other inhabitants stared at him as if he'd done something terrible to them. "Can't really expect people to trust me yet, hey?"

He followed Carl into the fort's main building, its interior almost pitch black. A small flame flickered in the distance, moving toward them. A woman with a candle met them and led them farther along, past dozens of small, door-less rooms on either side, frowning faces floating in the dark.

Carl turned to him and wiped a bit of dirt from his eye. "I take it you don't remember much of the old world, yet?"

"Almost nothing," Blaze admitted.

"Well, you let me know when you remember. I'm mighty curious to find out where you learned to fight like that."

"Same here."

Being led through the narrow and warped corridors, past smirking faces, Blaze had never felt so vulnerable in his life. Their shadows surrounded him— lost souls searching for a home, trapping him like starving children waiting for the dinner bell. Yearning for whatever he had to offer.

And he had no idea how to get back out again. He'd tried to keep track of where he was, but kept losing himself in his dark surroundings.

Yet they continued on, past more dwellings and passages. The fort looked a lot smaller from the outside. They finally entered a spacious meeting hall in what he believed to be the center of the fort, a large tree stump holding up the high ceiling. Large rectangular gaps running across it allowed more of the outside gloom to sneak through.

Several people sat around a crude table beside the tree, seemingly nodding their approval. Almost licking their lips. Blaze hoped he had only *imagined* that last bit.

Carl stopped and turned to Blaze before they reached the men, only to notice Houston had followed them. He approached Houston and whispered a command in his ear.

Houston snarled something back and the two men exchanged more heated words.

Blaze eyed the other men. He couldn't help but feel this display was a trap to draw his attention while others snuck up from behind to kill him.

Houston retreated beyond the doorway, barely visible but still there. Carl's smile returned so fast Blaze could only deem it fake.

Just as Blaze thought he'd made the biggest mistake since his arrival in this world, *she* entered the room.

"Ah, there you are," Carl said. "Blaze, this is Magdalene. She'll be your . . . host for the evening."

An unusual calm washed over Blaze. He wasn't sure why, but the older woman, nearly grey and clearly in her late forties or early fifties, reminded him of someone—someone he must've known from his previous life.

"Well," Carl said smacking his lips, "try to get some sleep . . . We'll meet here in the morning for a chat. Take care now."

Blaze nodded, unsure how to react to the hint of sarcasm in Carl's voice.

"Over here," Magdalene ushered him to a crude chair beside the table.

Blaze sat down, forced to turn his back to the others, and the woman started dusting off his pants with a dry cloth—an old T-shirt or something similar.

The men around the table continued their conversations about the ugliest zombies they've ever seen.

Are women only here to serve? Shit, this can't be a good sign.

Blaze searched his mind for conversation starters, and even though the situation was clearly awkward, he felt more and more at ease with every passing moment. "What . . . what are you doing?"

"Just checking for bites or scratches. Scratches can still be treated with some human blood, but bites . . . damn, that's a whole other problem."

"Feels more like you're measuring my muscles for something unpleasant."

Magdalene laughed. "Like eating you? No thanks."

Blaze forced a laugh.

Human blood? Fuck, from where?

"What do you do to still the hunger?"

"Mmm?" she mumbled through pursed lips, her concentration fixed on cleaning and inspecting his person.

She'd better not stumble onto that blade.

"I mean, it doesn't look like any of you are hungry or thirsty. Have you found a way around the hunger?"

She looked up into his eyes for a moment, then smiled. "Unfortunately not, my dear. But, after a while, you adapt to it, if you abstain from killing, of course."

"Killing makes it worse?"

"Of course. Killing is the tool of the hunter, those who seek to fight a way out of here. But if you submit and live in peace . . . Let's just say the hunger gets turned down to a whisper, but it'll never truly disappear. It's like being on drugs. You miss it less when you're no longer hooked, but you'll always have a craving." She stood up and took a step back, observing him.

"Makes sense." Blaze stretched out his shoulders and back.

Magdalene stood up and dusted her own knees before tucking the cloth into her belt. "All right then. Follow me."

Blaze accompanied her down another narrow hallway, constantly peeking over his shoulder, expecting only the worst. The passed a few guards patrolling the passages, each with a candle in hand.

Damn, I hope that's animal fat in those candles.

Just as it started to feel like he was trapped in the reeds again, his attention was diverted to the not-so-distant screams emanating from the mountains. He hadn't realized it before, but the screams had been sounding since he arrived. "Aren't we a bit close to the caves? Is it safe here?"

"You'll get used to it. You'll be surprised how much you can get used to after a while in this place. *Believe me.*"

"What do you—"

"Magdalene!" a guard called from behind.

"Coming!" She turned her attention to Blaze and pointed down the hallway. "You'll find your chamber second door to the right. I'll be back in a bit."

***

Several hours had passed before Blaze dared peek out of his room, not that time had any relevance anymore.

He had waited for the last stragglers to come back to their rooms and settle in for a few hours' sleep. There would still be guards on duty, but this would be his best opportunity to either escape or sneak around. His feeling of dread was still unconfirmed, and a little snooping might be exactly what he needed. He'd definitely feel more at ease if he knew the way out.

With his shoes back on, he snuck out the room. He moved past the first room, hoping the dark figure on the cot was asleep.

Silence.

Blaze moved past the next one and heard a faint snore drift from the darkness within, then continued in what he believed to be the direction of the meeting hall.

He listened to the fall of his own footsteps crossing what felt like some sort of carpet, wondering whether anyone else could hear him. Snores creaked and croaked from all sides.

Voices ahead.

He stopped short of an intersecting hallway and peered around the corner, where a guard stood with his back toward Blaze as he leaned into a room. The other voice belonged to a girl.

He'd have to sneak by unnoticed. He couldn't risk getting lost trying a different route, and he was pretty sure he was on the right path.

Not wanting to waste time and be caught by another guard from behind, Blaze skulked one step closer.

"A guard is always on duty," the man spoke.

Another step. Although he was 'dead,' he could swear his heart was still beating against his chest.

The woman mumbled.

Shit, he'll hear me. Then everyone will come charging out of their rooms.

"I'm at the service of the people, you know?" the man flirted.

Blaze crouched down, almost directly behind the guard. Hopefully the girl wouldn't be able to spot him, the guard's candle shining in her eyes.

"I'll be back in a little bit," the guard said, half turning toward Blaze.

Blaze didn't know if he should lie down for cover or somehow kill the guard and his lady friend without a single word escaping their lips.

He fumbled for the throwing blade in his shoe, rubbing it with his forefingers to test its weight. He'd sit still and wait, only to strike if the guard noticed him. If he had to, he'd plunge the blade into the guy's throat and then whirl it through the air and into the woman's forehead. If luck would have it.

"I thought you said you're here to *service* the people." The flirtatious tone of her voice made it clear that her words were accompanied by some sort of physical gesture, as well.

The guard turned back to her and entered the room.

Blaze snuck past, trying not to look.

Some things will always be more important.

He carried on toward the meeting hall, where perhaps he'd get his hands on a more combat-ready knife, preferably his own, and sneak out of the fort. Even better, he could try to get hold of Magdalene and find out what was really happening.

Was he leaving too soon?

Was this sense of distrust something he'd brought from his old life, or the result of his dearly departed friends Bones and Scrubs?

A light at the end of the tunnel signaled what he believed to be the first of his destinations. Voices crept from the meeting hall.

" . . . just too good to lose," a voice sounding like Houston's said as Blaze inched closer.

"He must have had some sort of military training. It's not like he'd be the first soldier we've ever lost." It was Carl. "What if he was a serial killer? He did end up here, after all."

"Exactly," Houston said. "With all the rest of us. He would fit right in."

"What if his memories come back? Then what? What if he figures he'd rather kill us all in our sleep? Nothing will stop him then. And his memory *will* come back."

"I just think we'd be better off keeping him."

"What the hell?" Carl said. "You're the one who almost didn't let him in."

"Why are you being such an asshole about this?"

"Calm yourself," Carl spat. "I'm still in charge around here. Make no mistake about that. It's my choice."

"No, it's our choice. All of us. Our lives are at stake. And there's too much that can go wrong. We need to keep him."

"Don't you get it? He's the perfect sacrifice," Carl said. "I see what's going on here. If we go your way, you'll probably kill him in his sleep for his strength. Do you really think you're the only one who's thought of that?"

Blaze's throat tightened. *Sacrifice?*

"He's definitely better than the other sacrifices below," Houston reluctantly said.

Below? Another level below us?

Blaze looked down at the carpet-like fabric below him before sneaking closer. He could see the two men seated at the table, contemplating.

They didn't seem in a hurry to go to bed, and the room was just too well lit to sneak through unnoticed.

Hoping to find another way out, through the basement perhaps, Blaze turned to sneak back to the intersecting hallways, and looked up at a dark shadow standing before him, and the fist that followed.

The punch landed on his temple, slamming the side of his head against the wall. He slumped down but forced himself up, only to be knocked down with a kick.

Blaze grabbed a leg and punched the small blade into the man's groin. The screaming man's body shuddered and crashed to the ground.

Blaze tried to stand, but someone tackled him from behind and pinned him down, his blade-wielding arm now trapped beneath his chest.

"Hold him down," Carl shouted. "Don't give him room!"

It was Houston lying on top of him, and Blaze relished at the opportunity of killing the man.

A sharp pain shot through his side. He could feel a blade scrape against his ribs.

More footsteps rushed toward him.

Another kick in the face.

A barrage of fists and sharp cuts across the tendons of his knees, arms, and elbows.

Even above his feet.

All he could do was cover up and take it.

A women screamed in the distance.

After a few more attacks they picked him up, but his limp hand was no longer able to hold the blade. They slammed him against the wall and continued the beating. Blaze stared down at the blood oozing from his wounds.

The woman screamed again, her voice closer yet still far away.

Houston raised his elbow high and brought it crashing down on Blaze.

Blaze could do little more than flinch, falling deeper and deeper into a world of hurt, and when he opened his eyes again he was back home, a mere teenager hiding in his closet, listening to the dying screams of his mother. He could hear his father shouting at her to shut up. Over and over as dull thuds silences her screams. He couldn't move, could do nothing to save his mother and sister.

The house fell silent.

The young boy tried to calm his breathing, to silence the air gushing noisily in and out of his mouth.

The sound of footsteps and a grown man crying preceded his father's journey down the hallway.

A young Jason clasped his hand over his mouth and closed his eyes. Too scared to beg or pray. Once again, too scared to do anything, but save himself.

"Where are you!" his father shouted. "Please, son. I . . . We need to talk."

He remained quiet.

His father entered the room, rummaged around,

and then stopped. The deafening gunshot brought Blaze back to his current fight for survival.

But the fight was already over, and he'd lost.

Blaze caught glimpses of the floor as they carried him away and tossed him into a dark pit beneath a trap door. He spat sand from his mouth and crawled across the dark sand,, away from death and pain. All he could think of was the memory of what had happened in his real life. The guilt of being too scared. The guilt, which had stayed with him his entire life. His memory of not being there that night was a lie he'd used all his life. A lie he later believed.

***

Blaze opened his eyes, but the world remained black—tainted in pain that crawled up and down his body like a purring cat looking for the perfect spot.

He tried to move but cringed in pain. His energy levels were nearly depleted.

Had anyone ever been this close to death? One more punch or kick surely would've ended it.

Magdalene! Why?

Had she known all along?

Of course she did. Fuck!

But Blaze should've known. It was his punishment. He deserved this betrayal for abandoning his mother.

A cough sounded from within the surrounding darkness, leaving Blaze to hold his breath. So he wasn't alone, he knew that much, but were the others in the same state he was?

And who were they?

What felt like ages passed before Blaze assured himself there were no monsters coming to tear him apart. The others were probably just like him, prisoners who were once lured into The Commons. He wondered if Bones and Scrubs knew about this. Perhaps this had been their plan all along?

He sank deeper into the darkness, closed his eyes, and waited to die.

What a horrible place this world has turned out to be.

A light ripped him from his reverie.

Voices around him stirred, crying in fear.

A candle descended down a ladder in the center of the basement, a room he could now distinguish as roughly the same size as the meeting hall. Several men traversed the ladder, mumbling as they pointed at some of the other figures who, just like Blaze, were lying against the wall, waiting to die.

"No," the men mumbled, yet they hardly had the strength to raise an arm in defiance. "Please."

"This one will do," one of the men ordered as he pointed to someone in the far corner.

The man could barely speak as they dragged him by his feet and lifted him up through the trapdoor. The light moved away until the trapdoor was bolted shut, and darkness crept back in. Darkness and silence.

"Oh, fuck! Fuck me!"

"Relax," a voice spoke close to him. "You're still too strong for them to risk moving you."

"Who's there?"

"Just an old man. Nothing special."

"What are you talking about? Move me where?"

"Outside the fort somewhere. From what I've gathered, they sacrifice us to the Gatherers, then use the bones and other leftovers for tools and utensils. Weapons and so forth. Our blood for medicine."

"Fuck me," Blaze said.

"That's pretty much what they do, yeah. They take the weakest ones first. Less of a risk or something."

"No wonder they're not scared of them. Or as hungry as the rest of us. Damn, so they'd rather live in this world forever than take a chance to get out of here?"

"You ask me, they're a bunch of scared assholes. They'd rather pay tribute to those Gatherers than put up a fight. I'm an old man, and just a bit of defiance is enough to keep me alive."

Blaze gathered his strength and pushed himself closer to the old man. "Good for you."

"Yeah, well. It's so damn boring down here, I'll probably just let them take me."

Blaze chuckled. "I guess not everyone's as chatty as me."

"No one wants to get attached, the old man said. "Whatever. I don't have much strength left, anyway. My time's pretty much out."

"I just have one question. Why didn't they let me in immediately? Why did they refuse me until they saw me fight?"

"Probably a smoke screen. Can't be too easy to get in here, otherwise they'd be swarmed. My guess is they send someone to track you down after you leave, then drag you down here with the rest of us. It's pretty crowded down here."

"Not crowded enough to start a revolt."

"Not with these guys, but that's actually not a bad idea."

The old man fell silent. Blaze heard a shuffle and felt the man's musty breath on his skin. The old man swallowed audibly. "You need to kill me," he whispered. "Kill all of us."

"What are you talking about?"

"Quiet . . . You said you can fight, right?"

"Yeah, pretty damn good, actually. Not sure how, but yeah."

"Don't worry about that. It takes a lot longer for that memory to come back. But now, now you have us to feed on. Take our strength and fight your way out of this place. Take these bastards down from the inside."

"Uh, it's . . . it's a good plan, but I'm not going to kill you."

"You hardly even know me. I'm going to die soon, anyway."

"I can take you with me."

"No. I'm done. And you'll need all the strength you can get."

"Fuck me," Blaze said.

"Go ahead. It'll be all right."

Blaze knew he had to do it, but wanted to hold it off for as long as possible.

"You need to fight back, my friend. Now. I'll be fine."

Blaze gazed through the darkness at the old man. "Any last words?"

"Kill me. Then kill them, and embrace who you *really* are. We all deserve to be here. Remember that, and you'll make it out of here."

Blaze gathered what little strength he had left and sat up, turning toward the old man.

"Go ahead, before they come. You need to be ready."

For the first time since his true death, Blaze

struggled to finish off a kill. Such an easy kill at that, even with his diminished strength. For some reason he'd grown quite fond of the old man in their short time together. "Good luck, my friend, wherever you end up."

"And to you."

He shifted toward the old man and cradled his head with both arms, half smothering him. Blaze pulled him closer to his chest, and using the last of his strength, fell forward at an angle, his weight snapping the old man's neck.

He hoped it was at least painless.

And as the old man's energy flowed through Blaze's body, awakening his vigor for life, he regretted not asking the old man for his name.

With the renewed strength of the kill came the revelation of who he used to be. He was a city detective and martial arts instructor to stunt men, and although he'd fought crime on a daily basis, he had a dark side which kept calling out to him. He never followed his dark thoughts, but always wondered what it would feel like to give in to his desire . . . to kill in cold blood. Looks like evil thoughts were enough to send him to this horrible place in the shadow of the mountain.

In that moment of recognition, the veil of resistance that had shrouded his dark side lifted. The little bit of restraint or guilt that he had felt with each kill disappeared, and the joy he felt multiplied, becoming orgasmic, tantric!

He thought about who he was and who he'd be from now on; although he used to be Jason back on earth, deep down he knew he was now a combination of the old and the new him. He was Blaze, a warrior who would never again hide or retreat—the perfect killer.

The old man's limp body fell from his grasp. Blaze rose to his feet and stepped forward, his eyesight unhindered by the dark.

"Time to go to work."

A smile curled across his cheeks as he plunged into an orgy of death and blood topped off with even more strength . . . Power! It took all his willpower not to shout in pure ecstasy.

****

When the last body gave its final shudder, Blaze stomped and pulled until an arm ripped from a nearby dead body. He yanked the meat off until he could break off a small piece of bone, about a finger's length. He eased his own finger over its sharp edge.

Only then did he hear the commotion outside. While Blaze was killing, he'd planned on breaking through the trapdoor to kill the guards off one by one, but he felt ready for whatever they had in store.

A large section of the wall began to rise. The normally dim light from outside suddenly seemed like a sunny day.

Blaze readied himself for whatever would come through. All he spotted were the ropes from above raising the door, and the dirt incline that lead up and out of this hole. Warm air brushed his cheeks.

"You can take them all if that one won't do," Carl shouted, his voice shaky. "Please. We've got plenty down there."

Blaze walked up the ramp to face the wall of zombies, at least a thousand strong, standing between The Commons and the mountain. In the lead stood their leader—a Gatherer—at nearly seven feet tall it was a beast on two legs, draped in black.

Between The Commons wall and the Gatherer sat the skinny man they'd pulled dragged off earlier.

The men above Blaze gasped at the blood and guts all over his body, but all Blaze could do was stare at the fiery gaze of the Gatherer.

"Where are the others?" Carl screamed. "What have you done?"

"They're dead," Blaze said, "just like you'll be soon. You and that dick of a Houston."

"You son of a bitch!" Houston hollered.

"Leave it," Carl said. "It's clearly interested in him."

Behind the Gatherer, the ocean of the undead swayed from side to side, awaiting the command of one of their masters. They didn't dare attack without its consent.

"You see, Great One," Carl spoke, "this offering is much more than just a man. He's a great warrior. Probably the best you've ever had."

"A wonderful sacrifice," Houston squeaked.

The Gatherer turned toward Blaze and raised its head to sniff the air in short, ragged intakes. An impossibly low voice reverberated from its throat, "Perhaps."

The trapdoor slammed behind Blaze, echoing like a starting bell of a boxing match.

Ding-ding, motherfucker!

Blaze approached the Gatherer with cruel intent, the surrounding zombie horde stepping closer, enclosing them like a human barrier during a school yard brawl.

The Gatherer pointed a bony finger at Blaze and took a giant step forward.

A few feet from his opponent, Blaze lost himself once more in the beast's fireball stare. It was fearless.

The creature reached with long arms and grasped Blaze by the neck. It raised him up, but Blaze refused to dangle his legs like a hanging man, or show any signs of pain.

"You fool," the creature said through the charcoal hair inching over its brimstone skull. It tried to laugh, but it sounded more like a drowning gurgle.

Blaze reached his right arm over to grab hold of the creature's middle finger and curled it back slightly. He hoped the beast would be able to read his thoughts: *How dare you try and rule me?*

With one quick movement he pulled the finger back, which forced the creature to focus on its grip instead of its opponent.

The beast only laughed.

Blaze smiled and thrust the short arm bone he'd salvaged into the Gatherer's neck. It's skin was tough and leathery, too thick for a mere man to pierce, but with the power Blaze had obtained from the massacre in the pit, he succeeded to plunge it through the skin and up into the burning red ball beyond the creature's eyes.

The following events occurred in mere seconds: The Gatherer's ear-piercing screech spread like a tidal wave through the zombie wall. A rumbling growl emanated from the monster, who was still holding onto Blaze's neck, swinging him from side to side. Steam whistled from the gash in its neck and scorched Blaze's arm.

Blaze screamed.

The Gatherer's red brain pulsed brighter then

faded, grew brighter then faded, faster and faster until it exploded in a ball of fire that instantly ran along the creature's long hair and down Blaze's right arm. The Gatherer let go and crumpled to the dirt.

Blaze hit the ground with a thud. His right arm was burnt beyond recognition, withered and in terrible pain. He hardly heard Carl's shriek, but quickly noticed the spear flying toward him. Blaze rolled sideways to dodge it.

The zombies moaned and trampled around, unsure of what to do. They had clearly never seen one of their masters fall. It didn't take the zombies long to decide who their first target would be, and their steps quickly directed toward Blaze.

Blaze struggled to stand. The first wave of zombies reached Blaze. He ducked below their outstretched fingers, the icy cold pain in his arm too excruciating to fight with.

The zombies encircled him, reaching out.

The Gatherer gave one last final ear shattering cry, and died.

The zombies stopped.

A wave of life force crashed into Blaze's body, his skin moments away from ripping apart.

The surge stopped.

Blaze pushed himself up and looked at his arm again. It was no longer burnt or shriveled. His entire body radiated with supernatural strength.

The eerie cries of the other Gatherers echoed from the mountain caves. Their screeches filled with anger and pain.

Blaze jumped up, plucked the spear out of the ground, and hurled it toward Houston, whose attention was drawn to the mountains. The spear torpedoed through the man's shoulder, sending the wide-eyed henchman toppling from the walkway.

The zombies still swayed as they stared at him. Just waiting.

With his newly acquired unnatural strength, Blaze grabbed hold of a zombie and flung it through the air, watching it crash through The Commons' barricade. The zombie hardly cared being picked up, so Blaze tossed a second one and threw it even farther, watching it penetrate the center of the fort.

The people inside screamed.

Blaze looked at the opening in the fort's fence, then at the zombies waiting for him. He pointed a finger at the fence and shouted, "Attack!"

A thousand zombies turned in unison upon the Commons, shambling their way toward the opening.

Blaze continued to fling nearby zombies over the fence into the guards on the walkway and into the fort itself. He grabbed hold of one last zombie, hurling it toward Carl, the fearless leader who now just stood mouth agape. "Have a nice day, motherfucker!"

The two bodies smacked together and disappeared beyond the wall.

"Fire!" someone shouted from inside The Commons.

The fire, perhaps caused by a zombie falling through the fort and onto a candle carrying guard, spread faster than the swarm of zombies charging the weakened fortress.

Screeches from the approaching Gatherers stung Blaze's ears. He looked toward the mountains and the forest below, where thousands more zombies made their way forward. They joined his own army, but instead of charging The Commons, they pushed and clawed their way through to reach him, following the commands of their own Gatherer leaders.

Shit. They're not under my control.

Blaze turned back to the screaming Commoners. Black smoke tumbled through the air like angry hornets. The Commons was fully ablaze now, along with a few dozen zombies who'd ventured too close to the welcoming heat for a taste of cooked meat.

Magdalene!

No, she's one of them!

How could he be certain she wasn't in on it from the start? She had to have known what her people did with newcomers. Of course she had. She was probably dead already . . . and he was alone once again.

But he had to try. In this life he had to go back and at least try.

"Finally," a voice spoke from behind him.

Blaze turned to meet his next opponent, knowing full well who it would be. The hunter, who had earlier slain the small group Blaze tried to help, waved him closer.

If Blaze could only remember who this man had been back on earth. Somewhere their paths had to have crossed. He was certain of it.

The two men eased into their fighting stances, skulked forward just beyond striking distance, and circled each other . . .

"Why me?" Blaze asked? "Why did you slaughter those people to get to me?"

"You're special, of course."

"Do I know you?"

The hunter lurched forward and into combat, Blaze skillfully ducking and dodging as the two men exchanged blows. Although his opponent was faster, Blaze quickly realized he was a lot stronger. Stronger than the man who ripped out a spinal column!

Still Blaze could not get past the man to save Magdalene, his desperation costing him a few cuts on his arm and torso.

Blaze peered over the hunter at the inferno The Commons had become.

It was too late to save her.

Just like in his old life, he had failed to save the woman.

It's all my fault. Everything.

But why? Is it really all my fault?

Then he realized it. Just like this hunter had just stopped him from saving Magdalene, his father would've stopped him, as well. Even though he'd spent his entire life learning how to fight, he was just too young that day. He would've failed miserably, no matter what. It might be too late to save Magdalene now, but he could still take down the man standing in his way.

He blocked the hunter's overhand attack, faked a punch and charged forward, tackling his opponent. The force sent them both to the ground.

Blaze pushed his elbow against the man's chin, pinning one arm under his knee and the other in his free hand. "Who are you? Why are you after me?"

"Because you're good," he grunted. "Rumors were spreading about you and I wanted to be the one to take you down. That's all."

"Liar!" Blaze shouted without thinking "You killed her. You killed my mother."

"What are you talking about?"

A part of Blaze wanted to believe this man was his father, but he knew it couldn't be. His father's soul had travelled through this place long ago. But now he could finally fight back by taking down the hunter.

The hunter slipped out the side, taking advantage of Blaze's momentary distraction. They rolled across the sand, over rocks and brush until the hunter pinned Blaze.

He pressed his forearm against Blaze's throat and leaned forward with all his weight.

The pressure on Blaze's throat tightened, the hunter's bloody teeth grinning down at him.

Something forced the hunter to look up, and his smile turned into a frown, his eyes widening. "No, it's not fair." He rolled off Blaze.

Blaze, fighting to regain his breath, turned to see the other Gatherers approaching, like giants cutting through the zombie horde. All around him the zombies stood, and waited.

"He's mine! His powers are mine!" the hunter shouted.

Blaze spat blood onto the dry dirt and rushed forward. A dropkick to his chest sent the hunter sprawling into a wall of zombies, who didn't waste any time ripping the man apart.

Blaze stood, watching the Gatherers as they surrounded him. There were twelve of them. Clearly he'd killed their lucky number thirteen, and he was about to pay for it.

He should've killed the hunter himself, instead of offering him to the zombies. He was going to need the extra strength.

One of the Gatherers circled Blaze like an encroaching predator sizing up its prey, perhaps wary of underestimating a mortal like the other one had.

It lunged forward with a massive right foot torpedoing toward Blaze's chest. It moved so fast Blaze hardly had a chance to dodge it, the heel of its foot crashing into his shoulder. It was a blow that would've ripped the arm of a normal man, but Blaze managed to strike out with his left fist. His fist glided off the Gatherers skull, and both warriors stepped back to reevaluate each other.

The Gatherer inched forward.

Then stopped.

It straightened, and dropped its guard.

Blaze caught the hint of a smile upon the creature's lips before it turned toward the mountain. The other Gatherers followed and the group started marching, forcing Blaze, stuck in the middle of this group, to keep up.

At first, he thought to strike the Gatherer when it dropped its guard, or even refuse to follow them, but he suddenly didn't feel wrath emanating from his opponents. He hardly felt forced to follow them.

Have I proven myself worthy?

They're leading me back to the real world.

Earth?

Reincarnation!

As they left he took one final glance back at the smoke billowing from the remains of The Commons. The fort was gone, and so were the screams. At least he'd leave the plains behind a little bit safer. Give everyone a better shot at surviving.

The zombies stepped back to make space for the

procession, turning their attention to other food sources supplied by the barren plains.

They entered the forest, the Gatherers gliding effortlessly and silently through the trees. The heat resonating from the cave entrance increased. It was a lot hotter on this side than where he'd entered days before. Even the trees and scrubs had died in front of the entrance.

Once inside the tunnel he fell in line with the Gatherers. Except for what Blaze thought to be illuminating fungi, the tunnels were dark, but he had little trouble following the fireball skulls of the Gatherers. They crossed several side tunnels on their journey. A journey no man would've been able to complete without a guide.

The screams within the tunnels were deafening. The air filled with the stench of burnt meat and blood. And hot death.

He could see the orange glow of the real world pulsing from another opening ahead.

He was almost there.

The Gatherers stopped, their bony fingers pointing for him to continue.

Blaze glanced back several times as he walked on, checking that they weren't about to kill him from behind.

The smile on his face cracked his dry lips and the crusted blood on his cheeks. He could hardly wait.

The orange glow grew bigger and brighter . . . then it darkened into a fiery red.

A wave of heat washed over Blaze's bare skin. He stepped to the cliff of a world basked in fire, a world worse than anything the men on the plain could ever have imagined: A lake of fire, and dozens of winged demons sitting atop fire-breathing dragons that soared through the air.

Trudging knee-deep through the fiery lake marched legions of chained zombies. Whips cracked the air as the army of blazing zombies composed of great warriors like himself marched to the orders of their demon keepers.

The ground beneath his feet crumpled away, sending a helpless Blaze sliding down the slope toward the lake, and his undetermined future . . . in the lake of fire.

Fuck me!

INTO THE VOID

ARMAND ROSAMILIA

BLAZE COULD HEAR the crowd chanting through the concrete walls of the arena as he sat in silence, ignoring the other men around him.

"You're up, Joe," one of the handlers said, opening the dressing room door.

"Let them wait" Blaze/Joe said. "This is what they've come for, right?"

The handler shook his head. "The boss is going to be pissed. You shoulda been in Gorilla Position ten minutes ago."

"Let him get mad. The only reason this is a sellout tonight is because I'm in the main event." Joe lifted the gold title belt on the table next to him. "He can send every guy in this locker room against me. It doesn't matter. None of them can beat me." Joe looked around the room at the other wrestlers but none met his gaze. "That's what I thought."

The handler shook his head again. "Joe, you're just asking for trouble."

***

Blaze woke with a start.

He was about to roll over and try to go back to sleep when a shadow passed over his body. Without thinking, instinct kicked in and he lashed out, striking Bones in the face with his heel.

He was on his feet and pivoted just as Scrubs came at him with his own newly-acquired knife. Bones began crawling away, out of the hole they'd been hiding in.

"What are you doing?" Blaze asked. He may have been weaponless, but knew what he was capable of. The dream hadn't merely been a dream; it was a flashback to something important. He had been a professional wrestler, a good one as far as he knew. A title holder. Someone the fans cheered for.

"Nothing personal, Blaze. It's just dog eat dog out here. There isn't enough food and water for everyone," Scrubs said. He glanced at Bones, who moaned. "Shut up or you'll call a hundred zombies to our spot, idiot."

"Give me back my knife and let me leave. And my name is Joe."

Scrubs shook his head. "Sorry, I can't do that. If we let you go you'll just circle back in a day or two and kill us in our sleep."

"Like you were trying to do to me?"

Scrubs shrugged. "Again . . . nothing personal. You seem like a nice guy. You're big and you can fight. Which is why I wanted to kill you before you woke, but dumbass screwed that up. I think you broke his nose."

"Thee bloke my nothe," Bones repeated, covering his face with his hands, blood spurting between his fingers.

"I'll do worse if you don't let me walk away," Joe said.

Scrubs shook the knife in his hand. "What makes you think you can make the rules? If you drop to your knees and bow your head I'll make your death quick, I promise. Bones and I decided when we met, we'd work together. Just the two of us. We've taken advantage of quite a few newbies over the last few weeks. It's no coincidence we hang out near the caves where everyone begins. We sucker them in as they stumble around and can't remember who they are. Before they remember and become dangerous."

"I know who I am," Joe said. He tried to seem casual, but he was ready to spring into action at any moment. "I think you're in trouble."

"I know who you are. You're a killer like the rest of us—a thief, a liar, a bad person. It's no sin to get rid of you. Or anyone else who gets in my way," Scrubs said.

Joe smiled. "Did you ever watch pro wrestling?"

Scrubs looked confused. "Not since I was a kid."

"You're about to get your ass whooped by the World Heavyweight Champion . . . Big Chuck Wagon."

"That's a stupid name," Scrubs said.

"Holy Thith . . . I thoughth he loothed familiar," Bones said. "He's the Unstoppable Forth."

"Huh?" Scrubs asked.

"They call me the Unstoppable Force, because no one can beat me. No one. Especially not someone like you," Joe said.

Scrubs grinned. "Wait a minute, I know you now. You were in the news. You killed that guy in the ring in Madison Square Garden. Broke his neck and then wouldn't stop kicking him. You were so high on drugs you thought wrestling was real."

"You think it's all fake?" Joe asked and suddenly shifted to his left, his wrestling training taking over. When Scrubs tried to follow the move, Joe went right and drove his arm into Scrubs'. It was almost too easy for Joe. The crack echoed across the plain.

Scrubs fell to the ground, holding his broken arm. "You're fast for a big guy," he said. "I'm about to be killed by a celebrity." he said through clenched teeth.

"Better me than Paris Hilton," Joe said and retrieved his knife.

"We've seen her," Scrubs said.

Joe made quick work of both men, who had resigned themselves to their fate. At each death he felt invigorated, like he'd just slept and had a great meal all at once. He liked the feeling.

***

"What do you have to offer?" Big Chuck Wagon asked the giant of a man. "I only fight if there is something in it for me. You know the rules."

"Rules? There are no rules. We're in Purgatory. It's kill or be killed. And I'm going to kill you," the man said. He stood a head taller than Chuck and was broader in the shoulders. Chuck had filled out in the last few weeks of fighting and gaining power from the victories.

He was no longer Joe and Blaze. Those personas were a distant memory to him.

He'd learned to practice his moves on the zombies roaming the plain. When he'd reached The Commons he'd taken on their champion and defeated him in no time. Then, he defeated the next five men, killing them with his bare hands, even though weapons were allowed.

This man was one of the warriors who fought at The Inferno, the killing field closer to the caves the Gatherers lived at. Chuck had heard a rumor that he had killed thirteen men so far. Obviously he was undefeated, since he was still alive. Chuck had killed ten since he'd begun—those two nameless guys in the catacombs, Scrubs and Bones, and six others. Each time he killed, his thirst for food and drink had been quenched, his need to sleep gone for a time. The more he killed the stronger he would get. If he could keep ahead of it he'd never feel tired or hungry

Chuck put his arms out and looked at the gathered crowd. "This little boy thinks he's still fighting old men in The Inferno. Don't you know where you are? You're in my world now. There are rules." Chuck pointed at a woman standing nearby. "Woman, can you explain the rules to this fool?"

She folded her arms across her overlarge chest and frowned. "Who are you calling woman, you steroid punk bitch?"

The crowd roared and Chuck grinned. "Do you think you're so bad you can talk to the champion like that?"

"You're no champion. Just a lucky guy who hasn't met me in combat yet," she said. Though, she was a thick girl Chuck wouldn't underestimate her strength or speed because of her extra weight. He'd wrestled men close to four hundred pounds that were as graceful as ballerinas.

"You are on shaky ground, Chubby Warrior."

The crowd roared again.

"You're nothing but big talk. I've watched you fight. You're not as good as you think you are," she said. "This Chubby Warrior is going to squash you like a grape."

"Not so fast." The large man shook his hands. "I challenged him. I am known as Samson."

"Ha! Then I will cut off your hair and shove it down your throat before I break your neck," Chuck said.

"I'll fight both of you," she said.

Chuck smiled. Two opponents? This would be a great challenge. When he defeated two fighters the rest would fear him more. He looked at the hushed crowd. "What do the people say? Should your champion fight these two and spill their blood for your enjoyment?"

The crowd cheered like his wrestling fans had done for all those years. "Chuck! Wagon! Chuck! Wagon!"

"Then it's settled. We fight to the death," Chuck said.

All three fighters stepped into the rock circle. As far as Chuck could tell, the makeshift arena had been here long before anyone in The Commons had lived here, and the oldest surviving members say it looked weathered back then. The Inferno was miles long. People came to either die or test their skills in killing. This was the designated spot to fight. Not that it stopped anyone from killing anyone else in other places, especially with no real law, but it gave people something to do.

Chuck decided the crowd would want to see Samson go down first. Then, after that was done, he'd toy with the woman. He'd never faced a female in the ring before. The only women he'd worked with in pro wrestling had been divas and eye candy half-dressed bimbos he'd try to grab a quick feel on *accidentally* if he could.

Since eliminating Bones and Scrubs, his past life had come back to him in broken fragments: The constant traveling, endless lines of groupies, drinking to go to sleep, doing drugs to stay awake, shooting steroids and popping pills to maintain muscles and stamina If he wanted to go to a club and drink all night for free, he could. Chuck could snap his fingers and every two-bit local drug dealer would be giving him coke and heroin for free, just for bragging-rights. Guys would offer up their girlfriends for sex. There was nothing in life Chuck couldn't get. And he got all of it in excess.

Until that fateful night.

Chuck almost missed the woman's quick attack, who had lunged for his kneecap, due to his reminiscing. He jumped up and backed out of her range.

"Nice moves, honey," he said. "I think I'll kill your boyfriend first and then wrestle your clothes off."

"Big talk for a little man," Samson said.

The three circled while the crowd chanted and clapped.

Chuck saw he'd unnerved her by his comments. He decided to push her into making a fatal mistake. "Tell me, Chubby Warrior . . . are your boobs real? They must be. They droop so low."

She looked pissed and went on the offensive but didn't protect her side well. Samson stepped up and punched her in her side, knocking her into the dirt.

"No more games. I came to fight a Champion, not some fat chick," Samson said.

"That's pretty mean," Chuck said as he maneuvered his way between Samson and the woman. "Especially for a guy who probably has a small weapon in his shorts."

Samson smiled. "I see what you're trying to do and it won't work. That cow was stupid, attacking in blind rage. I'm going to methodically rip you apart and claim the title for myself."

Chuck stopped moving and held up two fingers. "You're missing two key points."

Samson stopped moving. His hands were still ready to throw a punch as he stared at Chuck.

Chuck held up one finger and played to the crowd. "His first mistake? Underestimating his foe."

"I doubt I've underestimated you," Samson scoffed.

Chuck shook his head. "It's not me you've underestimated." Chuck held up a second finger.

The woman punched Samson in the groin from a kneeling position behind him, connecting solidly. As he fell forward she stood and drove her foot into his back over and over, watching Chuck as she did.

"Number two: Never turn your back on an opponent, no matter how insignificant you think they are," Chuck said.

When it was obvious he wasn't getting back up anytime soon, she stopped putting the boot to Samson with a final kick to the head. "Enough talking. I'm here to fight."

"I'm here to spank your fat ass," Chuck said and grinned.

She looked mad for a second before a calm washed over her features. She grinned. "You won't fool me again. Trash-talk all you want. I'm a big girl and I'm damn proud of it. In fact, I'm going to sit on you with this fat ass and break your ribs. How does that sound?" She slapped her ass cheeks and the crowd cheered.

Chuck had to laugh. He was actually enjoying himself. So far, most of the opponents were cowards who wanted to die but were too afraid to kill themselves, or they were men who thought they had something to prove. Taking out the Alpha Male on this world was the quickest way to do it. Unfortunately, Chuck had destroyed the top tier of them, and he was firmly in control.

"You can claim all of his items," Chuck said and pointed at the dead Samson. "It will make it easier for me when I claim everything you have, too. Then I can take it all in one shot. Isn't that the law?"

"You're even stupider than you look. There is no law. Only ruin and zombies. My name is Macaria and I bring you blessed death."

"Fancy. I'm sure your real name is something stupid like Amber, though. Every Amber I've ever known was a fat girl."

He'd pushed the right button. She charged him.

Chuck sidestepped at the last moment and tripped her. She went sprawling into the sand, scrambling to stand and right herself.

He lunged, driving a knee onto her back as he used his weight and momentum to pounce, hearing a satisfying crack. She spasmed and screamed. He'd broken her back.

"Finish her," someone from the crowd shouted.

Chuck stalked around the woman, laughing as the crowd's noise rose in volume. This is what he lived for. This is what he'd died for, too. And Chuck was getting comfortable with it. If he died on this battlefield he'd die like a man.

"Kill her," another person yelled.

Chuck took a few steps back. The woman was broken, panting and trying to breathe through her cracked ribs. He'd destroyed her body and as he walked in front of her and bent down, he could see the pain and fear in her eyes. She was completely lost.

"Finish me," she whispered, and coughed.

Chuck walked around her again, waving his arms so the crowd chanted his name.

He pulled his knife and knelt over her body, reaching around her dramatically and slicing through her neck. As the blood hissed in the hot sand, Chuck stood and licked the blade clean.

***

There was nowhere to hide from the sun.

Chuck wrapped his head with Samson's shirt and used the woman's shirt across his back to block the heat.

He was bored. Since killing the woman, word had spread he'd vanquished two opponents at once. His legend went to the far reaches of this plain. Chuck hadn't had a challenger in days, and he spent his time keeping in shape by going further and further away from The Commons and killing zombies, who offered no threat.

Chuck came across three men wielding long browned clubs. "Where did you find those weapons?" He pulled his knife. He'd enjoy fighting three armed men. It would be quite a challenge.

"You are the champion." One of the men tossed the club on the ground. He turned and ran, and his companions stumbled backwards before fleeing in opposite directions.

Chuck picked up the weapon and realized it was a bone, but it wasn't like anything he'd ever seen. It was as long as his forearm but thicker by twice its girth, and he had big arms. Whatever kind of creature had bones this big and thick was one Chuck didn't want to run into.

The men were still dots on the horizon when Chuck saw something different in this never-ending land of sand: A makeshift hut built into the side of a mound. It looked unnatural. Someone had been building.

"Hello?" Chuck called out.

He didn't want to get attacked by anyone, and wondered if the three men lived here. If they had, since they'd fled, he could claim it for his own.

The hut, made of sticks and dried mud with an air hole on the top, looked like a hornet's nest. Chuck took another step forward, surveying his surroundings. He noticed no footprints except his own. The three men had given the hut a wide berth when they ran. Had they even seen it? Only when Chuck had been nearly on top of it, had he seen the dwelling.

"Is there anyone inside?"

He circled warily, perplexed by the randomness of a hut in the middle of the desert plains.

Apart for the air hole on top, there was no entrance.

Was it an insect hive? A relic from a century ago? Something new? Chuck wanted to investigate but he was fearful for the first time in a long time.

Going back to The Commons to ask questions wouldn't work, either. The people feared him. They kept their distance except when he fought, cheering him on. As soon as the fight was over they scattered. He realized he hadn't spoken with anyone in weeks, except to taunt them before he killed them in the ring.

Chuck walked slowly to the hut, brandishing the

bone club. He spun around, feeling like twenty eyes were searing into his skin. He was alone, though.

His mind screamed for him to turn and run, but he took another step to the hut. He didn't shy away from a confrontation.

Chuck had been in Purgatory long enough to regain his full memories. He remembered being a small, weak child who'd been picked on as a kid at school. He'd spent middle school lifting weights and using protein shakes and supplements, chiseling his body from the little fat kid into a ripped monster. The steroids began in tenth grade, to gain more mass and muscle, and he'd gone to the State Championship in the eleventh and twelfth grades for wrestling—and won.

College had been one long party and wrestling meet, he'd excelled at both aspects. Unfortunately, he couldn't be bothered with the academic side of college and had flunked out, even though he'd had ample chances to pass. Hell, college chicks had even done most of his homework for him and he'd still managed to flunk out.

That's when the pro wrestling companies came knocking.

He was offered a six month tryout period for two hundred bucks a week, which soon turned into a two hundred thousand dollar a year contract. His steady march to wrestling heel and champion.

Chuck was arrogant and crude in the ring, and he didn't care. He loved the booing from the crowd. After a while, the boos turned to cheers, because even his haters respected him. In the ring he knew what his next five moves were going to be.

But now . . .

Chuck tested the side of the hut, expecting it to collapse at a mere touch. Instead, it felt hard and strong. He used both hands to push against it. The structure didn't budge.

Chuck used the myriad of sticks as hand-holds and scaled to the top of the twelve foot hut. He looked down, into the hole, but the darkness concealed the interior.

"Come inside," a booming voice called, startling Chuck. He slid down the side of the hut, landed on his feet at the bottom, and put the bone in front of his body.

He saw an opening on the side of the hut, which was not there before. Chuck was sure.

Inside, pitch black darkness greeted him.

"Who's there?" he asked.

A small fire in a pit lit up, and a cross-legged robed figure sat on the opposite side. "Come inside," it repeated.

Chuck stood tall. He was afraid of no man, so he walked inside and stood over the fire. "Who are you?"

"Sit."

"I think I'll stand," Chuck said.

"Then we will not speak. It is rude to ignore a host's command, even from a guest as esteemed as The Unstoppable Force," the figure said.

Chuck grinned. Once again someone knew who he was, but who was this robed person? "Take off your hood so we can have a face-to-face conversation." Chuck sat down on his knees, so he could easily jump into a standing position if the situation required it.

"That is not possible."

"Why not?"

"Because, to see my true face would drive you to madness. It is for your own good. Trust me," the figure said.

"Then what do I call you?"

"I am a Gatherer."

Chuck was confused. "Everyone tells me the Gatherers live in the caves and come out to hunt humans. You torture and kill us. Isn't that true?"

"Very much so."

"Are you planning on trying to capture me?" Chuck asked, casually gripping the bone club. He gauged the distance between them and knew he'd have to lunge forward to execute a strike.

The Gatherer put up a gray, skeletal hand. "No need for violence . . . just yet. I came to talk with you. That is all. If you feel the need to attack, I will not stop you."

"Is this a trick?"

"No, simply reality. The hut is surrounded by twelve of my brothers. At my mental command they will annihilate the space we sit in. There will be nothing left. While my life, if you want to call it, is not important . . . your life is. For now. But no one is so important they cannot be destroyed. Do you understand?"

Chuck grinned. "You need me for something."

"For now we need you to stay alive. No more fighting."

"No way," Chuck said. "Fighting is all I have now."

"I can offer you so much more if you show patience. Think about it. If you die you will be tossed into a fiery pit to spend the rest of your days," The Gatherer said. "And if anyone kills you they will become the Chosen One. The strongest will truly survive."

"Why me?"

"Because you are a survivor, and you have the skills to continue to survive. This plain is simply a rest-stop for your true placement. What you do here affects the rest of your journey. Your soul is the only thing you have left now. We intend to help you on your voyage, but in order to do this there is only one steadfast rule: Do not die."

Chuck nodded. "How long until you get me out of here?"

"Soon enough. Now go, and hide if you must, but stay alive," The Gatherer said.

"What about my strength? I need to kill in order to stay awake, not die of hunger or thirst."

The Gatherer laughed harshly. "If you die, hunger, thirst, and exhaustion will be the least of your worries. Take no risks."

***

Chuck was sprawled on his stomach, watching from the top of a sand dune at the men fighting below. He'd been gone for, what he assumed was, four days. Time was hard to tell, but he'd slept three times so far. His stomach groaned.

When it was obvious he wasn't coming back, the fighters had grown tired of waiting and began to battle. Within two days a large man with a shaved head and long goatee, bearing many scars across his torso, had started to destroy the competition.

Chuck held himself back, but he wanted so badly to run down the dune and challenge him. The warrior was nearly as good as Chuck. He used his strength to attack his foe, clubbing them to death with only his huge forearms and large hands. Man after man was beat into submission this way. No battle lasted more than a couple of minutes.

Chuck was growing impatient. He'd done as The Gatherer had told him, walking away from The Commons to hide. He knew when the time came they'd find him no matter where he hid, but the only thing he'd found was desert and zombies.

He'd dispatched the undead with ease.

They were more a nuisance than a threat, really. A couple of times he'd ignored them altogether, simply walking by as they reached out for him. Chuck feared no man, especially those who were already dead. The thrill of killing a zombie was nonexistent now, and he sometimes thought of going into the forest where the zombies congregated to see how many he could kill with his bare hands.

With nothing better to do than watch the pseudo-champion killing his competition, Chuck decided to take a long stroll to see just how many zombies he could find.

***

They were the first real trees he'd seen since he'd awoken in the cave, even if the trees were bare and stunted. The large grove, perhaps a mile long and half a mile thick, was covered with the dead.

Zombies stood silent, staring with bloodshot eyes into space. They didn't move, an unnerving sight for anyone still breathing.

Chuck covered himself in sand with only his head showing on the side of a nearby dune and watched . . . Nothing happened.

An hour passed. Not a single zombie moved. Chuck wanted to take a closer look but if he got too close he was afraid some silent call would go out and thousands of zombies would hone in on him. An army of zombies, marching along the desert, would not be fun or fair.

Chuck smiled, pulled himself from the hot sand, and began the long trek back to The Commons.

He formulated the plan in his mind as he moved, ignoring the zombies crisscrossing the desert in front of him. Quite a few were moving in the general direction of the forest, and he wondered if the ones he saw walking were just on their way to the rendezvous.

He decided to test a theory but it would involve something even he wouldn't be proud to do.

***

The man was old, and feeble. He was obviously new here, because he looked like a frightened little bird.

Chuck had been hanging around the cave system where he'd first entered Purgatory for two days until the man appeared, bewildered.

"Hey, friend, are you lost?" Chuck approached casually, trying not to frighten the old man. He was sure there was no danger of him running away successfully, but Chuck didn't feel like working too hard. The lack of food and water in his system, made him weaker and his skin was crisp, burning too many spots. As the champion, he'd been able to scare people into giving him their meager possessions, like the clothes they came in with or anything semi-edible. Now he was fighting to stand on two feet.

The old man looked wary but he finally waved at Chuck. "Where am I?"

Chuck approached and shook his head. "Where did you come from? What's your name?"

The old man looked like he was concentrating but

then shook his head, a tear in his eye. "I don't really know."

Chuck lifted his arm and pointed behind the old man. "You see that bus station? You can get on there."

The old man turned. "What bus station?"

Chuck stabbed him between the shoulder blades and turned the knife. "I just need you to die for me and turn into a zombie. No big deal."

There was a small spot near the cave that offered shade. Chuck knew it was dangerous being this close but he needed to watch the body of the old man to see what happened, if anything. He didn't really know if this was how you created zombies. What if the zombies weren't the dead people? Everyone who killed someone made sure they lopped off the head just in case.

Chuck tried to stay awake as he watched the unmoving body. He thought of his former life, and all the bad things he'd done to get to the top. The backstabbing deals he'd made against other wrestlers. Friends in the business he'd come up with. His former trainers who he'd screwed over at the first sign of a bigger payday. The men in the ring he'd hurt for spite or just for fun.

The many women he'd used. At first it was for their money and a place to crash because he was broke. Later, it was for the sake of having arm candy for publicity and media gossip. Later, it was for how much he could degrade them . . . if he thought about it, he was glad he hadn't just ended up in Hell. It was where he belonged.

He must've dozed off because he woke with a start. He'd been dreaming and there was a scratching noise.

At first he was disoriented, but then saw the disturbed ground where the old man had been. As well as the footprints that led away.

Chuck smiled.

The tracks led in the direction of the forest of zombies.

***

He was pissed.

It had been weeks since he'd spoken to the Gatherer. He roamed the area where he thought he'd first found the hut, looking for answers. How long was he supposed to act like a coward? He just wanted to leave this retched place. Chuck had never been weaker in his life, and the hunger pains were eating him alive.

Zombies roamed the area but he no longer tried to kill them. In fact, he went out of his way to steer clear of them. He would watch them move slowly in one direction, unless they were provoked or if they spotted him, but once he was out of range they'd go back to their journey.

And Chuck kept going back to The Commons to watch the people there without being seen. Until . . .

"Holy shit, is that him?"

Chuck rolled over and cupped his eyes to block the sun. Three men and a woman stood about fifty feet away from him.

"Can I help you?" Chuck asked, standing and showing them his bone club. "Or do you just want to do the sensible thing and go away?"

"We thought you were dead. Taken in the night by Clubber," one of the men said.

"Who's Clubber?" Chuck asked but he already knew—the new champion who'd taken his spot when

209

he disappeared. "That fat, bald bastard? I could crush him within minutes. Tell him to enjoy his brief reign."

The woman stepped forward. "Why don't you challenge him? We want to see you fight again. It's all we had to live for. Reclaim your championship. Clubber is just an animal. There is no show. He catches his opponent and beats him into submission and then kills him. No drama. No showboating. Nothing."

Chuck shook his head. "I'm done for now. I can't fight."

"Are you hurt?"

"I have sworn not to fight until they come for me," Chuck said.

"Until who comes for you?" the woman asked.

"The Gatherer told me to stay alive and I will go to the next plain."

All four people began to laugh.

"The only ones to ever talk to the Gatherers are dead people. How do you think the zombies are created? By talking to the Gatherers. I think you've been in the sun too long. It's starting to affect what little brain you had," a man said.

They all laughed but stopped when Chuck raised the bone weapon.

"What are you going to do with that?" another man said and grinned. "Didn't the Gatherers tell you not to fight?"

"No. They told me not to die." Chuck took two lightning steps forward and crushed the man's head in with the bone. "There's no chance any of you could stop me, even fighting together." Chuck felt the rush of adrenaline coursing through his body. It had been too long since he'd killed.

A man tripped as he tried to run backwards and Chuck simply slammed him in the face as he went by. "Two down . . . "

The woman and remaining man were running together, trying in vain to get away from Chuck.

If they'd split up they would have had a small chance for one of them to escape, but running side by side . . . they would both die.

Chuck jogged after them, enjoying his renewed vigor. He was still following the law of The Gatherer: Don't die.

The two people finally got their wits and separated, the woman heading toward The Commons. Chuck knew the man had told her he'd sacrifice himself so she could warn the others. How chivalrous of him. Chuck admired the man, who would do something so noble, even in a place like this.

For a brief second Chuck thought about going after the man and killing him quickly, but then turned and began running as fast as he could in the direction of the woman.

Out here there was only one rule . . . kill or be killed.

If he was lucky he could double back and find the man again.

***

The woman tried to beg for her life, but Chuck ended her pleading quickly. He wasn't into torturing people, especially women. He took his time killing only when he had an audience who appreciated what he was doing. The power surged through him.

Chuck made sure not to damage the head and left her sprawled in the sand before following her footsteps back to where the two people had finally split. The man was moving at what looked to be a fast walk but as Chuck jogged in his direction he saw the man had veered and looped back around, heading toward The Commons. Obviously he'd seen Chuck not following and knew the woman was his target.

It felt good to be running now, keeping stride with the man. He hadn't looked like he was in great shape, so Chuck knew he could catch up.

Chuck wasn't even winded yet.

He crested a large sand dune and went to shoot down the other side when he stopped.

Below him was a large gathering of people, and they all looked up when the man he'd been chasing pointed and shouted.

Their new champion, grinning, pointed at Chuck and then made a motion with his hand to join them. Chuck stood on the dune. He glanced back the way he'd come, knowing he could outrun most of them.

But could he outrun the entire group?

What if he grew tired and they caught up. If he wasn't one hundred percent in fighting shape someone could get lucky and take him out. He didn't want to take the chance.

Knowing he needed to conserve energy and bide his time, Chuck walked slowly, at a diagonal angle down the sloping sand dune so he couldn't be surrounded easily.

He wasn't surprised when he saw their champion angling with him. "So, you're the big bad Chuck Wagon, huh? I used to watch you on television when I was a kid. I even had a picture ripped from a wrestling magazine in my gym locker. I hung my four State Champion medals on the door, too."

This close, Chuck got a better look at the guy. He actually looked familiar.

The man idly put his fingers through his tangled beard. "I won several competitions in college. I could've done anything I wanted at that point, and I did. I followed my hero into the ranks of pro wrestling, first at a wrestling school and then doing independent shows in the circuit from New Jersey to Maine. I learned to use my body like you do. I learned to move like a lighter man in the ring, and copied your moves but made them more powerful. You know what they billed me back then?"

Chuck sighed. He recognized the man under that straggly beard. "They called you Meat Wagon, the son of Chuck Wagon."

"And what did you do?"

Chuck smiled. "I had my lawyers sue you and the company you worked for."

The man stabbed a finger in the air at Chuck. "You destroyed my livelihood. You took away a huge contract and buried me."

"You could've changed your name and worked anywhere else. Don't put that on me," Chuck said. He remembered all the articles written about the man. Truthfully, Chuck had thought it was kind of cool to have someone copy him. When his bosses saw it, however, they wanted to bring the guy in and match him up with Chuck. Chuck wasn't interested. This guy was too hungry, much younger and had the look in his eyes Chuck used to have. The kid would've embarrassed Chuck in the ring. "You still had a viable career, but you chose to make stupid decisions, like beating your girlfriend in Vegas and working for piss-poor promotions. You tarnished your own name."

The man was hot, pacing back and forth now as the crowd watched him. "I can defeat you. You know it and I know it."

"In the ring? Hardly. Even at my weakest and you in your prime, you would've never taken me," Chuck said.

"Prove it." The man stopped pacing and grinned.

Damn ego, Chuck thought. It had gotten the better of him. He didn't want to take the chance of being killed and losing out on the Gatherers' promise. He supposed dying would put him out of his misery, anyway, but once again it was the ego that took hold. "I don't want to fight you."

The crowd began to murmur.

"You can't be serious. By rights, you're still the champion, unless you're afraid of Meat Wagon defeating you once and for all."

Chuck shook his head. "I'm not afraid of you. I just..."

The man he'd been hunting pushed through the crowd. "He says the Gatherers spoke to him and said not to fight."

"They told me not to die," Chuck corrected.

Now everyone was laughing, especially Meat.

"This is a joke, right? Even I know the Gatherers don't talk to us. They hunt us. They kill us. Unless I kill you first, of course," Meat said. "Enough with the ridiculous heat-induced ramblings. The Gatherers aren't interested in you anymore than they're interested in us. We are here to fight."

"I'm not interested in facing you right now," Chuck said. "Someday soon, though. You can count on it."

"You're serious?" Meat asked. "You won't fight me?"

Chuck wanted to smash the man's teeth down his throat, but he hesitated. What if this was a test? Even now The Gatherer could be watching to see what he did. "I will meet you in three days in the center of The Commons and we will square off," Chuck lied. He knew if he didn't at least promise Meat something he'd be set upon, the crowd blocking his escape. It was worth the gamble.

"How do I know you'll come back?" Meat asked.

"You don't. You only have my word, which is all a man really has out here, right? If I don't come back in three days feel free to bring the mob and rip me to pieces," Chuck said, knowing every word of it was a lie.

"Not good enough. I want to face you in combat. Man versus man."

"Then I will see you in three days. And Meat . . . once I destroy you and you're lying on the ground about to die, I will reclaim the championship and the Wagon name once and for all."

***

Chuck stomped off to the zombie forest, his anger and embarrassment feeding him as he walked away. He'd backed down from Meat in front of everyone, even if he defeated him in three days (which he had no intention of doing), the living will remember his reluctance. No one would respect him anymore.

He was so deep in thought over what had transpired he nearly walked into the waiting arms of the zombies in the Bamboo grove.

He got within twenty feet of the tree-line. Some of the zombies began to moan quietly, all bloodshot eyes staring hungrily. Other zombies crowded forward, but none stepped onto the sand.

"What are you waiting for?" Chuck asked. "I'm right here. Fresh meat. All you have to do is follow me and I can show you where all the good food is. Come on."

Chuck waved his hand but not one zombie stepped out. He looked up and down the line, awed once more by the sheer number of undead. There must be thousands upon thousands of them, all pushing to get a look at him.

He needed to figure out what it would take for them to follow. Chuck walked up and down the line, feeling like a general addressing his troops before a great battle. "Aren't you hungry? Aren't you interested in a free meal? I can take you to a place where hundreds of living and breathing people await you. All you have to do is keep pace with me. I am willing to give this to you. Can't you see it?"

When the noise of someone or something stepping into sand behind him came to his ears, Chuck smiled. He turned to see one zombie, an older man with one ruined eye socket and a missing an arm, out of the forest and facing him.

Chuck pointed but kept a safe distance. "You see? It can be done. We can do this together. We can help each other. This is a win-win situation."

As five more zombies stepped onto the sand, Chuck began backpedaling, grinning. By the time he turned and walked over the first sand dune, trying to not walk too fast, though staying out of reach, perhaps a thousand of walking corpses had begun to follow his lead.

***

No one witnessed the majesty of so many zombies marching slowly across the sands, one slow step at a time. The stench of rotting flesh brought tears to Chuck's eyes when the wind shifted slightly.

The Commons wasn't too far, but at this shambling pace the horde wouldn't arrive in time. What's more, Chuck needed to rest at some point. But how could he?

All Chuck could do was to keep walking. Every now and then he'd stop, turn back, and make sure he wasn't too far ahead. If he was, he'd wave his arms and jump up and down a few times to make sure the zombies stayed on course.

***

Chuck strode into The Commons; all eyes turned to him.

Someone ran off, but Chuck ignored it.

He wanted the thousands of people in The Commons to gather in this spot.

"Where is your false champion?" Chuck asked the crowd. "Has he run off scared?"

Meat appeared, walking through the crowd, slapping his shoulders in preparation for battle. "You are the chicken. You were supposed to be here yesterday. I assumed you came to your senses and tried to run as far away from me as you could. Tomorrow I would've hunted you down like the animal you are," Meat said.

The crowd cheered. Chuck noticed that many of his former fans now booed him.

Not that it mattered, because Chuck was going to make them all pay soon enough. "I'll fight you all. I'll battle and kill every person standing," he yelled.

Meat laughed. "Big words for such a coward. Why don't you come here and face me like the man you aren't? I'll crush you in front of everyone."

"I'm not going to fight you. I want to kill you last." Chuck turned to everyone around the area. "The first one who can catch me gets a free punch. How does that sound?"

Meat frowned. "Is this a game to you?"

"Life or death, asshole. I guess someone as big and stupid as you can't really run." Chuck looked at the others. "And everyone else is so pathetic. No wonder you're here. What a bunch of losers. The Gatherer was wrong when he said whoever could kill me would be free from this place, because none of you have the balls to do it."

It took a while for Chuck's words to sink in. When they had, the first man ran at Chuck, with a few others trailing behind. Chuck scampered up the sand dune, laughing and mocking them for being too slow. He got to the top. A few were only steps behind.

He'd planned it perfectly.

Just as Chuck got to the top, he veered right and ran as the zombies marched forward, the first group of men and women coming over the ridge were swiftly grabbed by the undead and dragged into their ranks.

Chuck slipped down the dune, a few hundred feet away, and backed up, watching as zombies ripped apart the people on top of the ridge and fell onto those trying to get up.

It was a massacre.

But Meat was nowhere to be found.

Chuck kept his distance, watching as many men and women ran from the melee, but more than half of them were killed and eaten by the zombies. Zombies slid and fell down the dune, before righting themselves and continuing to walk.

He knew most of the people would survive since the zombies were slow, but they'd be scattered in every direction. Many had been caught unawares, though, and Chuck decided that the plan had been successful. He was quite proud of himself.

Three zombies slid down the embankment and fixed on Chuck, moaning as they shuffled to get at him.

"After all I've done for you?" Chuck used his bone club to pummel them to the ground before splitting their heads like melons. He kept circling to make sure no one got the jump on him, zombies or the living.

He saw Meat, wading through the throng of undead, punching and knocking them over with ease. His eyes were locked on Chuck as he strode through the horde.

Chuck grinned and motioned with his hand to keep coming. He hoped Meat would be overwhelmed, but knew it wasn't likely.

People ran past him, too far to take a cheap shot and bash their heads in. Chuck kept one eye on Meat and the other on the zombies and living in the area.

These people have no loyalty to their heroes, Chuck thought. You step away from the spotlight for a few days and you're replaced. It was the same sad story in pro wrestling. He had no idea how long he'd actually been gone, but he knew his legacy had already been tarnished with the accidental killing in the ring, as well as his subsequent trial and suicide.

Chuck stopped dead in his tracks.

He hadn't thought about taking all the pills with

the bottle of vodka, when he was sitting in his beach condo. At that time, he had two days to report to prison. He'd planned to throw a going away party that night, where all his fake friends would be—those who were left. None of his wrestling buddies would show, according to their vague excuses. Chuck knew the wrestling company had told the men and women in the locker room to distance themselves from him and the situation.

He'd be stricken from the commercials and his action figure would be pulled from the shelves. His *Best Of . . . Big Chuck Wagon* DVD was going out of circulation, and the book deal had already been taken off the table. Even his own agent, who'd made a ton of money off Chuck over the years, wasn't returning his phone calls.

"You ready to die?" Meat asked when he got within twenty feet, pulling Chuck out of his memories and into the present. "This is going to be a dream come true for me."

"You're not only stupid, you're delusional," Chuck said. He swung the bone club in his hand and smiled.

"I don't need a weapon to break you, only these hands," Meat said. "I want your death to be very personal. I'll stare into your eyes as I strangle the life out of you."

A zombie walked between the two men and Meat grabbed it, breaking the neck in one move without taking his eyes off Chuck. "You're next."

"I'm not impressed."

The ground rumbled. The dune to the side shook and a stream of sand slid down, forcing both men to walk away without taking their eyes off the other.

Chuck watched as the zombie behind Meat fell to the ground, jerking like it'd been hit with a Taser. "What's happening?" he asked.

Blow holes of sand appeared all around them, throwing the living and undead into the air. They crashed to earth from twenty feet up and went quiet.

Neither Chuck nor Meat was touched, but they were both hesitant to take a step, either. All around them the sand erupted, washing them in a sand cloud but not hurting them.

It was over in seconds. The dust began to settle.

Chuck could see the silhouette of Meat, still standing a few paces away, but he wasn't on the attack just yet.

And as the sand fell back to the ground a third figure had joined the two men: A Gatherer.

***

Chuck straightened up.

The Gatherer was here to take him out of this horrible place. He smiled. He'd be doing it right in front of Meat, too. How fitting.

The Gatherer put up both of his bony hands, sliding out of the robe. "Welcome to the final test."

Meat grinned. "I'm looking forward to this."

"Wait . . . what?" Chuck asked incredulously.

The Gatherer turned toward Chuck, face still hidden in the robe. "Did you think you were the only one looking to leave this plain of existence?" Plane is correct in this instance, as in a level. Harkening back to my D&D days.

"I've been biding my time as well, Chuck. Doing the things I needed to do to get to this point. I've been gathering all of the living to the Commons with promises of a great fight between us." Meat nodded at The Gatherer. "Now I see what you did. You had Chuck bring the zombies and in one battle you wiped out thousands of the living and the dead. Brilliant."

"I brought the zombies. It was my idea," Chuck said.

"Was it?" The Gatherer asked. "Do you really believe you still have free will?"

Chuck said nothing. He'd been played, and so had Meat. Both men had been pawns in some horrific plot to annihilate thousands.

"Now what?" Meat asked.

"You are forever the impatient one," The Gatherer said. "For your parts in helping me and my brethren cull the population on this plain, you've been given a gift of sorts. You will fight one another to the death. No witnesses. No glory other than the chance for the one who survives to move onto the next plain."

Both men grinned.

***

"Are you planning on cheating with your toy?" Meat asked, pointing at the bone club. "I would if I were you. I won't blame you for trying to even the odds. After all, I'm stronger, younger and in better shape. You look like you've spent the last few days leading zombies across a desert. Oh, wait . . ."

"You don't look so good, either. I remember when you were a young puppy, trying to emulate your hero, you had much better bulk and a great shape. Now your arms aren't as big. I'm guessing not taking the juice has started to get you back to a smaller size. Too bad. I would've loved to have crushed you in your prime," Chuck said.

"Enough talk," Meat said.

Chuck threw the bone club to the side, within reach. He had no problem using it if need be. There was no way this guy was going to defeat him, and he'd had enough wrestling matches where he'd used a foreign object or substance on his opponent to gain the advantage. With no refs or spectators, no one would know how he'd won. As long as he won. Even The Gatherer had disappeared when they weren't looking.

Meat took a step forward and feigned an attack, but Chuck wasn't easily fooled.

"You want to dance all day in the hot sun, or get this going?" Chuck asked before taking a false step back and then charging Meat, who managed to get his arms up in time to lock hands together.

"You're slow. That move wouldn't fool an amateur wrestler," Chuck said, pushing against Meat as they struggled to get the other one onto the ground by force.

"You talk too much. I never liked that about you," Meat said, sweat popping onto his bald head. "I'm going to make sure I punch your teeth out before you die."

"You can try," Chuck said through gritted teeth. Meat was definitely strong, and Chuck had to take a step back before he was knocked down. As he went back Chuck suddenly pulled instead of pushed and kicked Meat in the exposed stomach, even though he was aiming for a groin kick.

When Meat released his grip and doubled over, Chuck gripped him in a headlock with his right hand and began punching him in the temple with his left, jerking Meat's head back and forth.

Meat reached out and locked his hands around

Chuck's back, squeezing him in a bear hug and finally lifting Chuck off the ground. He was forced to release the headlock.

Both men went to the ground, the hot sand spraying their faces. Meat was on top, using it to his advantage. He threw punches that Chuck blocked with his arms, but he was getting tired. Lack of food and water had weakened him.

A punch got through his defenses and cracked against his jaw. Chuck could taste blood in his mouth and tried to throw Meat, but the man was now sitting on Chuck's stomach and locking his legs behind him so he couldn't move.

The blows rained down on Chuck, who weakened quickly. Another punch to the face broke his nose, and Meat, straddling him, laughed as he got into a rhythm of punches.

Chuck put his right hand to the ground, exposing his side. Meat swung and connected with the side of Chuck's face, knocking teeth loose.

But Chuck had done it on purpose. When his hand came back up he was gripping sand, which he tossed into Meat's face—blinding him.

As Meat's hands went to his eyes, Chuck rolled over and expelled Meat, struggling to his feet.

"I'm going to torture you now," Meat said, rubbing his eyes.

Chuck was done with this fight. He spit three bloody teeth into the sand and stumbled away from his opponent.

"Get back here, you coward," Meat yelled.

Chuck fell to his knees in front of the bone club and sighed. He was out of breath and he could feel his right eye swelling where he'd taken the majority of Meat's blows.

Meat ran after him, half-blind, and Chuck made to stand but thought better of it. Instead, he set on one knee and drove the bone club up and into Meat's groin.

As Meat fell to the ground, Chuck stood on wobbly legs and looked down at his opponent. "You are a worthy adversary, but you'll never be The Unstoppable Force that is Big Chuck Wagon."

Chuck beat Meat with the club, finally stopping when the man was nothing more than a pile of bloody meat.

***

Chuck must've passed out.

When he opened his eyes he could see what was left of Meat a few feet away. He went to stand and a shadow fell over him. Chuck turned to see a dozen Gatherers, fifteen feet away.

"I won," Chuck said, his throat sore and dry. "Am I now free?"

A wicked chuckle arose from the Gatherers.

"As promised," one of them said. He lifted a bony hand and the earth began to rumble. Between Chuck and Meat a sinkhole formed, sand sliding into it at an alarming rate.

Chuck stood, backing up, until he was standing directly in front of the Gatherers.

The hole opened, a vast crevasse, and the heat coming from it was unbearable. Chuck could see flames far below, maybe three hundred feet, and a river of lava as the hole grew wider.

"I don't understand," he said, turning to the Gatherers. "I defeated him. I brought the zombies. I did as you asked."

They all nodded in unison.

"Exactly. You have wiped away years of survivors in one fell swoop. You've done our job for us, because we grew tired of finding new ways to kill them. We are weary of being the recruiters for Him Below. So we do this culling every now and then, once the population grows enough. Survivors will tell the newcomers about the zombies and the rules of this land, even though there aren't any."

"I don't get to leave?" Chuck asked, feeling duped.

A Gatherer grabbed him from behind and pushed Chuck to his knees, pushing a bony yet strong knee into his back. Another Gatherer gripped Chuck's arm and twisted it to the point of breaking.

"Of course you can leave. You had my word. You will move onto a better place. Below. To spend eternity as one of the worst men who have ever lived. You are truly elite. For that you get to burn forever."

The Gatherers dragged a kicking and fighting Chuck closer to the hole, the sand sliding away underneath his feet. His arm popped out of the socket from the pressure of the Gatherer. All the while the other Gatherers pushed him inexorably toward the fiery hole, and toward eternal damnation.

ONLY THE DEAD GO FREE

JOE MCKINNEY

CHOICES.

All of them bad.

Blaze woke before either of his companions, and though he still remembered absolutely nothing of his life before his death, before coming to this wasteland, this Purgatory, he sensed that waking early was a part of who he was.

Or rather, who he had been.

Scrubs had told him to do what comes naturally, that if he did, his memory would come back sooner.

He'd seen little of this land so far—the catacombs, the empty plain, cliffs in the distance, a lot of nothing—and Scrubs had talked quite a bit. Blaze wasn't sure why, but he was suspicious of his companions. Blaze wasn't even sure if he was alive or dead. Scrubs and Bones had been certain they were dead, just as they were certain there was a way, maybe several ways, to move beyond this land something else, but in Blaze's mind the jury was still out.

He was certain that rising early had just saved his ass, though, for a herd of zombies lumbered toward them, getting closer with every step.

Zombies.

At least Scrubs was right about one thing.

Blaze crouched behind a dead, tangled shrub. He wasn't sure if there was enough ambient light to backlight him against the landscape, but he wasn't prepared to take the chance.

He doubted it would last all that long.

The zombies were close now, and they seemed to be headed right for the little campsite he shared with Scrubs and Bones. They moved like the wounded, limping from a battlefield, bodies jerking and lurching with every step. At less than a hundred feet away, they were close enough so Blaze could see the holes in their faces and their bodies.

He'd scoffed when he first heard there were zombies in this new world. Like everybody else, he'd seen them on the TV and in bad movies, and he'd thought them little more than derivative byproducts of unimaginative storytelling. And yet here he was, standing on a low mound overlooking rugged terrain, watching a crowd of dead men and women approaching. No children, though. The TV shows always had children to bump up the creepy factor, he guessed, but there were none among the approaching horde—just a legion of nearly nude and filthy emaciated corpses, moaning like a chorus of damned souls.

Blaze wasn't scoffing now.

Far from it.

There was genuine fear curdling in his gut. It was one thing, he realized, to mock the dead when they were merely actors in makeup, but quite another to watch a herd of them approaching, moaning of insatiable hunger.

This was real, and it was time to get the hell out of Dodge.

His two traveling companions were still snoring away like fat dogs. They'd told him they were hunters, zombie killers bent on earning their freedom one zombie pelt at a time, but at the moment he found that hard to believe.

Once again, he was left with choices; none of them good.

He could run away. At this point he was certain he could easily outrun the herd.

If he really wanted to be a dick about it, he could hamstring his sleeping companions with the knife, and let them be a distraction for his escape.

Made tactical sense.

And so he was left with choices. Still, none of them good ones.

In the end he figured he wasn't quite up for that level of assholery. He turned to Scrubs and gave him a hard kick in the leg.

The man grunted in pain. "Hey, what gives?"

"Wake up, you idiot. Both of you."

Scrubs rolled over onto his knees, grinding the sleep from his eyes with the heels of his hands. Beside him, Bones managed only a groan. "What's going on?" Scrubs asked.

"We've got company," Blaze said. "Lots of it."

That got both men scrambling to their feet. Scrubs reached for his bag and pulled out a crude looking truncheon made from the remnants of a heavy branch. Bones took longer to react, but when he did, he dove into his belongings, throwing clothing and bits of trash onto the hard-packed earth like a man who'd lost his most treasured possession.

Eventually he came up with a stick about the size of his forearm, unremarkable except for a knot at the end that might give it a little punch, in the right hands.

Blaze looked from one man to the other in disgust. "I thought you two were supposed to be hunters."

"We are," said Bones, chin raised in defiance.

"Okay, well, time to put up or shut up." Blaze nodded at the three zombies coming around the cluster of shrubs behind Bones.

Bones made a little gasp of surprise and spun around.

The dead man closest to them, naked and rotting, stuck his yellowed hands in Bones' face. Bones slapped the man's hands away, but it was a weak gesture, kind of pathetic actually, and the zombie recovered quickly. The dead man righted himself with a groan and lunged forward, snapping at Bones with rotten teeth, eyes unblinking.

Bones whimpered and fell back.

"Do something," he screamed. "Jesus, fucking help me."

Blaze sensed eyes on him and glanced toward Scrubs. The man stood with his truncheon stretched out, jittering from one foot to the other in abject fear. He stared at Blaze nervously, waiting for him to take the lead.

"You're the hunter," Blaze said.

"Fucking help us," Scrubs said. "Do something."

So that's was the way it is, Blaze realized. These two. They'd spent so much time telling him how this world worked, giving their wisdom, but now he saw what their wisdom was worth.

They were cowards.

They were helpless fools in need of someone like him to carry them through this wasteland.

Blaze pushed Bones to one side and got in the zombie's face. At first the dead man didn't seem to know how to react, but the zombie didn't take long to correct itself. With a growl the dead man righted himself and lunged.

Blaze pushed the zombie's hands aside easily and jammed his heel into the back of the dead man's left leg.

The zombie folded to its knees, bent over backward so its face was pointed up at Blaze.

He grabbed the zombie's chin with one hand and a clump of its hair in the other. The dead man gnawed at the air while Blaze started to twist, wrenching the zombie's head around until he heard the neck snap.

The zombie went limp in his arms and sagged to the ground, but didn't stop moaning. It landed on its back, though its face pointed downward, chewing on the dirt.

Blaze left it there.

There was no point in bothering with it anymore. It wouldn't be a threat.

There were two other zombies right behind that one, though, and one of them held a heavy metal pipe. The zombie swung the pipe and hit Scrubs on the arm. Scrubs let out a whimpering cry and sank to one knee. Blaze grabbed Scrubs by the back of his shirt and pulled him out of the way before the zombie had a chance to swing the pipe a second time.

Scrubs landed hard in the dust and rolled over, his hands over his face.

With a shake of his head Blaze turned back to the

zombie with the pipe and pulled the knife from his waistband. The zombie raised the pipe over his head, his movements slow and drunkenly awkward, giving Blaze time to jump forward and slash the knife deep into the zombie's throat.

Blaze hadn't anticipated the zombie's flesh to be so yielding. The knife went all the way to the spine and wedged in one of the vertebrae. The zombie's head fell back, its rotted scalp almost resting on its spine before it collapsed to the ground.

It didn't quite stop moving, though.

Its mouth opened and closed in silent gulps, like a fish out of water. Its eyes followed Blaze as he circled around it, putting the fallen zombie between himself and the third one, which was having trouble trying to get through a tangled screen of dead vegetation.

Blaze took advantage of the zombie's confusion and darted forward to get the knife. He tried to pull it loose, but only managed to drag the zombie along with it.

"Come on," he grunted, trying to pull the knife loose.

It wouldn't budge.

Finally, he had to step on the zombie's chin so he could yank the knife loose.

It came away with a snap of bone. The zombie's head rolled away from the rest of the body. Blaze wiped the blade clean on the sole of his shoes and sheathed it. Lesson learned. Cutting weapons did little good against zombies, especially when they got stuck.

The metal pipe, on the other hand, held promise.

He tested its heft, and liked it. Good control, nice and solid.

He crossed behind the third zombie, and before the thing could extricate itself from the dead shrub, he teed off on the back of the dead man's head, dropping the zombie with one blow.

With all three zombies down, Blaze turned to the approaching horde. The closest of them were less than thirty feet away, close enough to be on them in another few seconds.

"I suggest you get your shit together and head out," he said to Scrubs. "Both of you."

"But wait," Scrubs said. "Dude, you can't just leave us here."

"I'm not leaving you anywhere. I'm telling you to hit the road."

"You're not coming with us?"

"Why on earth would I do that?"

"Because we're not on Earth!" Bones said. "Please, man, come with us. We need you."

"Yeah, a lot more than I need you."

Blaze turned to the advancing zombie herd and briefly considered fighting them. They were easy kills, when separated, and he was already feeling the ecstasy that came from killing coursing through his veins. It was like a drug, that warmth, addicting enough to make him do dumb, impulsive things.

No, he couldn't stay and fight. For as good as it felt to kill, he had to be smart about this.

"Maybe I'll see you around," he said, and turned and trotted off.

From somewhere behind him, Bones and Scrubs whimpered and yelled at each other as they ran off in the opposite direction.

Blaze was left on the open road.

With choices.

None of them good.

***

He needed more information.

After watching Scrubs and Bones wallow in their own cowardice, he realized he couldn't trust anything they'd told him. Maybe they'd told been truthful—they certainly didn't lie about the zombies—but maybe they'd also fed him a lot of horseshit just so he'd stay with them as their protector.

That wasn't going to happen.

He wasn't going to be anybody's protector.

The Commons, though, might prove more interesting. Scrubs had said they practiced nonviolence there, that they lived right under the noses of the Gatherers, seemingly exempt from predation. If any of that was true, if even some of it was true, he wanted to know why. Anything that helped him survive was good, and so he headed toward The Commons.

This new land wasn't particularly large. The sky above him was a ghastly blackish-purple, like a fresh bruise. Stretching off in every direction, the land was a dusty, arid desert; a featureless plain broken only by dead shrubs and skeletal trees and an occasional crack in the earth. The wind was cold, the air smelled stale. If this was Hell, or even Purgatory, it was closer to Samuel Beckett's version than anything out of Dante or Milton.

But at least it wasn't all that big.

He set out on a worn patch of dirt, which passed for roads, and wandered until he came to the dirty little gathering of lean-to sheds surrounded by a crude wooden fence.

All told, a trip of about four hours.

He stood on the road, outside the wall, studying the largest community in this land. Blaze just had to laugh. This was no city. Even the name, Commons, was a bit of a stretch. What he was looking at was a joke. He'd seen bigger villages in West Africa, and in the mountains of Afghanistan.

And that thought stopped him cold.

Afghanistan? West Africa?

Had he been there?

He must have been there. The thought was fresh in his mind, even though there was no memory to go with it. He tried to reach deep into his own head and found only an uncertain darkness.

Struggling with his missing memory got him worked up. He felt upset, angry, and more than a little scared. That bothered him. Eventually he had to will himself to stop thinking about it. Instead, he focused on circling the little cluster of wooden sheds, looking for a way in. He made his way carefully, scanning the wall and the surrounding landscape, looking for any signs of movement. Scrubs had warned him about the dead forest, saying it was basically Grand Central Station for this world's zombie population. But for all the spiritual glow he felt after killing a zombie, he really had no desire to wade into a zombie army. Discretion was, here at least, the better part of valor. Valor was something he felt he prized very much, more so even than the spiritual afterglow that came with a kill.

He turned inward again, desperately searching for something like a memory, yet it was still a haze in his mind.

He did feel a little closer, though.

Afghanistan.

Valor.

Perhaps he'd been a soldier?

Yeah, he thought. *Maybe.*

Blaze was surprised to realize he'd been holding his breath. He gasped, the air burning his lungs. He forced himself to breathe again. His fingers tingled. His heart beat so fast it hurt.

Gradually, he mastered the pain and turned his attention back to the surrounding landscape. The dead forest was thick with dried and thorny underbrush. Everything had a gray, dusty veneer. Everything, save, for a large, gallows-like structure midway between The Commons and the dead forest.

That stood out.

Curious, he approached it. Behind the fence that encircled the village, heads poked into view. Lots of eyes, watching him, studying him.

He saw a large platform about ten feet off the ground, an eight by eight feet square. There was a wide, wooden staircase that led up to the platform, the foot of which faced the dead forest. He climbed the stairs and faced a wooden wall, stained with old, dried blood. He walked closer, staring at the matching pairs of leather straps attached to the top and bottom edges of the wall.

Something caught his eye.

One of the straps had a streak of blue on it.

He stepped closer, held the length of it in his palm, only to realize the streak of blue was a tattoo.

He dropped the strap, vomit rising in the back of his throat. Blaze tried to hold it in check, but couldn't.

He turned on his heel and vomited on the top of the stairs.

Blaze stayed like that, bent over, his head swimming with the awful realization of what he'd just held in his hand.

When he caught his wind again, he stood, smoothed his clothes, wiped his lips clean, and turned back to the wall.

A pair of straps up top, another pair at the bottom: It all made a sick, awful sense. This platform, facing the dead forest, was some kind of sacrificial altar. The victim would be strapped to this wall—with leather made from human skin—and made to play offering to . . .

. . . to what?

Blaze studied the dead forest. Nothing moved out there. What could possibly be at the root of all this? What weird sort of relationship existed here?

Scrubs had said the people of The Commons lived right in the shadow of the Gatherers, immune from their depredations. Were these leather straps the ties that bound some kind of contract, some kind of totally wrong, totally fucked up relationship?

Confused, but disgusted beyond measure, Blaze vacated the platform and made his way toward The Commons.

After circling the perimeter, he found a section of the wall that had been knocked down, trampled more likely, fairly recently. There were still a lot of footprints in the dust, and the broken edges of the wood were clean. No dust had gathered there, like it had everywhere else.

Blaze climbed over the ruined section of wall, entering the town. A dozen buildings, all of which looked like they'd collapse in a hard wind, stood in silence.

He looked around, and listened.

The town seemed to be deserted.

Nothing moved.

It felt wrong, somehow. He'd been in situations like this before—he could remember the feeling, the creeping dread of it, even if the specific memories had yet to develop—and they'd all been traps.

Perhaps in another time, in his previous life, he might have tensed, every nerve on high alert, but this place, this strange land, was like a dream world.

And he felt like a dreamer.

He stood in one of the lanes and looked around, not scared, not worried, just curious and impatient for some answers.

Then, two definitive answers staggered around the corner of one of the sheds and headed his way. Their hands came up, clenching for him like they were begging for food.

Behind them, three more, then five more, then nine, appeared. All of them naked and rotting away, but still on their feet.

"Damn it," he said, and brought up the metal pipe. If he was going to have to fight, he'd fight. He'd give them what they wanted. He could handle a small crowd like this with no problem.

Hell, he might even enjoy it.

Something snapped behind him. Blaze wheeled around and saw a large crowd of zombies forcing their way through the hole in the wall. Instinctively he tried to count them, but there were too many.

Where had they all come from? He'd been careful

on his approach to The Commons. He'd scanned the area completely and moved quietly. True, he'd been unable to look inside the dead forest behind the town, but he'd watched the tree line for movement, and had seen nothing.

Yet, here they were, closing on him.

In dreams, one could accept a strange turn of events with relaxed ease. Blaze took everything in with that same degree of forgiveness. Even though he could smell the rot coming off the horde; even though his ears ached from their constant moaning; even for all that, Blaze shrugged it off as the stuff of dreams.

He couldn't make a break for it. There were too many behind him, and the wall around the town, though flimsy-looking, was tall enough to make it impossible to scale it before the horde closed on him.

He scanned the buildings around him, looking for cover, and saw movement inside one of the sheds.

So it isn't deserted, he thought.

He went to the wooden door where he'd seen the movement and pounded on it. "Open up," he shouted. "I'm one of you." The crudely constructed door shook when he banged on it. In the darkness behind the slats a man backed away into the darkness. "Let me in."

"No," a voice said. "Go away. Take them with you."

"The hell I will."

"We don't want trouble," the man said.

"You don't?" Blaze answered back. "Well, guess what you just got." He kicked the door, which gave a little, but didn't open.

He'd kicked doors down before, he was sure of it. What he recognized as training came back to him. Picture the lock on the door. Kick with your heel, not with your toe. Break the deadbolt. It may take two or three strikes, but it'll give.

Just use the heel.

Two more strikes broke the door apart.

As it swung open, he heard the gasps of a dozen people, some of them women. Blaze stepped inside and closed the door behind him. "Help me barricade this," he demanded. No one moved. "Help me, damn it! We have to move."

A zombie stumbled through the doorway behind him. The people inside the shack shrank into the corners, terrified.

"Get up and fight," Blaze commanded. "Help me!"

One of the men shook his head. Blaze looked from one to the other, their faces dirty, their clothes little more than rags. They looked utterly terrified. Blaze felt the fear coming off them like heat from a radiator, and it made him angry. He felt disgusted and enraged.

No wonder killing felt so good here, he thought. He wanted nothing more in that moment than to kill the lot of them.

"What's wrong with you people?" The zombie in the doorway put a withered, skeletal hand on Blaze's shoulder. He spun around, knocking the zombie's hand away. "Get off me, you son of a bitch!"

He swung the metal pipe at the zombie's head and sent it tumbling into a corner, where it collapsed in a heap and didn't get up. There were more behind it, though. Blaze kicked the one closest to him and sent it flying backwards into the others. Then he slammed the door closed and held it there with his back. The zombies fell on the door, but they were weak; their hands slapped uselessly against the other side.

Blaze felt stronger by the moment, a surge of energy coursing through him, like a drug doling out its first rush.

His legs felt like tree trunks rooting into the ground, strong and sturdy. There were muscles in his back he never knew he had. His teeth clenched and ground together so forcefully he could hear them.

He would hold the door, but the villagers at the back of the shed didn't notice.

They were clustered around a trapdoor in the ground. Already, several of them had made their way down, and the rest were pushing their way toward the entrance.

"Where are you going?" Blaze demanded. "Stand and fight!"

The last man climbed into the hole, gave him an inscrutable look, and closed the hatch door as he sank out of sight.

Blaze was left alone in the room, the zombies beating at his back.

He glanced around and realized for the first time there was almost no furniture. How did these people live? There were three mats to his right, what passed for beds, he guessed, but they were little more than finely chopped dead leaves poking out from under a sheet stitched together from old clothes. These villagers were so Spartan, their material lives so utterly bereft of content, almost like they were merely placeholders. They may be surviving against the odds, but at what cost? What kind of life was this?

The only other furniture in the room was a crudely fashioned bench and table to his left. The bench looked weak, but the table was a heavy piece of wood. He could use that.

He jammed his metal pipe against the door and stuck the other end in the dirt. The zombies pounded on the door, and it shook in its frame, but held.

Blaze ran over to the table and kicked the legs off it. He then dragged it over and propped it up against the door, wedging it into the ground just as he'd done with the pipe. With the door secure, he grabbed his pipe and made his way to the trapdoor. It was locked from the underside, but the lock was flimsy and he was able to wedge the pipe under the lip of the door and pry it apart.

There was a short ladder under the trapdoor. Blaze climbed down it until the passageway opened up to a tunnel, tall enough for grown men to walk down without stooping.

So this was how they did it, he thought. This was how they survived. Scrubs had told him The Commons preached non-violence, which was somehow the secret to their survival.

That wasn't true, was it?

They survived by playing turtle. The zombies encroached on the walls, and the people of The Commons went down into their tunnels.

Not too bad, he thought. *Actually, pretty damn smart.*

For a moment, he thought of going after them. Asking questions, but then he heard . . . not really singing . . . more like chanting. A low, steady sound drowned out the moaning crowds of zombies, and then silenced them entirely.

"What the . . . ?" he said.

He listened for a moment longer, and was surprised to hear the crowds of zombies moving away from the door. He couldn't be certain, because the moans were all but gone, but hundreds of bodies made a lot of noise moving about. It sounded almost like they were leaving the village.

The chanting was fading, too.

Something told him to stay low, he was safe here. The smart thing to do was to stay where he was, but his curiosity was overpowering. The chanting . . . it seemed to be leading the zombies away. That meant it was either an ally, or at least a potential ally, or it was a far worse threat than the zombies.

Either way, he wanted to see what it was.

And he had come here for answers.

Blaze climbed the ladder, crawled across the floor, and found a crack in the wall to peer through.

He listened and heard nothing.

The chanting, or whatever it had been, was gone. He looked up and down the lane as far as he could see, but there was just a settling haze of dust the zombie hordes had kicked up.

This world was insane.

He rose to his feet and dusted himself off. There really seemed no point in going on with this charade. Whatever he was doing here, whatever crime he was supposedly serving penance for, he didn't see the point. The killing made no sense. The reward for the killing made even less sense. He just wanted to remember.

Maybe that was the catch, though. Maybe that was what he was supposed to grasp. Maybe the punishment came from that, from reclaiming memory. And maybe, just maybe, he could cheat his tormentors.

Maybe he could take the knife from his belt and run himself through.

Certainly he could die down here, or at least transition to some other state. Surely Scrubs and Bones wouldn't have feared the zombies so unless they believed that, and even if he doubted them, the villagers had shown the same kind of fear when they crawled down into their holes.

Maybe he could cheat Death through death.

Or at least deny Death his sting.

He tossed the metal pipe to one side, spread his feet shoulder width apart for balance, and pulled the knife from his belt.

Blaze stared at the knife, a rusted, dented, ages-old hunting knife. He was seriously considering jamming it into his heart. He wondered if he could really do it. His body tingled all over, but the thought of suicide was somehow satisfying, almost calming.

He pointed the tip of the blade to his chest and suddenly, the calm that had nagged at the corners of his thoughts took over.

This was the right thing to do.

He felt certain of that now.

His breathing slowed. His heart stopped thundering in his chest. There had been a roaring in his ears that was so loud he'd stopped noticing it, but that was gone now. He was left with echoing silence, acceptance and calm.

All of which disappeared when the door exploded inward.

Blaze stood there, stupidly, staring at a cloaked figure in the doorway.

A Gatherer.

The Gatherer was surprised, too. He'd listened to Scrubs and Bones talk about what the Gatherers looked like, and he'd known right away they were full of shit. Bones had said they were insubstantial beings made of smoke and glowing eyes, but even then Blaze had known what to make of that. He remembered all too well the cold, powerful hands that had carried him from the catacombs to this new world. He knew there was substance under those robes, that a corporeal being existed there.

Now, looking the Gatherer in the eyes, he knew they were just men, like himself.

Clearly they didn't have absolute control down here, for this Gatherer obviously didn't know Blaze would be waiting for him on the other side of the door. He'd blasted down the door without the slightest effort. He stood in the cloud of settling splinters and dust with his hands at his sides, his purple robe smooth along the flanks of his tall, gaunt frame.

The moment of surprise ended, and at seeing Blaze, his hands came up defensively.

That was all Blaze needed to see.

There was a moment when the fight could have gone either way, but seeing the Gatherer's surprise was enough to wake the killer in Blaze. He took the knife from his chest and lunged for the Gatherer, thrusting the blade deep into the man's mouth. He felt it sink into the palate. The Gatherer went limp at once, choking and gurgling on his own blood as he sagged to his knees.

Blaze didn't let up, though. He jammed the knife deeper, twisting it to maximize the damage. The Gatherer responded with a series of violent spasms, his body jerking and convulsing. Finally, the Gatherer withered and wasted away to something that looked like a man-size, pale and puckered apple. Blaze stood there with the robes still hanging from the tip of his knife, disbelieving.

The shock didn't last long, though, for the energy, the pleasure and the pain, the thrill and the fear, the body-racking waves of confusion and lust that coursed through him were so overpowering they caused him to fold to the ground in a heap next to his kill. His body curled into a fetal position. More waves of pleasure and pain gripped him. It felt like an enormous fist had reached inside his chest and squeezed his heart. He could barely breathe one moment, and the next his lungs felt like they might burst with all the sweet thrill they were taking in.

There were no thoughts in his head. Panic, fear, surprise, hunger; they all shrank into nothingness, leaving only the experience of taking on of the dead Gatherer's power.

***

Eventually, the overwhelming rush of the power-transfer subsided.

Blaze was left a twitching and convulsing ball on the floor. He tried to get up, but it wasn't going to happen. He could barely keep his eyes open. When he did open them, the world was a vibrating blur.

He could, however, sense people gathering around him.

He could hear their voices, their whispers.

He sensed their shock, their hushed and fearful reverence for the new being born into their midst. They were terrified.

And he felt glorious.

***

As the ecstasy faded, Blaze stood up.

He looked around at the sudden rush of activity. The villagers fell over themselves to back away from him, as though they feared what he might do.

Blaze had a pretty good idea of what he wanted to do to them.

His eyes narrowed at the ring of faces shrinking from him.

He'd never felt such disgust for anyone. The dark clouds where his memory was breaking apart, and while he still couldn't put together the pieces of what had been his life before this place, he felt with absolute certainty he'd never felt such revulsion for anyone. Their cowardice made him want to spit at their feet.

"Hey," a desperate voice from outside the wall cried. "Hey, anyone!"

A woman off to Blaze's right grew suddenly hopeful. "That's Scrubs," she said to another woman. "He's okay. He made it back."

Blaze growled under his breath. "What is this?"

He got his answer a moment later.

Scrubs and Bones came sprinting through the hole in the wall, out of breath and wild-eyed. "We got a whole mess of trouble coming this way," Bones said to the assembled villagers. "We got to move."

The pair finally saw Blaze. "What are you doing here?" Scrubs said.

"He killed one of the Gatherers," the woman to Blaze's right said.

"You did what?" Scrubs said.

"He did," the woman said. "With that knife. Look at the robe. He's got one of their robes." She turned to Blaze. "You took on the Gatherer's power, didn't you?

I can see it in your face. You could protect us." She ran to Scrubs and grabbed his arm. At a glance, Blaze could tell there was history there—some kind of romantic history. "We wouldn't need the sacrifices anymore," she said. "We'd be free."

Scrubs pushed her away. "Be quiet, Linda."

"But he could change things for us."

"You talk too much, woman. Zip it."

Linda shrank from him, hurt and obviously afraid.

Bones stood behind Scrubs. He shook so violently he could barely contain himself. "We don't have time for this," he said, still winded. "We have to get down into the tunnels."

"He's right," Scrubs said. "There isn't time for this. We've got a massive horde coming out of the forest. They're right behind us. We need to get out of here, and fast."

Blaze looked around and saw a few of the villagers moving toward the shacks. There were, he figured, tunnel entrances under most of the buildings in The Commons.

Cowards, he thought.

Blaze turned to Scrubs. "They were already here. They've come and gone."

"You mean that little group you chased off?" Scrubs answered. "Not by a long shot. We saw thousands of them coming this way. Maybe even tens of thousands."

Finally, Blaze's disgust got the better of him and he spit at Scrubs' feet. Scrubs flinched from the spray like it was a bullet.

"I've developed some serious doubts about every word that comes out your mouth," Blaze said.

"Yeah?" Scrubs asked.

"Yeah."

"Well, if you don't believe me, check out the tree line. Go ahead."

"They're coming up from the forest," Bones concurred. "More of them than we could count."

"Is that right?" Blaze said. "This from the man who told me the Gatherers were made of smoke?"

"Look, we were just—"

"Shut up," Scrubs said. "We don't have time for this. We need to get into the tunnels."

Scrubs grabbed his girlfriend by the arm and tried to pull her toward one of the sheds, but Blaze reached out a hand and caught him by the throat. Scrubs struggled, but he was no match for Blaze's iron grip.

Blaze pushed him up against the wall and squeezed until Scrubs' eyes bulged, then he eased up.

He kept his grip on the man's neck, though. "Not so fast," he said.

"We have to go," Scrubs managed to wheeze out.

"Answers first. You live here. You lied to me. You're no hunter."

Scrubs shook his head.

Blaze squeezed again, making Scrubs choke. His lips turned blue, but rather than let him go, Blaze picked him up, letting his feet dangle six inches from the dusty road.

Scrubs tried to scream, but no words came out.

"Mister, please!" Linda said. "Please."

Blaze glanced her way then turned back to Scrubs.

Gradually, he lowered him to the ground and released the pressure.

Scrubs doubled over, spitting and coughing. He tried to speak but couldn't. He finally managed to stand up, not straight, but more or less upright, and turned his bloodshot eyes toward Blaze.

"Tell me the truth," Blaze said.

"You want the truth? Okay, I'll give you the truth. If we don't get out of here right now, we're all gonna be zombie chow. They've got three Gatherers leading them. They'll kill us all."

"Why?" Blaze asked. "Why now?"

"It's because of you," the woman said. "You were meant to keep them away."

"Be quiet, Linda," Scrubs said.

Blaze grabbed Scrubs by the throat again and squeezed. Not hard enough to choke him, but hard enough to keep him from talking.

He turned to the woman and said, "You're name is Linda?"

She nodded.

"Okay, Linda. Listen to your boyfriend here. Shut the fuck up. I want to hear the truth from this son of a bitch."

He turned back to Scrubs and was about to question him further when someone from the crowd shouted, "Here they come! We gotta go!"

"We gotta go, man," said Bones.

"You go," said Blaze. "Scrubs and I have a few things to discuss."

Even with Blaze's fingers wrapped around his throat, Scrubs managed to shake his head.

"Mister, please," said Linda. "Let him go."

"What does she mean?" Blaze asked. "How was I supposed to keep them away?"

The rest of the villagers ran to the shacks, slipping behind closed doors, leaving only Scrubs, Blaze and

Linda, and the first of the zombie army stepping through the crashed section of wall.

Blaze turned Scrubs head so he could see the dead army getting closer. "Better talk fast."

"The platform," Scrubs choked out. "You were going to be our sacrifice."

Sacrifice.

Something in the word held power for Blaze. He released his grip on Scrubs' throat and let the man fall to the ground.

"What do you mean . . . sacrifice?"

"Just that," Scrubs said, rising to his knees, one hand rubbing his aching throat.

"Tell me," Blaze demanded.

Scrubs looked right, toward the first zombies climbing over the rubble that had once been The Commons wall. "There's no time," he said.

"Make time," Blaze said. "Spit it out."

Linda stepped forward then and said, "He's telling you the truth. He and Bones are hunters. We send them to the plain whenever the Gatherers bring in somebody new. If they can, they bring them back here."

"And you tie them to that wall on the platform," Blaze said, filling in the rest. "What for?"

"As sacrifice," Scrubs said. "Like we said."

"To whom?"

"The zombies in the forest. They feed on the sacrifice. In return, they leave us alone."

"How is that possible? I thought you said there were thousands of them out there."

"More than that," Scrubs said. Four zombies climbed through the breach. Another nine were right behind them. "We have to get out of here."

"You'll die here if I don't get my answers."

Scrubs laughed at him. "We're already dead, you fool! Haven't you figured that out yet? The killing. It's the only thing that lets us live again. It's the only thing we have down here. There's no way out. There's nothing beyond this." He held up his hands as though to take in everything, the whole world. "This is all there is. When you remember your crimes, you'll understand."

One of the zombies put a hand on Blaze's shoulder.

Blaze pushed the thing away and crushed its skull into a pulp with the metal pipe.

"You feel that rush?" Scrubs asked. "Feels good, doesn't it? That's your life now, killer. That's what you got to live for. The zombies feel it more than anyone. That's why the sacrifice works. Even a drop of blood is enough to bring back what it felt like to be alive. And that's the real hell that awaits us all."

Before Blaze could respond, a whole section of the wall burst apart and a flood of naked, blood-smeared bodies tumbled over themselves.

"They're all around us," Linda shouted.

"I don't want to die," Bones said. "Oh God, no!"

Scrubs jumped to his feet. He grabbed Linda and pulled her toward one of the shacks. "Help us," he screamed at Blaze as he ran passed. "Do something."

Blaze nearly grabbed Scrubs by the throat again. He wanted to. He wanted to choke the ever loving shit out of the man, but even as his hands reached for the little coward, his mind hiccupped.

"You better go," Blaze said quietly.

Scrubs and Linda didn't wait for more. They ran down the main lane of the little village and ducked into the first shack they came to.

Bones was slower to react. He said, "Hey, thanks man," and then ran for the same shack Scrubs and Linda had disappeared into. He stopped at the door. "What are you doing? You need to get in the tunnels."

"No," Blaze said. "I'm getting out of here."

***

What that meant, Blaze didn't know.

He stepped over the busted wall and out on the plain. The dead forest was a dark, hulking line in the near distance. Closer, a ghastly silhouette against the horizon, stood the sacrificial platform. Blaze felt anger swell inside him. They were going to tie him with straps made from human skin. They were going to give him to the zombies.

What would such a sacrifice buy the villagers, he wondered.

A week of peace?

A month?

Of course, it didn't really matter now, did it? The zombies, a teeming ocean of them, surged out of the forest, the three Gatherers in the lead.

He smiled grimly.

The way they moved . . . so slowly. Every single one of them was either nude or wearing nothing but soiled rags that looked like they might slip from their emaciated frames at any second. He could run right past them, like he was Walter Payton, slipping through the secondary.

He would hardly even need to fight.

Only the Gatherers would present a problem.

Already he could feel them reaching out to him, trying to touch his mind with theirs. They wanted him to come to them, to join them. To be one of them.

Blaze raised the metal pipe and tensed to run through the crowd, when he saw a figure moving through the naked dead. It was a man in full combat gear. He wore a look of terrified panic. The man panted and whined, spittle flying from his mouth, his eyes full of terror.

Blaze went cold with dread, for he recognized the man.

He was looking at himself.

The soldier, the man Blaze had once been, weaved through the legion of zombies without once raising his rifle. He was so scared, he looked like he barely knew he had a weapon in his hands. A voice inside Blaze's head yelled at him to run, just as his other self was doing, but he held his ground.

Suddenly, the soldier froze in his tracks.

He threw his chest out, his arms spreading wide, and a look of surprise, pain and terror flashed across his face as he sank to his knees, falling over.

Blaze gasped.

A zombie stepped in front of him, but it was like all the rest, wan and wasted. He grabbed the thing by the chin and the back of its head, twisting to break its neck. It fell to the ground, still groaning, but unable to move.

That was the impetus he needed.

Blaze advanced through the crowd of zombies, striking them with his metal pipe when they got too close, crushing their skulls like overripe pumpkins. He hacked and slashed, kicked and screamed, and finally made his way to the dead soldier's side.

He reached down and wrangled with the chinstrap on the helmet.

A zombie put its hand on his back and he jumped

up, delirious now with a new fear he couldn't quite articulate.

"Back the fuck off," he screamed at the dead woman, and swung the pipe at her face. The metal connected with her jaw, knocking the bottom half of her face off her head. Her separated jaw hit the ground a few yards away, but she didn't go down. "I said, back the fuck off," he roared again, and this time brought the pipe down like a hatchet on the top of her head.

That put her down.

He turned in a slow circle, studying the zombies closing in around him. He was going to have to fight, but he needed to do something first.

Blaze knelt at the soldier's side and wrenched his helmet off his head.

It was exactly as he feared. He was looking at himself.

Blaze's gaze wandered to the insignia on the soldier's shoulder and suddenly he remembered it all. He and his platoon had been caught in an overgrown ditch by Taliban elements. They'd thought they were getting the drop on a shack fifty meters north of the ditch, but once they'd opened fire, the Taliban had closed the barn door behind them. Before they knew it, they had incoming fire from every side, mortars and small arms fire.

His brain slipped from reality into memory, and he found himself back there, in that overgrown ditch outside of Sarwan Qala Village, his nerves once again jangling with the rattle of guns and the piercing shriek of bullets flying past his ears.

Another soldier slid down beside him, the branches

above him chewed to chowder by bullets. "Looks like we're fucked! They're bounding."

"Where's that God damn air support?"

"Four minutes out!"

"Shit, we'll be fucking dead in two."

"Here they come."

The soldier next to Blaze rolled over onto his belly and crawled up to the lip of the ditch.

Blaze watched the man raise his rifle and fire, heard the constant popping of automatic weapons and the low grumbling roar of mortars. It was like some kind of out of body experience. Like déjà vu. He knew what was going to happen, and yet he was powerless to do anything about it.

He watched the soldier poke his head above the lip of the ditch, and before he could shout at the man to get down, a bullet punched into the man's face, twisting his head around.

The next instant the soldier slid back down the side of the ditch, coming to final rest just inches from Blaze's side. The 7.62 mm round had done its work. The man, the soldier, his friend, was dead. His face was a half-exploded flower of blood and meat and pieces of bone.

"They're bounding again! Twenty meters!"

"Gimme some suppressive fire up here! McGuire, where the fuck are you?"

Blaze looked up. In his memory he could see a young lieutenant screaming at him. Other soldiers were scrambling up the side of the ditch, firing in all directions.

"Get the fuck up, McGuire! Up here!"

Sean McGuire. That was his name; his real name.

Blaze felt the air run out his lungs. His face flushed with heat. Every single nerve in his body pulsed with fear. The bullets ripped through the vegetation above him, and with every snapping twig, with every scream of an injured man, he felt his fear grow a little stronger.

"McGuire," the lieutenant screamed again. "Get up here!"

And then his fear overwhelmed him. He jumped to his feet, the breath catching in his throat as he scrambled up the far side of the ditch and ran from the fight.

"McGuire! Get back here!"

He ran the other way. Even as he fled the firefight he knew he had nowhere to run. He was writing his own death sentence. Still, he couldn't stop. His fear was so great he was all but blind to everything. He had to get away. He had to put the rattle of the guns and the screams of the dying as far behind as he could.

He had to run.

And then the bullet bit into his back, piercing his body armor and punching through to his spine, perforating his heart.

His chest pushed out.

His arms spread wide.

McGuire fell to his knees then sagged into a heap in the dirt.

Full of shame, Blaze looked down at where the dead soldier had once been. There was nothing there now. Zombies closed in around him, but he didn't care. He had learned the truth about his life before coming here, and it was awful. Dante had reserved the deepest level of hell for betrayers, for Judas and Brutus and Cassius, the worst of the worst.

Until now.

Now, Blaze could count himself among that number. He had betrayed his fellow soldiers. He had run the other way.

He was the coward.

He turned toward The Commons, and realized he'd come home. He had hated them for their cowardice. He'd seen them cower in fear and he'd been disgusted beyond measure, but now he realized that disgust for what it really was, and he knew where he was.

He was on the circle of hell he deserved.

The shame of his new knowledge weighed so heavily upon him he sank to his knees, unable to even lift his head to the moaning dead men crowding around him.

"Blaze! Hey man, get up!"

There were hands on him, and at first he thought they were zombies, but then he saw Scrubs and Bones trying to pull him to his feet.

"Get up, man," Scrubs shouted at him. "Come on!"

"Let's go!" Bones said.

Scrubs leaned down next to Blaze and said, "Come on, buddy, we have to go. We have to hide."

Blaze looked up at him, his eyes full of tears. "What was it you told me?" Blaze asked. He spoke with utter calm, not a trace of fear in his voice. "The killing. It's all we have down here. It's what we live for."

"What?" Scrubs hooked a hand under Blaze's arm and tried to pull him to his feet. "Yeah, sure. The killing. And with you," he said, "we're finally gonna have a chance to come out on top."

"No," Blaze said.

"What? Come on!"

"No," Blaze said again. He stood up on his own and straightened his clothes with a sweep of his hands. "You and Bones go back to The Commons. I have something I need to do."

"What are you talking about? You have to come with us."

Blaze didn't answer him. He knew Scrubs didn't understand. Not the way he did. The zombies had stopped. They'd turned, as a single body, and they were watching him. A voice—no, not a voice, but a chorus, like the chanting he'd heard earlier in the village, before he'd killed the fourth Gatherer—filled his head. Cocking his head to listen, he realized he could hear the message contained within. This legion of rotting, naked corpses was at his command. Each of the Gatherers had their share of the dead, and they could do with them as they pleased, but this column, this part of the army, was his.

They were waiting for him to give them marching orders.

He made his way through the legion of dead men surrounding them, until he got to the sacrificial platform.

"What are you doing?" Scrubs yelled at his back.

"Getting out of here," he answered.

Beyond the throng of the dead, he could see the other Gatherers watching him, waiting to see what he would do. He could feel them reaching for his mind with theirs, begging him to take his place among them.

He could be a god here.

He could have real power.

If he could only live with himself.

There was the rub. To live here, even as a god, was

to live inside his own head. To live with the knowledge of what he once was.

And once a man knew himself to be a betrayer, could he ever be anything but?

Somehow, Blaze doubted it.

"There is no getting out of here," Scrubs shouted. "There's just the killing, nothing more."

That wasn't true, was it? Even in the deepest level of hell, a man could face his crimes. A man could answer for his cowardice.

He climbed the stairs, went to the wall, and wrapped the human leather around his fists. From the wall he could see the zombie army watching him, waiting at the foot of the platform.

"You can be more than this," a voice inside his head shouted at him.

Blaze looked over the crowd of dead men and saw the Gatherers watching him. He knew the pain on their faces. They were truly gods down here, but they too had their demons they were powerless to shake.

"Blaze, please!" Scrubs shouted.

Blaze turned toward Scrubs, and saw yet another terrified cockroach of a man, hiding from the light of honesty.

Blaze didn't want any part of it.

He was left with more choices. Join the Gatherers, and be a tortured god among tortured souls, or live as a groveling worm, but a shadow of the man he'd wanted to be in life.

Not all of his choices were bad, this time.

He could take charge of his fate. He couldn't shake the sting of death, but he could turn his back to the shame it hoped to saddle him with. He could deny the grave its lasting torments.

He closed his eyes and sent out orders to his zombie army.

Come to me. Devour your god.

When he opened his eyes again, the zombies were clamoring toward the platform, the first few already mounting the steps.

"What are you doing?" the Gatherers demanded of him. "Stop them."

Blaze had no intention of doing so.

Within seconds, they'd mount the platform, and tear him apart bit by bit.

In the process, perhaps they'd free his soul.

The End?

Not at all.

If you enjoyed this book or ever thought of becoming an author, I can highly recommend these books:

The Outsiders Lovecraftian shared-world anthology—They'll do anything to protect their way of life. Anything. Welcome to Priory, a small gated community in the UK, where the only thing worse than an ancient monster is the group worshipping it. Is that which slithers below true evil, or does evil reside in the people of Priory? Includes stories by Stephen Bacon, James Everington, Rosanne Rabinowitz, V.H. Leslie, and Gary Fry.

Tales from The Lake Vol.1 anthology—Remember those dark and scary nights spent telling ghost stories and other campfire stories? With the *Tales from The Lake* horror anthologies, you can relive some of those memories by reading the best Dark Fiction stories around. Includes Dark Fiction stories and poems by horror greats such as Graham Masterton, Bev Vincent, Tim Curran, Tim Waggoner, Elizabeth Massie, and many more. Be sure to check out our website for future *Tales from The Lake* volumes.

Fear the Reaper anthology—Did you know Death was a girl? Ever wondered if it was possible to cheat death? To kill Death? Or that it's possible to escape and even become death? Includes Grim Reapers stories by legends like Rick Hautala, Gary A. Braunbeck, Joe McKinney, Richard Thomas, Jeremy C Shipp, Jeff Strand, and many more.

Sleeper(s) by Paul Kane —An entire city falls asleep, and when Doctor Andrew Strauss and the army move in to investigate, the sleepers stand up to defend a single woman as a cohesive group, and mind. As Strauss' covert past and foretold future clash, the twisted fairytale truth behind this event will leave you breathless.

If you ever thought of becoming an author, I'd also like to recommend these non-fiction titles:

Writers On Writing: An Author's Guide—Your favorite authors share their secrets in the ultimate guide to becoming and being and author. With your support, *Writers On Writing* will become an ongoing eBook series with original 'On Writing' essays by writing professionals. A new edition will be launched every few months, featuring four or five essays per edition, so be sure to check out the webpage regularly for updates.

Horror 101: The Way Forward—a comprehensive overview of the Horror fiction genre and career opportunities available to established and aspiring authors, including Jack Ketchum, Graham Masterton, Edward Lee, Lisa Morton, Ellen Datlow, Ramsey Campbell, and many more.

Modern Mythmakers: 35 interviews with Horror and Science Fiction Writers and Filmmakers by Michael McCarty—Ever wanted to hang out with legends like Ray Bradbury, Richard Matheson, and Dean Koontz? *Modern Mythmakers* is your chance to hear fun anecdotes and career advice from authors and filmmakers like Forrest J. Ackerman, Ray Bradbury, Ramsey Campbell, John Carpenter, Dan Curtis, Elvira, Neil Gaiman, Mick Garris, Laurell K. Hamilton, Jack Ketchum, Dean Koontz, Graham Masterton, Richard Matheson, John Russo, William F. Nolan, John Saul, Peter Straub, and many more.

Or check out other Crystal Lake Publishing books for your Dark Fiction, Horror, Suspense, and Thriller needs.

Biographies

Tonia Brown is a southern author with a penchant for Victorian dead things. She lives in the backwoods of North Carolina with her genius husband and an ever fluctuating number of cats. She likes fudgesicles and coffee, though not always together. When not writing she raises unicorns and fights crime with her husband under the code names Dr. Weird and his sexy sidekick Butternut. You can learn more about her at: www.toniabrownauthor.com

Joe McKinney has his feet in several different worlds. In his day job, he has worked as a patrol officer for the San Antonio Police Department, a DWI Enforcement officer, a disaster mitigation specialist, a homicide detective, the director of the City of San Antonio's 911 Call Center, and a patrol supervisor. He played college baseball for Trinity University, where he graduated with a Bachelor's Degree in American History, and went on to earn a Master's Degree in English Literature from the University of Texas at San Antonio. He was the manager of a Barnes & Noble for a while, where he indulged a lifelong obsession with books. He published his first novel, *Dead City,* in 2006, a book that has since been recognized as a seminal work in the Horror genre, and one of the cornerstones of zombie literature. Since then, he has gone on to win two Bram Stoker Awards and expanded his oeuvre to cover everything from true crime and writings on police procedure to science fiction to cooking and Texas history. The author of more than twenty books, he is a frequent guest at horror and mystery conventions. Joe and his wife Tina have two lovely daughters and make their home in a little town just outside of San Antonio, where he indulges his passion for cooking and makes what some consider to be the finest batch of chili in Texas. You can keep up with all of Joe's latest releases by friending him on Facebook.

Born and raised in the coastal English town Lowestoft, it should come as no surprise (to those that have the misfortune of knowing this place) that **Alex Laybourne** became a horror writer.

From an early age he was sent to schools which were at least 30 minutes' drive away and so spent most of his free time alone, as the friends he did have lived too far away for him to be able to hang out with them in the weekends or holidays.

He has been a writer as long as he can remember and has always had a vivid imagination. To this very day he finds it all too easy to just drift away into his own mind and explore the world he creates—where the conditions always seem to be just perfect for the cultivation of ideas, plots, scenes, characters and lines of dialogue.

He is married and has five wonderful children; James, Logan, Ashleigh, Damon and Riley. His biggest dream for them is that they grow up, and spend their lives doing what makes them happy, whatever that is.

For people who buy his work, he hopes that they enjoy what they read and that he can create something that takes them away from reality for a short time. For him, the greatest compliment he can receive is not based on rankings but by knowing that people enjoy what he produces, that they buy his work with pleasure and never once feel as though their money would have been better spent elsewhere.

Joe Mynhardt is a South African horror writer, publisher, editor and teacher. Joe is also the owner of Crystal Lake Publishing, which he started in August, 2012. He has published and edited short stories, novellas, interviews and essays by the likes of Neil Gaiman, Ramsey Campbell, Jack Ketchum, Graham Masterton, Adam Nevill, Lisa Morton, Elizabeth Massie, Joe McKinney, Edward Lee, Wes Craven, John Carpenter, George A. Romero, Mick Garris, and hundreds more.

Just like Crystal Lake Publishing, Joe believes in reaching out to all authors, new and experienced, and being a beacon of friendship and guidance in the Dark Fiction field.

In his non-fictional life, Joe is a primary school teacher who enjoys reading books and comics, watching movies, and collecting rare coins. After matriculating in 1998, he moved to Bloemfontein, South Africa (birthplace of J.R.R Tolkien), where he received an honors degree in Education Leadership and Management. Joe devotes himself to his wife, his work, and to feeding his two dogs. I'm sure if something happened, and he was incapacitated, he wouldn't mind if his dogs ate him. After all, it would be a shame to let all that talent go to waste.

You can read more about Joe and Crystal Lake Publishing at www.crystallakepub.com or find him on Facebook.

Aurelio Rico Lopez III is a scribble junkie whose addictions include books, horror movies, rock and roll, and coffee. He is the author of *Food for the Crows* (Crowded Quarantine Publications), *Cry Wolf* (Crowded Quarantine Publications), *No Grave Too Deep* (Short Scary Tales Publications), and *Night Mare* (Great Old Ones Publishing). He is also the co-author of *Night of the Kaiju* (Severed Press) and *Crawlers* (Great Old Ones Publishing). Aurelio hails from Iloilo City, Philippines.

Armand Rosamilia is a New Jersey boy currently living in sunny Florida, where he writes all day until his back hurts and then gets doted on by his wife Shelly. Who yells at him to get out of the chair every once in a while. He has over 150 releases to date, has two successful podcasts on Project iRadio (*Arm Cast: Dead Sexy Horror Podcast* and *Arm N Toof's Dead Time Podcast* with co-host Mark Tufo) as well as runs the *Authors Supporting Our Troops* event, collecting author-signed books for the soldiers in remote areas. He is a firm believer in karma and helps fellow authors as much as he can. http://armandrosamilia.com for more information.

Monique Snyman lives in Pretoria, South Africa with an adorable Chihuahua that keeps her company and a bloodthirsty lawyer who keeps her sane. She is a full-time author, part-time editor and in-between reviewer of all things entertaining. Her short fiction has been published in a number of small press anthologies, the Charming Incantations Series is published by Rainstorm Press, and she's working hard on a couple of other novels in her spare time.

We hope you enjoyed this title. If so, we'd be grateful if you could leave a review on your blog or any of the other websites and outlets open to book reviews. Reviews are like gold to writers and publishers, since word-of-mouth is and will always be the best way to market a great book. And remember to keep an eye out for more of our books.

Connect with Crystal Lake Publishing:

Website:
www.crystallakepub.com
(receive a free eBook if you join our mailing list)
Facebook:
www.facebook.com/Crystallakepublishing
Twitter:
https://twitter.com/crystallakepub

With unmatched success since 2012, Crystal Lake Publishing has quickly become one of the world's leading indie publishers of Mystery, Thriller, and Suspense books with a Dark Fiction edge.

Crystal Lake Publishing puts integrity, honor and respect at the forefront of our operations.

We strive for each book and outreach program that's launched to not only entertain and touch or comment on issues that affect our readers, but also to strengthen and support the Dark Fiction field and its authors.

Not only do we publish authors who are legends in the field and as hardworking as us, but we look for men and women who care about their readers and fellow human beings. We only publish the very best Dark Fiction, and look forward to launching many new careers.

We strive to know each and every one of our readers, while building personal relationships with our authors, reviewers, bloggers, pod-casters, bookstores and libraries.

Crystal Lake Publishing is and will always be a beacon of what passion and dedication, combined with overwhelming teamwork and respect, can accomplish: Unique fiction you can't find anywhere else.

We do not just publish books, we present you worlds within your world, doors within your mind, from talented authors who sacrifice so much for a moment of your time.

This is what we believe in. What we stand for. This will be our legacy.

Welcome to Crystal Lake Publishing.

* 9 7 8 0 9 9 4 6 6 2 6 3 7 *